'No! I said *no*.'

Silas leapt to his
with exasperation. '
will you listen to wh
you—?'

Before three words were out, Isolde was up and facing him, eye to eye. 'No, in God's name I shall do no such thing, sir! I do not need you to make any plans for me, nor do I need your assistance to reach York.' Her eyes were wide open and, this time, furiously unflinching.

Fascinated, Silas stuck his thumbs into the girdle that belted his hips. 'There now, wench, you've been wanting to let fly at me ever since you got here, haven't you? Feeling better now?'

'You mistake the matter, sir. I haven't given you a moment's thought.' She swung away from him and stalked towards the door, but in two strides he was there before her, presenting her with the clearest challenge she had ever faced. The look that passed between them, so unlike the enigmatic exchange at suppertime, was of unbridled hostility on her part and total resolution on his.

Juliet Landon lives in an ancient country village in the north of England with her retired scientist husband. Her keen interest in embroidery, art and history, together with a fertile imagination, make writing historical novels a favourite occupation. She finds the research particularly exciting, especially the early medieval period and the fascinating laws concerning women in particular, and their struggle for survival in a man's world.

Recent titles by the same author:

THE PASSIONATE PILGRIM

THE MAIDEN'S ABDUCTION

Juliet Landon

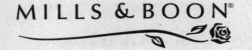

MILLS & BOON®

First published in Great Britain 2000
Harlequin Mills & Boon Limited,
Eton House, 18-24 Paradise Road, Richmond, Surrey TW9 1SR

© Juliet Landon 2000

ISBN 0 263 82334 2

Set in Times Roman 10½ on 12½ pt.
04-0101-73732

Printed and bound in Spain
by Litografía Rosés S.A., Barcelona

Chapter One

A crust of rooftops edged the distant horizon and, beyond them, a narrow sliver of shining sea suspended the last light of day above the dark, wine-rich tide that wafted its own unmistakable scent across the moorland. The three riders halted, held by its magic.

'Is that it?' Isolde whispered. 'The sea? That shining?'

The young man at her side smiled and eased his weight forward out of the saddle. 'That's it. Wait till tomorrow, then you'll see how big it is. Can you smell it?' He watched her take a deep lungful of air and hold it, savouring its essence.

She breathed out on a laugh and nodded. 'So that's Scarborough, then. What a trek, Bard.'

'I told you we'd get there in one day. Come on.'

'Only just.' Isolde turned to look over her shoulder, searching the rosy western sky and darkening wind-bent hawthorns. 'You don't think they'll—?'

'No! Course they won't. Come.'

The third rider pursed her lips, holding back the re-

tort which would have betrayed to her mistress a certain distrust of Bard La Vallon's optimism. A pessimist
she was not, but this wild goose-chase to Scarborough
was hardly the answer to their problem, such as it was.

For one thing, she did not believe Isolde thought any
more of La Vallon than she had about any of the other
bold young lads who sought to make an impression
month after month, year after year. Nor was it a yearning to see the sea that had drawn her all the way from
York in one day, though she was as good in the saddle
as any man. Mistress Cecily stayed a pace or two behind them on the stony track, caught by the pink halo
shimmering through Isolde's wild red curls, as fascinated by the girl's beauty after nineteen years as she
had been at her birth. The stifled retort gained momentum at each uncomfortable jolt of the hardy fell pony
beneath her. *Of course they'll come after us, child,
once they discover which direction we've taken.*

As if in reply to her maid's unspoken words, Isolde
called to her, holding a mass of wind-blown hair away
to one side, 'They'll think we've gone back home, Cecily, won't they?'

'Course, love. That'll be their first thought. Unless…'

'Unless what?'

Sensing that the matronly Mistress Cecily was about
to contribute some unnecessary logic to the serenity of
the moment, Bard drew Isolde's attention to the Norman castle silhouetted against the sea over to the left
of the town, making Cecily's reply redundant.

It had been this same Bardolph La Vallon whose

untimely interest in Isolde had caused her father, Sir Gillan Medwin, to pack her off in haste to York and there to remain in the safekeeping of Alderman Henry Fryde and his family. No explanation for this severe reaction was needed by anyone in the locality, for the feuding between the Medwins and the La Vallons spanned at least four generations, and the idea of any liaison between their members could not be evenly remotely considered. As soon as the days had begun to lengthen in the high northern dales and the sun to gain strength above the limestone hills, the reprisals had begun again: the stealing of sheep and oxen, the damming of the river above Medwin's mills, the firing of a new hayrick and, most recently, the near-killing of a La Vallon tenant.

On discovering that his daughter Isolde had actually given some encouragement to the younger La Vallon, Sir Gillan had acted with a predictable and terrifying swiftness to put a stop to it, not only because of the enmity, but also because the likelihood of Bard La Vallon's reputation as a lecher exceeding his father's was almost a certainty. Between them, Rider La Vallon and his younger son had fathered a crop of black-haired and merry-eyed bairns now residing with their single mothers in Sir Gillan's dales' villages. How many were being reared as La Vallon tenants, heaven only knew, but Sir Gillan did not intend his daughter to produce one of them. Though his second wife had died scarcely seven weeks earlier, in the middle of June, he was willing to lose his only daughter also, for her safety's sake.

Mistress Cecily sighed, noting how the slice of silver

in the distance had narrowed, darkening the sky still more in sympathy with her concerns.

'Nearly there, Cecily. Hold on,' came Isolde's assurance.

'Yes, love.'

She had not expected the young swain to come chasing after them, nor did she believe that Isolde had cared one way or the other until she had come to realise what lay behind her father's choice of Henry Fryde as her guardian, a choice that took the form of Henry Fryde's twenty-three-year-old son Martin. Then, Isolde's need for any form of rescue as long as it came quickly was justifiable: even the motherly Cecily had no quarrel with that. So, when two days ago young Bard had appeared behind them in the great minster at York during one of the Mercers' Guild's interminable thanksgiving ceremonies, the hand that had clutched hers had made her wince with the pain of it.

'He'll take us away from here, Cecily,' Isolde had whispered to her that night, in bed.

'Back home, you mean? He'd not—'

'No, not back to my father. I'd not go back there now. You'll never guess what he's done. Bard told me today.'

'Who's done? Bard, or your father?'

'My father. I think he's taken leave of his senses,' she added.

'Why, what is it?'

'Bard says he's taken his sister.'

Cecily frowned at that, unable to overcome the confusion. 'Felicia?' she ventured.

'Yes, Bard's younger sister, Felicia. Father's taken her.'

'Where to?'

'Home. To live with him. He's *abducted* her, Cecily. And do you know what I think?' She was clearly set to tell her. 'I think he intended it when he sent me here to York because he knows that Rider La Vallon will stop at nothing to get her back. No one's ever done anything quite as extreme as that, have they? He must have known that if I were there, they'd do their utmost to get me. And heaven help me if they did. I'd be a mother by this time next year, would I not? All the same, I think it's an over-reaction, taking a La Vallon woman just because Bard showed an interest in me. He's old enough to be her father, after all.'

'She's twenty-one.'

'Young enough to be his daughter, Cecily.'

'Mmm, so you think going off with Bard La Vallon will make everything all right, do you? I don't.'

'No, dearest.' In the dark, Isolde softened, kissing the ample cheek of her nurse and maid, the one who had helped her into the world and her mother out of it at the same time. 'But it's a chance to take control of my life, for a change, and I'll not let it slip. He sent me here to be groomed for marriage to that lout downstairs. You know that, don't you?'

'Yes, that's fairly obvious.'

'And would *you* marry him, dearest?'

The snorts of derision combined to render them both speechless for some time and, when they could draw breath, it was Isolde who found enough to speak.

'Well, then, the alternative is to get out of this awful place just as soon as we can.'

The question of ethics, however, was one which could not easily be put aside. Cecily manoeuvred her white-bonneted head on the pillow to see her companion by the light of the mean tallow candle. 'But listen, love. That young scallywag was the reason your father sent you away in the first place, and you surely wouldn't disobey your father so openly, would you? And what of Alderman Fryde? Think of the position it will put him in. After all, he's responsible for you.'

There was a silence during which Cecily hoped Isolde's mind was veering towards filial duty, but the answer, when it came, proved determination rather than any wavering. 'Alderman Fryde,' Isolde said, quietly, 'is one of the…no, *the* most objectionable men I've ever met. I would not marry his disgusting son if he owned the whole of York, nor shall I stay in this unhappy place a moment longer than I have to. Did you see Dame Margaret's face this morning?'

'Yes, I did.'

'He's been beating her again. The second time this week. I heard him.'

'You shouldn't have been listening, love.'

'I didn't have to listen. And that chaplain was smirking all over his chops, and I know for a fact that he's been telling Master Fryde what I said to him in confession about Bard.'

'No…oh, no! He couldn't. Wouldn't!'

'He has, Cecily. I know it. He's a troublemaker.'

There was another silence until Isolde continued. 'Bard has a cousin at Scarborough.'

'A likely story.'

'I believe him. He says we'll be able to stay there awhile and see the sea. He says they'll be pleased to see us.'

'The cousin is married?'

'Yes, with a family. I cannot go home, Cecily dearest, you know that.' She had heard disapproval in the flat voice, the refusal to share the excitement for its own sake. Cecily liked things cut and dried. 'I cannot. Not with Bard's sister a prisoner there and my father fearful for our safety. God knows what he's doing with her,' she whispered as an afterthought.

'Never mind what he's doing with her, child. What d'ye think young La Vallon's doing with *you*? Has it not occurred to ye once that he's come all this way to avenge his sister? I don't know how your father can explain the taking of a man's only daughter, even to prolong a feud, but allowing yourself to be stolen doesn't make much sense either, does it? You were talking just now of him being fearful of your safety, but just wait till he finds out who you're with, then he'll fear for sure. As for being a mother within the year—'

'Cecily!' The pillow squeaked under the sudden movement.

'Aye?' The voice was solid, uncompromising.

'We haven't got that far. Nowhere near.'

'*No*where near?'

'No.'

'Then that's another thing he'll have come for; to get a bit nearer.'

Isolde's smile came through her words as she nipped out the smoking candle. 'Stop worrying,' she said. 'I'm nineteen, remember?'

'And well in control, eh?'

'Yes. Goodnight, dear one.'

At last, Cecily smiled. 'Night, love.'

There had been no need to request Cecily's help for there had never been a time of withholding it but, even so, it was to the accompaniment of the maid's snores that Isolde's thoughts raced towards the morrow with the city's bells and the crier's assurances that all was well.

Apart from regretting the theft of Master Fryde's horses, all *had* been well, and since the Frydes believed she was visiting the nuns at Clementhorpe, just outside the city, there seemed to be no reason why anyone should miss her for some time. They had dressed simply to avoid attention taking a packhorse for their luggage and food from the kitchen which, to the Fryde household, had all the appearance of almsgivings to be passed on to the poor. It had not been a difficult deception, their clothes being what they were, unfashionable, plain and serviceable, reflecting a country lifestyle whose nearest town was Schepeton, which usually had more sheep than people.

Until they had reached York, neither of them had had any inkling of what wealthy merchants' wives were wearing, nor of the mercers' shops full of colourful fabrics that Isolde had seen only in her dreams.

Ships bearing cargoes of wine, spices, flax, grain, timber and exotic foods sailed up the rivers past Hull and Selby as far as York, but Isolde had so far been kept well away from the merchants' busy wharves. Nor had she been allowed a chance to complete her metamorphosis from chrysalis to butterfly, for the money that her father had given her was, at Master Fryde's insistence, placed in his money chest for safekeeping, and now a few gold pieces in her belt-purse was all she had. The faded blue high-waisted bodice and skirt was of good Halifax wool, but not to be compared to the velvets and richly patterned brocades that had so nearly been within her reach, had she stayed longer. Her fur trims were of coney instead of squirrel and the modest heart-shaped roll and embroidered side-pieces into which she had tucked her red hair for her arrival in York was a proclamation to all and sundry that she was a country lass sadly out of touch with fashion. Her longing for gauze streamers, jewelled cauls, horns and butterflies with wires was still unfulfilled, her eyebrows and hairline still unplucked for want of a pair of tweezers and some privacy.

Leaving the outskirts of York in the early-morning sunshine, she had tied up her hair into a thick bunch, but Bard had soon pulled it free to fly in the wind and over her face, laughing as she had to spit it out with her scolding. Her dark-lashed green-brown eyes, petite nose and exquisite cheekbones reminded Bard of his main reason for coming and, leaning towards her, he whispered in her ear, 'When do I get to kiss that beautiful mouth, my lady? Must I die of lust before we reach Scarborough?'

If he had mentioned love instead of lust, her heart might have softened, but she was not so innocent that she believed the two to be synonymous, nor did Bard La Vallon melt her heart or occupy her thoughts night and day as the lasses back home had described. Lacking an extensive vocabulary, they had defined the state of being in love more by giggles than by facts, giving Isolde no reason to suppose that it could be anything other than pleasurable. But Bard had presented her with a convenient means of escape from a bleak future, that was all; he was not suitable husband material. How long he would stay by her once he discovered the state of her mind was anyone's guess, but Cecily had said to take one step at a time without elaborating on the speed.

The attire which had caused so much self-consciousness in York could hardly have been more suitable for the small town of Scarborough on the North Sea coast of Yorkshire; though it was by no means a sleepy place, it bore no comparison to the ever-wakeful minster city where ships swept up the river and docked with well-oiled smoothness against the accommodating quayside. In the dusk, they passed with quickened steps the gibbet upon which an unidentifiable grey body swayed heavily in the sea breeze and then, looming ahead across a deep ditch and rampart, appeared the great square tower in the town wall through which they must pass.

'Newburgh Gate,' Bard told them. 'I'll go through first with the packhorse; you follow.'

'Just in time, young man,' the gatekeeper told him. 'Sun's nearly down.'

Bard thanked him and gave him a penny as the massive door was slammed into place behind them and barred for the night. He led them through the main street littered with the debris of market day, where they slithered on offal by the butchers' shambles and scattered a pack of snarling dogs. Veering towards the eastern part of town, they glimpsed the grey shine of a calm sea and heard its lapping between the houses, smelt the mingled scents of fish and broth through the open doors and felt the curious stares of the occupants.

'You didn't tell me their name,' Isolde called to Bard.

'Brakespeare,' he said over his shoulder. 'John and Elizabeth. And a little 'un. At least, he was little thirteen years ago.'

'When you were ten? That's when you last saw them?'

'Aye, must have been.'

'Then he'll not be so little, will he?'

Bard smiled and said no more. Blithely, he had told Isolde of his cousin, John Brakespeare, merchant of Scarborough, giving her the impression that they were in constant, if sporadic, communication. But his promise of a warm welcome was founded only on hope after so long a silence: his father was not a man to foster family connections which his own behaviour had done so little to justify, and for all Bard knew they might have gone to live elsewhere.

The house he remembered as a ten-year-old was still there at the base of a steep-sided hill where a conglomeration of thatched and slated houses slithered down towards the harbour and the salt-smelling sea. As a merchant's house, it was one of the largest to have direct access to the quay, stone-tiled and narrow-fronted but three storeys high, each tier slightly overhanging the one below. Its corner position and courtyard allowed it more windows on its inner face than its outer, as if shying away from the full force of the wind. Dark and bulky boats were tethered at the far side of the cobbled quay, and lanterns swung and bobbed further out on the water, the black masts of ships piercing the deepening sky like spears.

The echo of the horses' hooves in the courtyard attracted the immediate attention of two well-built lads who emerged from the stable at one side. Clearly puzzled by the intrusion, they waited.

'Hey, lad!' Bard called. 'Is your master at home?'

The taller of the two glanced at the other, frowned, and regarded the waiting group without a word. Isolde was treated to a longer scrutiny.

'D'ye hear me? Where's your master, John Brakespeare, eh?'

The lad came forward at last to stand by Bard's side and, though he wore the plain dress of a servant, spoke with authority. 'How long is it since you were here in Scarborough, sir?'

Nonplussed, Bard sensed the relevance of the question. 'Thirteen years, or thereabouts. Am I mistaken? John Brakespeare no longer lives here?'

'Indeed he does, sir. I am John Brakespeare and this is my younger brother Francis. How can I be of service to you?'

Bard let out a long slow breath and dismounted. 'I beg your pardon, John. Your father…?'

'Died thirteen years ago. And you, sir?'

'Bardolph La Vallon at your service. Your cousin, lad.'

'Francis!' With a nod, John Brakespeare sent his brother off towards the largest of the iron-bound doors, but it opened before he reached it, silhouetting a man's large frame against the soft light from within. His head almost touched the top curve of the door frame and, when he stepped outside and laid an arm across the younger lad's shoulder in a protective gesture, the contrast with Bard's lightweight stature was made all the more apparent.

John Brakespeare was clearly relieved by this telepathy. 'Silas?' he said, stepping backwards.

Whilst being blessed with the deep voice and vibrant timbre of a harp's bass strings, the man called Silas had the curtest of greetings to hand. 'Bard. Well, well. What the hell are you doing here? So you've lost your wits, too?'

'Brother! *You* here? What—?'

'Aye, a good word, that. *What*. And who's this?' He glanced rudely, Isolde thought, towards herself and Cecily.

That in itself was enough. Stooping from the saddle,

she grabbed at the reins of the packhorse, dug her heels sharply into the flanks of her tired mare and hauled both animals' heads towards the entrance of the court-yard, pulling them into a clattering trot as she heard Cecily do the same. She got no further than the cobbled quay outside before she heard Cecily yelp.

'Let go! Let go, I say! I must follow my mistress!'

Grinding her teeth in anger, Isolde came to a halt and turned to face the arrested maid, the bridle of whose horse was firmly in the hands of Bard's large and unwelcoming brother. 'Let her go, sir! Mistress Cecily comes with me!' she called.

'Mistress Cecily stays here.'

Pause.

'Then I shall have to go without her.'

'As you please.' He led Cecily's horse back into the courtyard entrance without a second look, heedless of the rider's wail of despair.

'From the frying-pan into the fire,' Isolde muttered in fury, once again reversing direction to follow her maid. 'From one interfering and obnoxiously over-bearing host to another. And this one a La Vallon, of all things. What in God's name have I done to deserve this, I wonder?' She was still muttering the last plain-tive enquiry when her bridle was caught and she was brought back to face the indignation of the younger La Vallon.

'Where are you off to, for pity's sake?' Bard de-manded. 'We've only just got here and you fly off the handle like—'

'I did not ask to come here,' she snapped, attempting

to yank the reins out of Silas La Vallon's hands without success. 'And it's quite clear we are not as welcome as you thought we'd be. There must be an inn somewhere in Scarborough. If it's my horse you want, Master La Vallon—' she leapt down from the wrong side of the saddle to avoid him '—you can take it. I'll take my panniers and my maid. Medwins do not willingly keep company with La Vallons.'

'You brought her here against her will, brother, did you?'

'Of course I didn't,' Bard said. 'She's tired, that's all.'

'That is not all,' Isolde insisted, attempting to unbuckle a pannier from the wooden frame of the packhorse. 'Oh! Drat this thing!' Her hair, still loose and unruly, had snagged on the prong of the buckle and was holding her captive in a position where she could not see how to loose it. Indifferent to the loss she would sustain, she pulled, but her wrist was held off by a powerful hand.

'Easy, lass! Calm down!' Silas La Vallon told her, holding her with one hand and lifting the taut strap with the other. 'There, loose it now. See? 'Twould be a small enough loss from *that* thatch,' he said, studying the wild red mass glowing in the light from the doorway, 'but a pity to waste it on a pannier. Now, come inside, if you will, and meet the lads' mother. She's probably never seen a real live Medwin before. Take the panniers inside, lads.'

Refusing to unbend, and smarting from the man's initial rudeness, she pulled her mop of hair back into some semblance of order with both hands, attempting to present a more dignified appearance before it was too late. In doing so, she had apparently no notion of the effect this had on at least three of the male audience, revealing the beautiful bones of her cheeks and chin, the lovely brow and graceful curve of her long neck, back and slender arms, the pile of brilliant hair that refused to be contained. Her dark lashes could not conceal the quick dart of anger in her eyes as young John Brakespeare dropped one side of the pannier and then the other with a crash, bouncing open the lid and spilling its contents.

'Thank you, but no. Your wife is clearly not expecting guests, and I would be the last one to impose—'

Young Francis Brakespeare, silent until now, exploded with laughter and nudged the elder La Vallon impudently. 'Eh, he's my mother's cousin, lady, not her *husband*. He's never stood still long enough to get himself wed, hasn't Silas.'

'I doubt if standing still would make a scrap of difference,' Isolde bit back at him, striding over to rescue the last of the contents from the cobbles. 'Your hero has a far greater problem than that, young man.' She stood to face Silas, her arms draped with old clothes. 'Now, despite your cousin's disappointment at not seeing a Medwin, after all, I bid you good evening, sir. I pray she will recover soon enough. Cecily, come!'

'Mistress...wait!' A lady's voice called from the doorway. 'Please stay.' From the other side of Bard's horse, a woman of Isolde's height stepped through the doorway into the courtyard and so, after all that, it was not the combined mass of the two La Vallon brothers that prevented Isolde's departure, but the genuine appeal in the woman's invitation that was the very nature of sincerity. Her hands were held out towards Isolde and her perplexed maid, and instantly their reaction was to go with her and to be led into a candle-lit hall where the air smelled warmly of lavender, beeswax, spices and new-baked bread.

'Dame Brakespeare?' Isolde said.

'Elizabeth,' the woman replied, smiling. 'You must be tired after such a long ride.'

Isolde did not pause to think how Dame Elizabeth knew the length of her journey, only that she could not, of course, have been Silas La Vallon's wife, for she was some years older than he, with two growing sons. Nevertheless, she was darkly attractive, her figure still shapely and supple, her dark eyes lit with a gentle kindness, like her voice. Her gown of soft madder-red linen hung in folds from an enamel link-girdle beneath her breasts and the deep V of her bodice was filled with the whitest embroidered chemise Isolde had ever seen. Her hair, except for dark tendrils upon her neck, was captured inside a huge swathed turban of shot blue-red silk that caught the light as she moved, changing colour, and Isolde was sure it must have been wired or weighted heavily.

'Dame Brakesp— Elizabeth,' Isolde corrected herself, 'may I present Mistress Cecily to you? She's been with me since I was born.' As the two women made their courtesies, Isolde took one more opportunity to extricate themselves from the situation. 'Dame Elizabeth, we cannot impose ourselves upon you like this. You see, I am Sir Gillan Medwin's daughter, and had I known that Bard's brother lived here, I would never have agreed to come.'

Silas La Vallon surged into the hall, bringing his brother and cousins with him like a shoal of fish. 'And Bard would not have come, either, if he'd known I was here. Would you, lad?' His initial surprise had turned to amusement.

Flushing with the effort of protest, Bard rose to the bait. 'Probably not, brother. Last time I heard of your whereabouts you were a freeman of York, a merchant, no less. But you can understand why I didn't spend time looking for you, surely? What do you do here at Scarborough?'

'I visit my cousins. What does it look like?'

In the light of the hall, Isolde could see more clearly than ever that Silas La Vallon had little in common with his younger brother except excessive good looks. It was, she thought, as if their mother had used up her best efforts on the first-born and from then on could manage only diluted versions. Whereas Bard was tall and willowy, Silas was tall and powerful, wide-shouldered, deep-chested and stronger of face. His chin was squarer than Bard's, the crinkles around his eyes supplanting his brother's beguiling air of innocence with an expression of extreme astuteness, which was only one of the reasons why Isolde found it impossible to meet them for more than a glance. Unlike his brother's stylish level trim, Silas's hair fell in silken

layers around his head where his fingers had no doubt
combed it back against its inclination, and somehow
Isolde knew that the look other men strived for was
here uncontrived, for his whole manner, despite the
well-cut clothes, exuded a complete lack of pretension.
Bard's cultivated seduction techniques drew women to
him like magnets: his brother's scorn of any such devices would leave many women baffled. *And hence the
unmarried state*, she thought sourly. She found herself
praying that Bard had not mentioned her father's abduction of their sister: things were bad enough; that
would only make them worse.

Dame Elizabeth was more forthcoming about the
reason for Silas's presence at her home, and the glance
she sent him was a clear rebuke for teasing his brother
with a false picture. She explained to Isolde. 'Silas was
my late husband's apprentice, you see, and I continue
his business as a Scarborough merchant.' She accepted
Isolde's astonishment with composure. 'Yes, we're a
select breed, but not unknown. There are several
women among the Merchant Adventurers of York, but
only myself at Scarborough. Now that Silas is a merchant in his own right, we assist each other as merchants do. He's been like a second husband in so many
ways.' She felt the sudden jerk of attention at the last
phrase and stammered an explanation. 'I mean, in putting trade my way, and...'

But it was too late. Silas's arm was about her shoulders, hugging her to his side with a soft laugh. 'Alas,
brother, she's as fickle as the rest. She'll not let me
near her. Besides, she has these two wolfhounds to

keep me at bay.' He ruffled the hair of the elder one, who dodged away from the affectionate hand and, keeping his eyes on Isolde, smoothed it down again.

'I shall take over the business eventually,' John said.

'Your father would be very proud to know that,' Isolde replied, gravely.

The courtesy of the gentle Brakespeare family was far removed from that of the Frydes in York, for all the latter's status and conspicuous wealth and, sensing the two women's unease and extreme tiredness, Dame Elizabeth insisted that further questions should be left until they had refreshed themselves. 'I always keep at least one room for guests,' she said, leading them out of the hall towards a flight of stairs. 'It's a large house, but we seem to fill it with ease nowadays.'

'Your sons are a credit to you, Dame Elizabeth,' Cecily said, following the lantern across a landing wide enough for several makeshift beds.

The proud mother threw a smile over her shoulder. 'I was carrying my little Francis when I lost my husband. A pity they never met; they're so alike. A great comfort. And Silas, of course. He's something between a father and an older brother to them, but I agree with you, Mistress Isolde, that one La Vallon at a time is more than enough for any woman. I'll try to keep him out of your way, if I can. Ah, here we are. Thank you, Emmie.'

A genial maid was laying out linen towels on the large canopied bed. She swiped a flat hand across the coverlet, bobbed a curtsy, and stepped through the door which was little more than a hole cut into the panelling.

Their shadows closed about them, and dissolved as they met the light from within that revealed a pot-pourri of floral colours spilling over the bed and on to the ankle-deep sheep's fleece at one side. After their days of mental and physical discomfort at York, the contrast was almost too much for Isolde, and her impulse was to embrace her hostess, who patted her back and assured them that hot water would be brought up and that supper would be ready as soon as they were.

Side by side, Isolde and Cecily sat upon the rug-covered chest at the end of the bed and looked about them at the details of comfort: the tiny jug of marigolds, the embroidered canopy of the bed, the cushioned prie-dieu in the corner and its leatherbound book of hours. Isolde placed a hand upon her cheek, still confused.

Cecily placed a finger to her lips. 'Keep your voice down,' she whispered. 'These walls are like paper.'

Isolde nodded. She had no intention of making the La Vallon brothers party to her thoughts. 'Did *you* know that there was an elder brother?'

'Yes, I knew. He was sent off when you were about six.'

'Doesn't appear to think much of his brother.'

Cecily's greying eyebrows lifted into her close-fitting head-dress. 'No, and nor do I. He was no more sure of a welcome here than we were, and he had no business putting you in this position. Or any of us,' she added. 'And we can't stay more than one night. We must leave here tomorrow. One La Vallon is bad enough, but two of 'em is dangerous, and that's a fact.'

'I'd have left tonight if I'd had my way.'

'Tomorrow. First thing.' Cecily held up the finger again. 'Now, don't you go being rude to that Silas. That would embarrass Dame Elizabeth and her sons.'

Isolde's face tightened as she poked one toe at the basketwork pannier. 'Monster! Did you notice his short jerkin? Hardly covered his bottom.'

The finger crooked and touched Isolde's chin. 'So, you had time to notice his bottom, did you? Come in!' she called to the door. 'Wait! I'll open it for you.' A maid waited outside to escort them to the hall.

Accordingly, Isolde's eyes were held well away from glimpses of heavily muscled buttocks to pay increasing attention to the array of food which, after their unsavoury days in York, was a feast worth sharing, even with monsters. The hall had been set with tables and was now busy with servants who arranged white linen cloths, pewter plates, silver knives and tall glass goblets. One man, older than the rest, stood at the huge silver-covered dresser, letting wine chortle merrily out of casks into pewter ewers, while the younger Brakespeare threw soft tapestries over the benches behind the table.

'We don't stand on ceremony at suppertime,' Dame Elizabeth said, coming across to meet them.

Ceremony or not, it was the best meal Isolde had had in weeks, only slightly marred by being seated next to an over-attentive John Brakespeare on one side and an unnecessarily possessive Bard on the other, whose hand seemed unable to find its way from her knee and thigh to the table. Finally, in exasperation, she took his hand forcibly in hers and slammed it heavily upon the table, thrusting a knife between its fingers. By some mischance, this was noticed by the elder La Vallon who, at that moment, had leaned forward from three places down the table to speak to his brother. But although she sensed the exchange of significant looks between them nothing was said, to Isolde's intense relief.

Under the watchful eyes of the steward, dish after dish was presented to the table, for the family had now swollen to include Dame Elizabeth's father and the other members of her household. Served by two apprentices and four kitchen servants, this made a household as large as the Frydes', a surprising revelation which gave Isolde some indication of Dame Elizabeth's success as a merchant. There was cabbage, onion and leek soup served with strands of crispy bacon, chicken pasties, cold salmon and fresh herrings in an egg sauce, mussels, whelks, cockles and oysters, cheeses, figs and raisins, manchets of finest white flour and crusty girdle breads yellowed with saffron for dipping into spiced sauces. It was the first time Isolde had eaten fresh herring.

'They come from Iceland,' John told her. 'Silas brings them.'

She would have liked to ask where Iceland was, but instead she mopped up the thick almondy sauce and wondered reluctantly which morsels to leave on her plate for the sake of politeness. The wine was of the finest, and her inclination was to watch the pale honey-coloured liquid bounce again into her glass from the servant's ewer, but something warned her to beware, and she place a hand over the rim, at the same time becoming aware of someone's eyes upon her, drawing her to meet them. From a corner of her eye, she noticed Dame Elizabeth lean towards her aged father, the servants' white napkins, the glint of light on glass and silver, but her eyes were held by two steady dark-brown ones beneath steeply angled brows, and for a timeless moment there was nothing in the room except that. No sound, no taste, no touch, no delicious smell of food. Then she remembered to breathe and found it difficult, for her lungs had forgotten how until her glance wavered and fell, her composure with it, and the bold stare she had practised so often upon younger men too far away to recall.

She turned to Bard, but he saw the signs of weariness there and took her hand. 'Bed, I think. Enough for one day, eh? We'll sort out what's to be done tomorrow, shall we?'

'We must go early,' she said with some urgency.

'Go?'

'Yes. Go back, Bard. Just go. Early.'

He blinked, but kept his voice low to her ear. 'He'll probably be going off tomorrow, sweetheart. Let's wait and see, shall we?'

She sighed, too weary to argue.

The warmth of the summer evening and the clinging heat of Cecily's ample body next to hers overrode Isolde's tiredness and forced her out of bed towards the window that chopped the pale moonlit sky into lozenges. Only the wealthiest people could afford to glaze their windows, and even the strips of lead were expensive. The catch was already undone; as she knelt upon the wooden clothes-chest to push it open wider, men's voices rose and fell on the still night air, below her on the quay. She leaned forward, easing the window out with one finger, recognising Bard's voice and its deep musical relative.

'Has it not occurred to you, lad?' Silas was saying, impatiently.

'She was with that—'

'I know who she was with. I have a house and servants in York who keep me informed of what's happening while I'm away. But have ye no care for Elizabeth and her lads? Have you any right to put her entire household at risk by chasing down here with her? God's truth, lad, you're as thoughtless as ever where a bit of skirt's involved.'

'That's not fair, Silas. He's not all that dangerous, surely?'

'Have you ever met him?'

'No. I saw him in the minster, though.'

'Then you'll have to take my word for it that Elizabeth had better not be on the receiving end of his attention. Nor must she know exactly who the lass was staying with, or she'll be worried sick.'

'Who will?'

'Elizabeth, you fool. Who d'ye think I mean? It's her safety I'm concerned about. Your lass has little to lose now, has she?'

'I wouldn't say that.'

There was a silence in which Isolde knew they were laughing.

'You must leave tomorrow, Bard, at first light.'

'But I've told her—'

'I don't care what you've told her. You leave at dawn and get back to York. I won't have that maniac chasing down here to reclaim either the girl or his bloody horses, just because your braies are afire.'

'Silas, it's not just—' Bard protested.

'Ssh…all right, all right. I suppose you can't help it if you take after Father. If I'd stayed longer I might have been the same, God knows.'

'But what the hell are we going to do in York, Silas? Can we stay at your house?'

'I'll help you out, lad. I've thought of a plan. Fool-proof. But you'll have to trust me, both of you.'

'I do, Silas, but I can't vouch for Isolde.'

A breeze lifted off the water and sent a dark line of ripples lapping at the harbour wall and Isolde's skin prickled beneath her hair.

'Come inside. I'll tell you about it.'

She waited, then tiptoed back to the bed and sat on its soft feathery edge until her mind began to quieten.

Chapter Two

Isolde's resentment, dormant only during the short bouts of sleep, surfaced again at the first screeching calls of the seagulls that swooped across the harbour, rising faster than the sun itself. From a belief that she was taking control of her life, she now saw that, after only a matter of hours, it was once more in someone else's hands. The two La Vallons, to be exact. Not a record to be proud of. In her heart, she had already made up her mind that a protracted stay at the Brakespeares' house was impossible, a decision that Bard's brother had endorsed in no uncertain terms, but to be packed off so unceremoniously back to York like a common servant—a bit of skirt, he had said—was humiliating to say the least. First a thorn in her father's side, next a potential trophy for a halfwit, and now an embarrassment.

Well, she would return to York with the remnants of her dignity, but not to stay. There was Allard at Cambridge, for instance, the older brother who had never once failed to mention on his visits home how

he wished she'd go and keep house for him. A student
of medicine in his final year at the university, he lived
in his lodgings where time to care for himself properly
had dwindled to nothing. Allard would welcome her
and Mistress Cecily, for hers was as kind an older
brother as anyone could wish for. Sean, their fifteen-
year-old half-brother, was like him in many ways, stu-
dious and mentally absent from much of what went on
around him, too preoccupied with copying books borrowed from the nearby abbeys to remember what day
it was. Isolde did not know whether Sean had been
distressed by his mother's recent death or whether he
had merely put a brave face on it for his father's sake.
He was not one to disclose his state of mind, as she
did, and she had often wondered whether his books
took him away from a world in which he felt at odds.
If she regretted leaving anyone, it was Sean. Who
would wash his hair for him now? Or his ears and neck,
for that matter? Should she return home, after all?

If she had thought to impress them by her dawn appearance, fully dressed and ready to begin her exodus
unbidden, the wind was removed from her sails by the
sight of a household already astir, well into its daily
preparations and not a hint of surprise at her eagerness
to be away. The plan outlined to Bard last night by his
overbearing brother no doubt concerned what he was
to do at York, once they arrived, and was of no real
interest to her at that moment. So when he drew her
forward into a small and comfortable parlour hung with
softly patterned rugs and deep with fresh rushes, she
was not best pleased to be joined by Silas La Vallon,

especially in the middle of a kiss that was neither expected nor welcome.

A servant followed him with a tray of bread rolls, cheese, ale, a dish of shrimps and a bowl of apples, one of which Silas threw up into the air, caught it without taking his eyes off the hastily separating pair, and noisily bit, enjoying Isolde's confusion as much as Bard's almost swaggering satisfaction.

Isolde scowled and took the mug of ale which the servant offered, observing Silas's ridiculous sleeves that dripped off the points of his elbows as far as his knees. His thigh-length gown was a miracle of pleats and padding that accentuated the width of his great shoulders, and in place of last night's pointed shoes he wore thigh-length travelling boots of softly wrinkled plum-coloured leather edged with olive-green, like his under-sleeves.

With a mouth full of apple, he invited her to sit and, with another ripping crunch at the unfortunate fruit, sat opposite her and leaned against the patterned rug.

Feeling the discomfort of his unrelenting perusal, she turned her attention to Bard and, with a businesslike coolness, said, 'What is all this about, Bard? We've a fair way to go, remember, and Mistress Cecily has barely recovered from yesterday.'

Bard swung a stool up with one hand and placed it near hers, sitting astride it. 'Yes, that's one of the reasons why Silas has agreed to help us out, sweetheart,' he said, taking one of her hands. 'We think it would be for the best if Mistress Cecily was given time to recover while I take the horses back to York alone.'

Without taking a moment to consider, Isolde countered, 'Oh, no. We shall not stay here. I'm resolved to leave immediately.'

Silas intervened, having no qualms about getting straight to the point and being less daunted by Isolde's fierceness. 'No, not to stay here, mistress. We all know you can't do that.'

'Thank you,' she murmured, throwing him a murderous glance.

'I shall take you and your maid to York by ship, I've—'

'That you will *not*!'

'I've got to go there to unload some cargo, and I've—'

'No!'

'I've told Bard that it'll take a few days, four at most, depending on the wind, to get up-river past Hull to York. Then I'll drop you off with your maid and baggage, and you can—'

'No! I said *no*.'

Silas slapped the half-eaten apple hard on to the bench at his side and leapt to his feet, his voice biting with exasperation. 'In God's name, woman, will you listen to what I have to say before you—?'

Before three words were out, Isolde was up and facing him, eye to eye, Bard's comforting hand thrown aside. 'No, in God's name, I shall do no such thing, sir! I do not need you to make any plans for me, nor do I need your assistance to reach York. I am quite aware that your first concern is for Dame Elizabeth and that you are using Mistress Cecily's fatigue to pull the wool over my eyes. You care no more about her than you do about me, so don't take me for a fool, either of you. And if Alderman Fryde should come to Scarborough to search for me it'll be a miracle worth two of St. William's, because he doesn't have the wit to look beyond his own pockets. The first thing he'll do is send home to see if I'm there.' Her eyes were wide open and, this time, furiously unflinching.

Fascinated, Silas stuck his thumbs into the girdle that belted his hips. 'There now, wench, you've been wanting to let fly at me ever since you got here, haven't you? Feeling better now?'

'You mistake the matter, sir. I haven't given you a moment's thought.' She swung away from him and stalked towards the door, but in two strides he was there before her, his head up, presenting her with the clearest challenge she had ever faced. The look that passed between them, so unlike the enigmatic exchange at suppertime, was of unbridled hostility on her part and total resolution on his, but, having no notion of the form this might take, and not willing to try it out there and then, she appealed to Bard for help.

'Well? Don't sit there grinning! Tell him to move.'

Bard went to her, having difficulty with his grin. 'Nay, he's bigger than me, sweetheart. Come, you haven't heard the whole argument yet, and what you say is not correct, you know. We both care greatly for your safety, and that's why Silas's plan is a sound one. I can reach York much faster than the three of us, without a chance of you being seen by anyone. Silas can smuggle you ashore at York and I'll meet you there and then you can make up your mind what to do, whether to stay or go on. And Mistress Cecily won't have to suffer another day in the saddle.'

'No, she'd be seasick instead. She'd prefer that, I'm sure.'

'No, she won't,' Silas said. 'We're only going down the coast and the sea's as calm as a millpond. The river doesn't make anyone seasick.'

'And what about the horses? You can't make good speed leading three.'

'Silas is lending me a lad.'

'Then what, when you've got them to York? You take them back to Fryde's, do you, and apologise?'

'Isolde!' Bard's tone was gently scolding. 'Course not. I leave them where his men will find them, tied up outside the Merchant Adventurers' Hall, most likely. He'll not know where they've been or how they were returned, will he?'

On the face of it, the plan seemed to be reasonable enough, but nagging doubts showed in her eyes and in the uneasy twitch of her brows. These two were La Vallons. Silas must know of Felicia's abduction by now, for surely Bard had told him, unless he had been informed of it beforehand, as he had been about her own arrival in York. What he had not known, apparently, was that Bard would bring her to Scarborough, and that had unnerved him more than anything else, otherwise he would by this time have made some re-mark about her father's wickedness and his own sister's welfare. Since they had not thought fit to brandish this latest Medwin villainy before her, nor even to hint at her own vulnerability, she could only assume that her association with Bard was protecting her from reprisals. The elder brother was clearly the dominant of the two but, judging from the conversation they'd had last night on the quay, there was no enmity between them. Silas was willing to help his brother since this also relieved his own concerns for his cousin, whatever they were. She could hardly blame him, though the thought kept alive a flame of pique which she could put no name to.

Her silence was watched carefully and, when Bard opened his mouth ready to hurry her decision, a frown from Silas quelled the opening word.

'You are La Vallons,' she said at last. 'And I am a Medwin. I would be a fool to trust you, would I not?'

It was Silas who answered her. 'My brother is prejudiced and would deny any foolishness as a matter of course. For myself, I think you may not have been offered too many options these last few weeks, but that doesn't make you a fool. A few days at sea, a change of air, would give you some time to make a better decision. I can recommend it, mistress.'

'The company is not what I would have chosen.'

'There are books to read on board. Your maid will be with you. Plenty to see. We shall be there before you notice the company.'

'You'll be there at York, Bard?'

'I'll be there, sweetheart. Trust me. I promise I'll be there waiting.'

She sighed heavily, turning her head. 'My panniers

are packed. You intend sailing today, sir?' she said to
the bowl of apples, taking one to caress its waxy skin.

'We sail immediately. The tide will be at its height
in half an hour and the captain is waiting. Bard is
packed and ready to be away.'

'I see. So it was already decided.'

Neither of the brothers denied it. She was right, of
course.

Having seen nothing of Scarborough in the daylight,
Isolde was almost on the point of changing her mind
about leaving so soon, and the surprise at what lay
beyond the windows and doors of the merchant's large
house turned to a sadness that Bard took, typically, to
be for his farewell. It had not been so difficult to see
him go, only to believe, with regard to his reputation,
that he was trustworthy. Now that she was alone with
Cecily, she could think of few reasons why she had
agreed to place a similar kind of trust in his disagree-
able brother, who saw no need to keep up any pretence
of liking her.

Despite the sadness and doubting, her spirits were
buoyed up by the nearness of Dame Elizabeth's house
to the harbour, the vast expanse of sparkling sea beyond, the swaying masts of ships and the brown water
that reflected every shape and threw it crazily askew.
Houses lined the quay in an arc on one side, enclosing
the harbour on the other side by a wall of stone and
timber that extended from the base of a massive natural
mound at one side of the town. It was on top of this
mound that the Norman castle perched, which they'd

seen against the evening sky. Now it was being mobbed by screaming seagulls, some of which came in to land at Isolde's feet with beady, enquiring eyes and bold, flat-footed advances.

'I'm going,' she told them, on the brink of tears. 'I'm going and I've only just arrived.'

The breeze that had brought a welcome coolness into her bedchamber overnight had now lifted the sea into more than Silas La Vallon's hypothetical millpond, causing Cecily to clutch at her skirts, her head-dress and shawl all at the same time. 'I hope you know what you're doing, love,' she said.

No, dear Cecily. I have not the slightest idea what I'm doing.

Silas La Vallon's ship was also a surprise to her, for she had thought he meant one of the squat northern cogs that piled cargo up and down the rivers, one-masted, cramped, and serviceably plain. She had seen them at York, loaded with bales of cloth and smelly commodities, and it had been a measure of her temporary madness that she had agreed to sail with him even in one of those. But this was not a cog; it was a four-hundred-ton carrack, a three-masted beauty that sat proudly on the high tide outside Dame Elizabeth's door almost, a towering thing with decorated castles fore and aft, swarming with men and more ropes than a ropemaker's shop.

The men grinned and nudged and pulled in their stomachs, then got on with their swarming as she and Cecily were led aboard and introduced to the master, whose aquamarine eyes sparkled with intrigue in a skin of creased and burnished leather. And she looked hard and with genuine regret at the three who stood waving and calling last-minute instructions on the quayside. The two boys watched in fascination the men who hauled in unison, the sails that squeaked upwards, cracking and billowing, the majestic swing of the bow, and it was only Dame Elizabeth who noticed the quick brush of fingers across one cheek as it received her wind-blown kiss.

Or perhaps there was another who saw, who came to lean on the bulwark by her side to wave, then to point out the Brakespeares' house and its adjacent warehouse, King Richard's House over there, the old Roman lighthouse, and there, over to the left, the town gate through which Bard would already have passed.

'Yes, I see,' she said, straining her eyes to scan the road.

The town nestled closer on to the hillside as they passed beyond the harbour entrance and out into the open sea, holding itself steady as the ship took its first pulling lunges into the swell like a swimmer lengthening his stroke. She felt the lurch as the sails cracked open and the corresponding rush of exhilaration in the pit of her stomach, as though she stood on a live beast, and found ever more to see as the distance between them and the land increased, the prominent headland at one side with never-ending cliffs on the other. Below the cliffs were beaches where white-edged surf broke and mended again, then raced in upon the rocks further along, determined to smash uninterrupted.

'We didn't see any of this on our way here,' she said.

'You'd not have seen the cliffs or the rocks because you were above them,' Silas told her. He turned round and pointed across the deck. 'That's what you'd have seen.'

The water was a pure shimmering blue, bouncing sunlight and seagulls into the clear morning air, and Isolde was spellbound.

'You can eat your apple now,' he said.

It was still there, in her hand, and so she did, but was unable to hear her own crunching for the multitude of creaks and groans underfoot and the crashing roar of waves hurtling past. Nor did she taste a thing.

He left her alone after that, as if, having made sure she would not jump overboard, he could relax his guard. That was the cynical view she took of things, which was, perhaps, an inefficient tool to guard against the wayward thoughts to do with his nearness as he had leaned across her to point; the tiny red mark on his chin where he had cut himself shaving, the way the cuffs of his white cotton shirt clung to his beautiful hands. Silly, inconsequential things. Irritably, she brushed back the memory of his intimidating manner, despite her own defence, but it returned with masochistic glee to taunt her with every detail of their argument.

Finally, she went aft towards the shallow stairway, where a cabin was built high on to the stern of the ship, its sloping roof decorated with gold-painted finials and cut-work edgings. It was large enough only for

a wide bed built above a cupboard, a shelf that served
as a table over their luggage, and two large boxes in a
corner. Cecily was sitting upon one of them, hugging
a basin to her chest and groaning. Her face was grey.
Isolde took a blanket and wrapped it around her maid's
shoulders, helping her outside to the deck. 'Deep
breaths, love,' she said. 'Stay in the corner and go to
sleep.'

Food and wine were brought to them mid-morning:
cold meats and mussels, delicious patties and cherries,
none of which Cecily could look at but which Isolde
devoured to the last crumb. The wind was strengthen-
ing and the sea bore dark patches, and the high head-
dress swathed with a fine veiling was no longer an
appropriate statement of restored dignity. It would have
to come off again. She took Cecily back to the cabin,
wondering why the crew needed to carry a supply of
live chickens and two piglets from Scarborough to
York.

The glass-paned window that looked out directly
over the ship's wake began to streak with rain long
before Isolde noticed it, for the constant pitching and
tossing had made Cecily's first voyage memorable for
all the wrong reasons, and Isolde was disinclined to
leave her so wretchedly helpless. When she did emerge
from the cabin to replenish her lungs with fresh air, the
deluge of fine rain made her screw up her face and
draw her cloak more tightly across her shoulders as she
made her way across the slippery deck to the bulwarks.

'Where are we?' she asked one of the crew as he

turned to watch, holding out a hand to steady her. 'Where's the land?'

The man looked out into the bank of cloud as he pointed. 'Over there, lady. It'll be hidden for a bit until this lot clears.'

She sat on a wet wooden crate for safety. 'I thought we'd be staying within sight of it, going south.'

'Nay.' He smiled. 'If we had a northerly, now that'd be different: that'd blow us due south in record time. But we don't get northerlies in summer, do we? So we have to fill our sails with whatever we can catch, and then go from side to side, see? Like that.' He zig-zagged with his hand. 'Your old maid taken bad, is she?'

That sounded like a perfectly reasonable explanation, and it satisfied Isolde, who knew little either of geography or navigation. Once again, she settled herself against Cecily's unhappily sleeping bulk, covered herself with blankets, and began an examination of the leatherbound books on the shelf above her. Silas La Vallon had an interesting collection, though she had not thought his taste would run to stories about King Arthur, *La Belle Dame sans Merci*, the *Legend of Ladies*, or a *Disputation between Hope and Despair*, which proved to be not quite the help she had expected. The possibility that these might have been selected for her benefit flashed through her mind, but was dismissed. Darkness came before supper that evening, and the bucking of the ship and the consequent swinging of the lantern made reading difficult. And Silas La Vallon, to please her, kept well out of sight.

* * *

Sleeping had been a fitful and precarious business, noisy with shouts and pounding feet, howling wind, clattering sails and the constant rush of water all around them. Using the close-stool had in itself been an unexpected peril, especially when trying to manoeuvre Cecily on and off it, and, by first light, Isolde had realised that sleep and ships were incompatible.

After watering her maid with some of their precious ration, then suffering the inevitable consequences only moments later, Isolde clutched a blanket tightly around herself and left the cabin in an attempt to reassure herself that land did exist. A fine line of blue stretched across the horizon below the clouds. 'There!' she called to the master. 'Look! Is that it?'

He came through the door beneath the forecastle where she understood his cabin to be and joined her, cheerily. 'That's a bit o' blue sky, mistress. We might get a bit o' sun later, and a good westerly, by the feel o' things.'

'But that will blow us away from Hull, won't it? I thought we'd have been within reach of Hull by now.'

'Eh…no. We shan't be seeing Hull today.' He laughed, not bothering to explain. 'I'll send ye some food up, mistress, seeing as you're awake already. Did ye not sleep so well?'

'Not much,' she said, frowning.

'Aye, well. It's always worse on't first night. Better tonight, eh?'

Disappointed, she returned to the cabin and made an effort to straighten it, and when the cabin boy brought the tray tried with her most beguiling smile and a toss of her glorious red hair to bedazzle him. 'Who does this ship belong to?' she said, sweetly, taking the tray from him.

'Master Silas Mariner, mistress. He's the owner.'

'Silas *Mariner*? Ah, easier to say than La Vallon, yes?'

'Yes, mistress.'

'And where did you berth before you went to Scarborough?'

Like a man, he took the full force of her green eyes, smiled, and said, 'Sorry, mistress. If I want to keep my job, I have to keep my mouth shut.' He bowed, and closed the door quietly.

It was mid-day when Isolde tried yet again to elicit some information regarding direction, distance, time of arrival—anything concerning land or the lack of it. She made another attempt mid-afternoon, and again in the evening, by which time Master Silas Mariner-La Vallon had failed to return to his cabin in the forecastle before she appeared on deck.

'I realise that you are doing your best to avoid me, Master La Vallon,' Isolde said, as he turned to make a polite bow, 'and I am grateful for that. However, there is a problem which I need to discuss.'

'You are mistaken, mistress. I was not avoiding you but waiting for you. And I am aware of your problem. My crew are well trained. They have to be.'

The fear and anger that she had tried since dawn to contain took another leap into her chest, making her feel as if she had bumped into something solid. Her legs felt weak, but she allowed herself to be led over coils of rope and across the drying deck into his cabin, which was not the master's, after all. It was larger than hers, but wedge-shaped, the table piled with papers and instruments, ledgers, quills and inkpots.

As the cabin dipped and rose again, she held on to a wooden pillar and waited until he had closed the door before turning to him. Her voice held more than a hint of panic, which she had not intended. 'For the fiftieth time of asking, sir, where *are* we?' The words seemed to come from far away, adding to the sense of unreality that had dogged her all day, and, in the exaggerated pause between question and answer, she saw that he, too, had discarded the earlier formal attire for the barest essentials of comfort. His shirt, a padded doublet of soft plum-coloured leather and tight hose were his only concessions to the North Sea's cutting edge.

'I will show you,' he said. He brought forward a roll of parchment from a pile on the table and weighted its corners with a sextant, a conch shell, a glass of wine and one hand. 'There…' he pointed to the eastern coastline '…there is Scarborough, and this is where we are now, down here, see?' His finger trailed south-wards, passing Hull, where Isolde had expected to enter the estuary of the River Humber in order to reach York on the Ouse. His finger stopped some distance from the coast of Norfolk, nowhere near land.

Isolde felt herself trembling, but pulled herself up as tall as she could despite the tightness in her lungs. 'No,' she said, 'I don't see. I don't see at all. What's happened? Have we been blown off course by the storm? Is that it?'

Silas allowed the roll to spring back, and she knew by his slow straightening, his watchful air, his whole stance, that he was preparing for her reaction. His shaking head confirmed that there was more to come. 'No, mistress, there was no storm last night. That was just weather. We are on course.'

'On course for where? Hull is behind us now.'

'Yes. We are heading for Flanders. We always were.'

The room swam.

'No,' she said, breathless now. 'No, sir. *You* may be, but I am *not* heading for Flanders. Turn this ship round immediately. *Immediately!* Do you hear me?' She whirled, heading for the door, the master, anybody. But once again he was there before her, and this time, with no one to witness, he caught her in a bear hug and swung her round to face him, wedging her against the door with his body. All the defences that she had been taught, which were supposed to be crippling to an attacker, were useless, for her feet were somewhere to the side, her hands were splayed above her head, and the shock had numbed her. Worse still, the reality which had been hovering out of reach all day now descended with cruel precision, wounding her, making this new and frightening restraint all the more unbearable.

She fought him with all her strength, refusing to call for help. This was his ship. These were his men. No one would interfere. She was more alone than she had ever been before, and her anger roared in her ears. 'I was a fool to trust you,' she snarled, twisting in his grip. 'I was a *fool*. You and your confounded brother. I should have seen what was happening. This is for Felicia, isn't it? And I walked straight into the trap. Fool…fool…what an *idiot*!'

'If that's what you want to believe, believe it,' he said, drawing her hands slowly down to the small of her back. 'It makes little difference what you believe, except that you're going to Flanders.'

'I'm not going *anywhere* with you!'

'You'd have gone anywhere with my brother.'

'I would not! I had no intention of staying in York with him: I was using him to get away from that place, that's all. Otherwise I would never consort with a La Vallon.'

'You'll consort with the La Vallons whether you like it or not, wench.' He lifted her easily, as he would have done a child. 'And you're wrong again. My brother is no part of my plans.'

'I don't believe you. Put me down! No…oh, no!' The soft bed hit her with a thud from behind and then, as she rolled away, the panelled wall cracked into her forehead. Stunned and utterly confused, she felt him pull her back and capture her wrist, tucking her other arm safely behind his back where she felt only a broad expanse of silky leather. Immediately his long legs and body were sprawled across her, holding her immobile and shaming her by their closeness. His brother had never been as close to her as this. Never.

With closed eyes and clenched jaws, she waited for

what she was sure would happen next, though she had no details to guide her. When all she experienced was the deep rocking of the ship nosing its way through the water and the rhythmic thud-thud on the sides, she opened them, warily.

He was leaning on one elbow and looking down at her face, his eyes wandering over hair and skin and finally coming to rest in hers. 'Well?' he whispered. 'You think I'm about to rape you?'

She gulped. 'Aren't you?'

To her relief, he did not smile. 'No. You'll come to me without that.'

His sentiment was so totally absurd that it was not worth an answer, and she looked away disdainfully. The memory of his regard at supper had scarcely left her, and the details of his contact over the last twenty-four hours had imprinted themselves upon almost every one of her waking thoughts. But the idea that she would ever give herself to him willingly after this unforgivable treatment was quite ridiculous. She would take the first opportunity to free herself.

She squirmed, and felt his legs tighten their hold. 'This is unworthy of you, sir. Let me go now. You must know that this is not the way to avenge your family for the abduction of your sister. You knew—?'

'About Felicia and your father? Of course I knew. Even before Bard told me.'

So. That was what she had thought. 'And he plotted with you to do the same?'

'No, he didn't. I've told you, Bard is not part of my plans. He never has been.'

Her green eyes flashed like sunlight over mossy waters. 'Rubbish! Don't tell me he'll be standing there on the quay at York waiting for you to deliver me, as you said you'd do.'

'He will. He'll wait and wait, and then he'll begin to ask questions, and he'll discover that I'm not due at York. We called there before Scarborough, so the cargo we're carrying is for Flanders. Poor Bard.' His tone was anything but concerned, and Isolde was tempted to believe him.

'I believed you before, but I'll not do it again, sir.'

'That's sad. Now I shall have to resort to more believable methods.'

She realised what he was about to do, and, when she thought about it later, knew that she could have made it more difficult for him, though not impossible. But his eyes held her every bit as surely as they had done before, and she could already feel the warmth of him on her skin, see his head blotting out the last of the dim light in the recessed bunk. Her eyelids closed under the infinitely slow exploration of his lips upon her face, and even then she wondered why she was doing nothing to resist it. Bard's kisses had always held more than a hint of selfishness, intended to impress but never to close her mind, as she felt his brother's doing.

Slowly, and with practised skill, he kept her mouth waiting until she moved her head to follow him, luring her on towards the sublime capture, the first taste of his mouth on hers. And with restraint, without even hinting that this moment was, for him, the assuaging of an ache that had threatened to devour him, he left the full impact of it until she moaned and softened under him, until he felt one hand move impatiently across his back. Then he released her wrist and slid an arm beneath her back to gather her up to him as he had done during that long look which had so puzzled and intrigued her.

The reality of it far surpassed anything either of them could have imagined in the hours since they had met, and there had been plenty of imagining on both sides. Yet there was a part of her that remained on an even keel, despite the weightlessness of her mind and the amazing sensations of her body. A part that reminded her of what she was about. Between his kisses came the cautionary voice, urging her to resist before it was too late. *La Vallon. The enemy. Abduction. Flanders. Revenge.* Obedient to the warning, she pushed at his shoulder, then his chin, tearing her mouth away. 'No…no…no!'

He gave her a chance to offer reasons, but she could remember nothing that would have convinced him of her unwillingness except a turn of her head and more denials. His voice was husky with wanting. 'It's no wonder my brother came after you so fast, maid, if that's how it was with him, too.'

It was, she thought, a particularly insensitive remark for him to have made, and she was at once angered and sobered by the need to rebut it. How could he kiss her so and believe that her response was common to both brothers? If she had been able to read his mind, she would have seen there the instant regret of one who had been as much shaken as she. But by then it was too late.

She turned back quickly to wound him. 'I see. So it's that too, is it? To prove that you can so easily take what he wants from under his nose. Well, well. With a ship and a crew of this size and a woman as naïve as me, who couldn't? But don't think you'll ever have my co-operation, Master Silas Mariner. Now let me go back to Mistress Cecily. She needs me.'

He twisted a hand into her hair. 'It was you, remember, who brought up Bard's name, not once, but twice. If you find comparisons hard to bear, then think on the boyish pecks he gave you while I try to win your co-operation.' His kiss this time was intended to teach her the difference between a man and a boy, but she had already discovered that, and needed no further demonstration of the power and scope of his artistry. For the next few moments she needed all her strength not to cry out or to fight for survival, and there were tears of anger in her eyes at its conclusion.

'Let me go,' she croaked. 'Let me go back to—'

'You're not going anywhere. You'll stay here tonight, where I can guard you.'

'Against what? Jumping overboard? Cecily needs me, I tell you.'

'She doesn't. The ship's physician is with her. You're staying with me.'

'And what d'ye think that lot out there will be thinking, after this?'

'My master and crew are paid to sail the ship. They do as they're told and keep their mouths shut.'

'I cannot stay here…please.'

'Hush, now, maid. You've had a long day and you need to sleep. I shall not harm you.' He removed her shoes and straightened her skirts, then pulled blankets over them both, enclosing her against the bend of his body, stroking back her hair and caressing her back with tender hands.

She had hardly slept last night and, after a nerve-racking day, she was exhausted. Now, within the safety and comfort of his arms and the rocking of the ship, there were no more choices to be made or decisions to be met. Nevertheless, she summoned her iciest tones to fire a last salvo over her shoulder, to where his smile was already settling in. 'You can't do this, you know. You simply cannot *do* this.'

She heard the smile broaden. 'Remind me, maid, if you will. What is it that I cannot do?' His voice almost melted her.

'You cannot insist on sleeping with a woman who dislikes you, for one. Nor can you take her somewhere she doesn't want to go.'

'Forgive me.' He grinned, sweeping his fingertips down her neck. 'But we merchants are an optimistic bunch. A law unto ourselves. Remind me again in a year, will you?' He yawned. 'And start calling me Silas.'

She woke once during the night, taking some time to recall where she was and why the large shape at her side was clearly not Cecily's. Then she remembered, and tried to sit up and take her bearings. The ship rolled, throwing her on to him, and she was instantly enclosed by strong arms that flung her back with a soft thud, his body bearing down on her as the cabin tipped in the opposite direction.

She tasted the silkiness of his hair against her lips, the warm musky smell of his skin, and was reminded of her duty to maintain anger. 'You planned it, didn't you?' she whispered. 'Right from the start, you knew what you were going to do.'

His reply touched her lips, with no distance for the words to go astray. 'Course I planned it. Course I knew what I was going to do. Don't blame yourself, lovely thing, there was nothing you could have done to prevent it. It would have made no difference whether you'd agreed to come or not; I would still have taken you.'

The last words merged into the kiss that he had tried, without success, to delay, and Isolde had neither the time nor the will to withhold her co-operation, as she had sworn to do. Even in half-sleep, the nagging voice returned with its doubts, forcing her to declare them. 'I don't want to go to Flanders,' she whispered, settling once more into his arms. It was all she could think of.

'Then go to sleep, maid,' he murmured.

'Ships do not turn round easily in mid-ocean,' Silas laughingly told her the next morning. 'They're not like horses. They're not even like rowing boats.'

Isolde had not seriously thought they were, but daytime resistance was obviously going to be more potent than any other, and he must not be allowed to think for one moment that he was going to get away lightly with this flagrant piracy, for that was what it was.

Mistress Cecily, recovered enough to sit in a corner of the deck and sip some weak ale, was even less amused by the idea of Flanders than Isolde was, but then, her sense of the absurd was presently at a low ebb, her only real concern being to place her two feet on dry land any time within the next half-hour. Which bit of land was of no immediate consequence as long as it stood still.

For Isolde's sake, she tried to take an interest, but this was predictably negative. 'They'll not speak our language, love. How shall we make ourselves understood? And what's your father going to say? And Master Fryde? There'll be such a to-do. We should never have…urgh!'

There was one thing guaranteed to halt the miseries of conjecture, albeit a drastic one, but there was something in what she said, even so. What *was* her father going to say?

Chapter Three

A tall graceful woman stood outside the stone porch of an elegant manor house, her eyes focussed to search along the valley where a river snaked a silver trail in the morning sunshine. Up on the far distant hillside, tree-darkened and just out of view, her father would be about his daily business, her mother perhaps doing exactly what *she* was doing, no doubt feeling helpless to intervene and wondering if the feuding could get any worse. God forbid.

She was about to go back inside when the clatter of hooves caught her attention, and she waited to watch the mounted party sweep through the stone gatehouse and into the courtyard, vaulting down from their saddles in a flurry of muted colours, tawny, madder, ochre and tan. One particular figure came to the fore and stood, looking across to where she waited, as if to check that she was still there.

He was a large and powerful man, old enough to be her father, certainly, but still a handsome creature whose deep auburn hair was now tinged with grey at the temples where it swept off a high forehead in thick waves. His eyes, like mossy stones, narrowed at the sight of her in warning rather than in recognition, and the woman held it as long as she dared, then turned away, hiding any trace of emotion.

'Mistress Felicia!'

She carried on walking across the busy hall with veils flowing and head held high, ignoring the plea.

'Mistress!' A young lad caught up with her. 'Please…'

Out of pity, she stopped.

'Mistress Felicia…'

'Mistress La Vallon, if you please,' she snapped. 'I have not lost my identity along with my honour. Yet.'

'I beg your pardon. Sir Gillan says that he expects you—'

'In the solar. Yes, I dare say he does.'

Stony as ever, her expression gave him no hope. She was very lonely, but her manner was proud for a woman in her position. The lad persisted, for he was of the same age, or thereabouts. 'Mistress, please…I dare not take him that as a message. Shall I say…?'

'Yes,' she replied, relenting for his sake. 'Say I'll come. Eventually.' She was a La Vallon in a Medwin household. They must be reminded of it.

The chaplain and two others were with him when she entered the solar, her beauty making them hesitate in mid-sentence and struggle to stay on course. Sir Gillan glared at her. 'At last,' he said. 'Did you keep your father waiting so long for your presence, lady?'

'Frequently, my lord,' she replied, crossing to the window.

The two men coughed discreetly behind their hands, hoping that there would be no scene this time. It was a frail hope, the news being so disturbing.

'I have news of your family,' Sir Gillan said. 'Does it interest you?'

Felicia came, picking up her long skirts and throwing them over one arm, a trace of eagerness in her large brown eyes at last. 'From my father? He's agreed a ransom?'

'No, lady. He has not. I haven't demanded one. The news partly concerns your rake of a brother, but you must be well used to his escapades by now, surely. He's disappeared, it seems.'

'Ah...with Isolde?' The eagerness changed to a triumph she could scarcely conceal.

Sir Gillan flared again, forbidding her to say a word in her brother's favour, and Felicia knew better than to flout him on this, knowing how he wanted only the best for his daughter. 'That's what we're presuming, since a messenger arrived from York only a moment ago to say that Isolde has also disappeared. How's that for revenge, eh? Makes you feel good, does it?'

Her concern at that news was obvious to all four men. 'No, my lord. Not revenge, surely? Bard and Isolde are—'

'I know my daughter, lady, and I know all about your brother. Whatever form his interest takes, it will not be to her advantage. We can all be sure of that. Revenge or not, your father must be laughing.'

'*He* might. My mother won't.' She tried to hold his eyes, but could not.

The chaplain came forward with a stool for her to sit on, placing himself nearby to speak to her on the same level. 'Mistress La Vallon, you are in a difficult position, I know, a position with which we symp—'

'Get on with it, man!' Sir Gillan barked.

'Sympathise. But you presumably hold no grudge against Sir Gillan's daughter?'

'No, none at all.'

'Then perhaps you could tell us if you think our trust in Alderman Fryde of York was misplaced. Does your father know him still?'

'I believe so.'

'And Master Fryde carries merchandise for the La Vallons, does he?'

Felicia sent him a scathing glance with an accompanying, 'Ich! Of course he doesn't, Sir Andrew. Fryde doesn't have ships of his own, and we have a merchant in the family with two.'

At this reminder, Sir Gillan sat more erect. 'Your brother Silas? A merchant already? Where? At York, is he?'

'Yes, but you need not think that Silas would have anything to do with Alderman Fryde, my lord. Far from it. Neither he nor my father can stand the man. My father would never have sent *his* daughter to such a man.'

Angrily, Sir Gillan stood up. 'Of course not. He guards his womenfolk more carefully, does he not, lady?'

Felicia had the grace to blush. She had gone too far. 'I did not mean that, my lord. I meant that, according to my father, Master Fryde has changed for the worse since his election to the council. He expects to be sheriff at the next election in January. Did you know that?'

'No, I didn't. I wondered if he and your father were…perhaps…?'

'There is no collusion there as far as I'm aware. From what I hear, anyone who colludes with Master Fryde needs a deep purse. He comes expensive, and my father does not seek the friendship of such men, whatever else he does.'

Glances were exchanged. They knew well what else Rider La Vallon did, particularly to swell the population hereabouts. One of the men took up the questioning. 'So, have you any suggestions, mistress, as to where your brother and Mistress Isolde might have gone, presuming, of course, that they are indeed together? Her honour is now at—' He jumped and frowned as his ankle was kicked by the seated chaplain.

'Her honour is at stake, is it?' said Felicia in her most sugary tones. 'Then she and I have more in common than ever I had thought.' Her eyes were downcast, unwilling to meet Sir Gillan's glare. 'But I have no idea where they might be.'

'Enough!' he snapped. 'Go, both of you. It's late, but you should be able to reach York some time tomorrow. Give the bloody man hell and tell him to get my daughter back into safekeeping or he can say goodbye to any sheriff's office. I'll bring the roof down on him: incompetent, self-seeking little toad. And I thought he was trustworthy. He promised me he'd take care of her, dammit!'

The two men bowed and left the room, leaving the chaplain still complacently seated until Sir Gillan bellowed at him, 'And you can draft a letter to Allard in Cambridge. I can't go to York, but he can. Time he made himself useful.'

The chaplain pulled forward his scrip, to take out his quills and ink, but was halted before he could reach for the parchment.

'Not here, man! Go and do it in the hall. Tell Allard he's to go to York and put the fear of God into Fryde. He's to deputise for me. Understand?'

The discomfited chaplain hesitated, unwilling to leave Felicia in the sole company of his volatile employer. But he was given little choice in the matter.

'Well? Go on. I'm not going to eat her!'

The door closed, leaving Sir Gillan Medwin with a scowl on his brow that reached only as far as the top of his captive's exaggerated head-dress. 'Take that contraption off your head, woman, and come here.'

Obediently, she went to stand before him and suffered him to unpin the huge inverted and padded horseshoe netted with gold and swathed with gauze, and to shake her hair free of its embroidered side-pieces. She would not help him, but kept her eyes lowered. 'My lord,' she said, 'it took me almost an hour to put that on.'

'So what would they talk about at dinner, d'ye think, if I let you walk out of here unmolested? Eh?' He took a deep fistful of her black hair and drew her face tenderly towards his own. 'And do not sail quite so close to the wind, wench, with your talk of honour and such. Do you understand me?'

'Yes, my lord.' Slowly, she raised her arms and linked them around his head, drawing his lips close to hers until they met. Then, as if time had run out on them, as if their bodies, stretched to breaking point, could bear the delay no longer, their mouths locked, searching desperately. Breathless, laughing with relief, and with barely enough space to reassure each other, they clung as long-lost lovers do. Felicia cupped his face in her hands to taste him again. 'Dearest… beloved…the pretence. I cannot keep it up…truly… I cannot.'

His laughter brought a flush to her cheeks. 'That problem, wench, is quite the reverse of mine. Just feel…' He took her hand and guided it.

Her attempt at shock was unconvincing. 'Sir Gillan, not only have you stolen your neighbour's daughter, but now you make indecent suggestions to her. Are you not—?'

'Ashamed? Aye, that I cannot keep my mind on its business for love of you. How long is it since you put your spell on me?'

'Years,' she whispered. 'Too many wasted years, God help us. Come, sweetheart, we must put Isolde first. My brother's morals are not of the purest, as you well know. We must see what's to be done about that first.'

He held her close, smoothing her hair. 'Good, and

beautiful, and caring. How did Rider La Vallon manage to spawn a woman like you?'

'Ah…' she caught his hand and kissed it '…he's not what you believe, dear heart. You used to fish together as lads, did you not? And ride, and fight, and go whoring too, I believe? Admit it!' She laughed, shaking the hand.

He did, sheepishly. 'A long time ago.'

'Not all *that* long ago. He's never been malicious, Gillan. He'd never approve of putting Isolde in danger. Nor would Bard. There has to be another explanation.'

'I hope to God you're right, my love. She's only a wee lass.'

'She's a woman, Gillan. Like me,' Felicia said.

For want of a more original approach, Isolde repeated her concern. 'What's my father going to say? Have you thought about that?'

'No, I cannot say I've given it too much thought.' Silas La Vallon braced his arms like buttresses against the ship's bulwarks and smiled, but whether at her question or at the appearance of land Isolde could not be sure. 'I'll concern myself with that when I have his reply in my hand.'

'Reply? You've sent him a message?' Yelping in alarm, the seagulls swooped round the rigging.

'I sent him a message. Yes.' He continued to study the horizon.

Isolde bit back her impatience. The man's composure was irritating, as was his complete command of the situation, his refusal to respond to her disquiet.

'Then since it probably concerns me, would you mind telling me what it contained? Or was it to do with the price of Halifax greens?'

Slowly, he swung his head to look at her, taking his time to drink in the reflection of the sea in her blazing green eyes and the fear mixed with anger. He knew she feared him, and why. 'I dare say it can do no harm,' he said. 'I told him I'd keep you as long as he keeps Felicia, that's all.' The slight lift of one eyebrow enhanced the amusement in his eyes at her dismay, and at the temper she was already learning not to waste on him. She was silent. Fuming, but silent. That was good. 'Well, maid?' he teased her. 'What d'ye think he'll say to that? You know him better than me.'

'Don't call me that,' she said.

'Maid? Why ever not? Are you telling me—' his smile was barely controlled and utterly disbelieving '—that you're not a maid? That young brother of mine—?'

'No! I'm telling you nothing of the sort,' she snapped in alarm, trying to push herself away from the bulwarks to avoid him, but too late. His arms were now braced on each side of her and the information for which she had pressed him had now swirled away on another current.

'No, maid, or you'd be lying. You've not been handled all that much, have you?'

'You are impertinent, sir! Let me go!'

'I'll let you go, but not too far. Once we reach land, you'll be safer staying close to me.'

'Safer?' She glared at him in open scorn. 'Safer than

what? You are a La Vallon and I am a Medwin; I've seen how safe that can be.'

The sea breeze lifted the dark silky overhang of hair from his brow, revealing a fine white scar that ran upwards like a cord and unravelled into his hair. 'Safe,' he repeated. 'You have little to fear from me, I assure you. I shall treat you well as long as you abide by the rules.'

'What rules?'

'Hostage rules. You don't need me to explain them, do you?'

No, she needed no explanation. Hostage rules were an unwritten acceptance of enforced hospitality; one person's good behaviour against another's safety. She had no doubts that, if need be, he would demand full payment, whatever that was. And so would her father. But what the latter would say in response was predictable. He would come to rescue her; she was convinced of that.

That, at least, was what her daytime voices assured her. It was all their doing: men's responsibility. The night voices hummed to a less strident tune when, over the rocking of the waves, her fears became confused with strange emotions that were all the more disturbing for being unidentifiable. Unnerved, and indignant at his too-familiar closeness, she had taken her pledge of non-co-operation to its limits but had found it to be insignificant against his arms, which were too strong, his kisses too skilled. Bristling, she had had to yield to his demands which, fortunately, had left her still intact but without any real defence against such an artful invasion. She had slept in his arms because he had given her no choice, but what if her father should come here to Flanders to claim her and return Felicia to the La Vallons? What then?

'No, sir,' she replied, unsmiling. 'Spare me rules, I beg you. You'd be hard-pressed, I'm sure, to remember any.'

Refusing her provocation, he smiled again, taking her shoulders and turning her to face the sea, holding her chin up with one forearm. He pointed to a narrow strip of land lying on the horizon beneath a bright eastern sky. 'See, there's where we'll come in. That's Sluys.'

'Slice?'

'Sluys. The harbour. That's where the cargo will be taken off and put on a barge for Brugge. We shall go ahead either by horseback or by boat. Which d'ye think Mistress Cecily would prefer?'

Isolde had to smile at that. 'That's all you can offer?'

'Afraid so. It's not far. The boat is flat calm; rivers and dykes, you see. Brugge is ringed with them. You'll like it. Friendly people. You can go and put your head-dress on again, if you wish.' His arm tightened across her, conveying his excitement.

Though she understood his suggestion to be for her own sake rather than his, the need for some dignifying accessories came before pique, and by the time she and her ineffectual maid emerged from the cabin she was able to present an outward appearance of composure that was convincing to almost everyone. Except for the foreign tongue that had been Cecily's first concern,

Isolde did not know what to expect but, having taken York in her stride despite her unfashionable appearance, she assumed that Flanders could be no better, for all the Flemish weavers she had encountered in England had been plain, well-scrubbed and homely creatures of no particular style.

The stately journey by barge from Sluys through the port of Damme and on towards Brugge gave her no reason to revise this impression, having been thoroughly stared at by everyone from small children and dockers to the brawny lightermen and their mates at every lock. Even their dogs had stared. And if the idea to escape had crossed her mind while her captor was otherwise engaged, it was quickly extinguished by three of the crew who hovered with decided intent.

Staring in her turn, she allowed the unintelligible burble of voices to isolate her and to focus her attention instead towards the prettily gabled houses packaged into tidy rows, the sparkling crispness of the ironed-out landscape, the willows and windmills that lined the waterway. The plunging and roaring of the wind-tossed carrack could not have been more different from this overwhelming sense of peace in which the sound of voices rose and fell with the swish of the barge through the water. Horizontal lines were reflected and multiplied, and even the clouds obediently followed the lie of the land. She could have asked for advance notice of this, had she not been too proud, but not even Master Silas could have described the tranquillity she inhaled like a healing balsam, or the hypnotic cut of the boat through sky-blue satin like newly sharpened shears. He could, however, understand the Flemish language.

Cecily leaned towards Isolde, pale and frowning. 'What are they saying?' she whispered loudly. 'Why are they staring? Is it your head-dress again?'

'Probably.' Isolde shrugged, glancing at the array of white wimples over plaits coiled like ship's ropes.

One matron, with a starched head-dress that looked ready to sail at any moment, leaned towards Silas with a grin that showed more gum than teeth. Indicating Isolde, she spoke, and he smiled a reply in Flemish.

Defensive, Cecily leaned from Isolde's other side. 'What?' she said.

'The dame says that my lady is very beautiful,' Silas told her without a glance at Isolde. 'And I agree with her.'

Regardless of the fact that the woman had hold of the wrong end of the stick, the compliment was enough to convince Mistress Cecily that the Flemings were, after all, people of discernment and should be treated with generosity, whether they were foreign or not. Accordingly, she removed herself unsteadily from Isolde's side, gestured to Silas to change places, and began a conversation with the starched lady by signs, gestures and like-sounding words as if she had known her for years.

Isolde was not so easily won, but saw no discreet way of removing the arm that came warmly across her back. 'You must not let them believe that,' she said. 'I am not your lady nor anyone else's.'

'That's Brugge,' Silas replied diverting the rebuke

with a finger that pointed towards the towers and spires appearing on the skyline. 'See, here are the first houses, and soon we'll be right in amongst them. And windmills, see. Dozens of them.'

'Did you hear what I said?'

'No, maid, I'm afraid I didn't. But I heard what the old crone said and it sounds as if her understanding is better than yours in some areas. Now, let me show you that tallest tower…that's the great belfry.'

'I cannot believe this is happening,' she said in some irritation.

'They're going to have to lower the mast to get under the bridge. Mind your head-dress.'

'I'm dreaming this.'

'There we go. Look, those smaller boats are called skiffs. That's how the people of Brugge get about. Turn back and look…the children are waving.'

'I shall wake any moment now.'

'You *are* awake. Wave to them.'

'No, I'm being abducted. This cannot be happening. Wake me,' she insisted.

His arm tightened across her shoulders as he turned his mouth toward her ear, overcoming the padded and embroidered barrier of the side-pieces. 'Courage,' he whispered. 'Most women would have swooned times over by now, but you have withstood—'

'Every hardship!' she whispered back, disguising her snarl beneath a smile. 'Don 't tell me I've withstood my ordeal like a man or I shall dive overboard.'

'Hardly like a man, if my memory serves me.' He grinned. 'Was it so very hard to bear, Isolde?'

'That was the worst part!' she hissed, understanding his reference.

'A dream, like the rest?'

'A nightmare!'

The warmth of his soft laugh caught her cheek and she blushed, turning her head away to hide the confusion in her eyes. But a warm firm finger eased her back to face him. 'It was no nightmare, maid, and you know it,' he softly rebuked her. 'Nor will your new life in Brugge be so, unless you refuse to be won over by what it has to offer you. Look around, see…is it not magical? Forget what you've left behind. You'll be perfectly safe here. I shall not shackle you, and you'll see more of life than ever you've seen before, and, what's more, you'll not be hidden from view as you have been so far. It's time others were allowed to see something of you.'

'Being stared at, you mean? Is that what I'll have to suffer?'

'Probably. I think you'll have to get used to plenty of that.'

'And the language, and the food, and you?'

The finger moved gently upon her cheek, and again she felt his slow smile. 'None of those have presented any real problems so far, have they? In fact, quite the contrary, eh?'

She tried to hide the reluctant smile but was only partly successful.

'That's better. Now, give in to this place and enjoy it. You'll have every comfort, I promise you. More than you had in York, and certainly more than you'd have with my brother.'

'That would not be difficult. Where are we going?'

'To my house. The boat takes us right to the door.'

She knew that to be an exaggeration. 'But surely no one will expect you to bring a woman back with you, will they?'

'I'm not taking a woman back, I'm taking a lady. The Flemings know the difference; they're a courteous people. And what my servants expect is irrelevant; they're paid to care for me, not to ask questions about my guests.'

'Like your crew?'

'Exactly.'

'You make a habit of abducting ladies, then?'

Slowly, like an owl, he blinked at her. 'Oh, I have one in every room, two in the attic, four in the cellars and one in the outhouse.'

'So where do I go?'

'Where you will, maid.'

She tried to terminate this facetiousness by looking away, but found it impossible. His eyes, deep and percipient, reflected his understanding of her anxieties as much as her secret thoughts, and his handsome head beneath the intricately untidy turban reminded her of a figure she had noticed in the Flemish *Book of Hours* in the room at Scarborough, an elegant figure that commanded the page and everyone on it by his presence. And, but for this quiet air of authority, his assurance and advice, Isolde might have continued to dwell on her plight, to overlook the first entrancing sights and sounds Brugge had to offer as they slid silently into its embrace.

The sun was still high, flooding the buildings and canals with a palette of rose-pinks, sand, mossy-greys and slate. Glimpses of gardens offered them the greens of trim bushes, well-behaved trees and the bright splash of flowers on balcony and sill. Windows hung precariously over the water or retired into rows, penetrating the tall stepped gables high above, and, swished by the constant wake of passing boats, the doors, gates, steps and arches appeared to lead directly into the buildings. Bricks, new to Isolde, made an apricot-coloured web over the walls to enclose a filigree of lancet windows, balustrades and cut stonework that reminded her of insets of lace. Beyond all that, massive buttresses of stone rose to assert some authority on a grander scale. Isolde was entranced.

Silas kept his commentary to a minimum, occasionally bringing his arm up to rest on her shoulder to point to the great towering belfry as they passed, then to St Donation's and the tall bristling spire of Our Lady's Church. 'We live opposite,' he whispered. His pointing hand turned to a wave as a shout of greeting came from the bridge ahead.

'Silas! Meester Silas! Ahoy!'

They swept beneath the happily waving man and found that, on the other side, the bridge was now lined with staring people. 'Pieter!' called Silas, waving.

'You're home!' A feathered hat waved at them as if it were alive.

'Go and tell them, then.'

Isolde lost count of the bridges. One of them, more like a tunnel, held houses suspended over the water, but the last one led them to a high wall bathed in sunshine where the boat drew up to a step below a wooden door arched into the mellow brickwork. Isolde looked at Silas in surprise.

'You didn't believe me, did you?' he smiled. 'Come, we're home.'

'I get the cellar?'

'No. That's only for special guests.'

'So, ordinary guests…?'

'Have to make do with the upper floors. Give me your hand.'

The door from the canal led them directly into a garden enclosed by the wall, the ends of two buildings and the elegant form of another. Sun-drenched lavender bushes, neatly squared lawns and cobbled pathways led them round the building on the right and into a sunny courtyard where two cats sprawled over the lips of a large yawning doorway. Tubs of gillyflowers and marigolds, mauve-tipped rosemary and bay trees softened the angular lines of a wooden trellis through which pink and white roses hung like heads through windows.

They had not reached the door before they were greeted by emerging figures dressed in tones of black, brown and plum, with white at head and breast reflecting light onto their beaming faces. 'Meester Silas… ah…*welkom*…*welkom*!'

Pieter of the feathered hat had beaten the boat by seconds.

* * *

Silas had known, of course, in those first few moments when she had responded with such immediacy to his surliness at Scarborough, that she would be a handful. Even in the dim light of the Brakespeares' courtyard he had seen the set of her jaw, the determination to take control and the quick reversal when she saw her maid's distress. That had hardly been because she couldn't manage without a maid. Her decisions were impulsive, perhaps too much so. The dash from York to Scarborough was not the well-considered act of a woman with a good reputation, but she was no hoyden and certainly no child; her anger at his familiarity had convinced him of that.

Wisely, though, she had chanelled her fears into a scornful anger which, after that first understandable over-reaction, he had been careful to deflect with some humour and more than a little tolerance. And now, too soon, the second test had arrived, when she would have to adapt to semi-confinement in a strange setting with few of the familiar essentials to ease the transition. Naturally he would do all he could to assist, but what followed would be a true test of her character. And already she was making a visible effort. He would have liked more time to warn his household and to prepare a room that would restore her to the comforts she must have longed for but had never once lamented. Ah, well, she would no doubt have her own ideas about how to do that.

Silas smiled to himself with a soupçon of satisfaction. To have achieved two such master strokes at once was nothing short of brilliant, though the possibility that Fryde might harass Elizabeth at Scarborough was the one cloud on the horizon that turned the smile quickly to a frown. But, no, Fryde would not link Isolde with a cousin of the La Vallons, and by the time Alderman Fryde's enquiries were under way his stolen horses would be back in York, together with an advance party of Sir Gillan's men to give him hell, Silas hoped. His mortification would be worth witnessing.

What disturbed Silas, however, was the degree of closeness between Isolde's father and Alderman Henry Fryde, which must initially have included enough trust to make York's most unscrupulous and ambitious merchant Isolde's temporary guardian. It could be, he mused, that, living in the far-flung hill country with only sheep for near-neighbours, one could know little of erstwhile friends in York or of the reputations that grew as fast as wealth. As for Felicia and Sir Gillan…? Silas's smile returned—they were both getting what they deserved. And so was his own father. And, for that matter, so was Bard. In fact, the only one not to do so was the lass herself, who would either have to stay with him or enter a convent. Only time would tell which she would choose.

The figure of a man entering the courtyard caught his attention. The man stooped to pick up one of the cats and drape it over his shoulder, his shape in the doorway blotting out the light.

But Silas was in no doubt of his visitor's identity. 'William…sir. I am honoured. What a treat. How did you—?'

'How did I know, Silas Mariner?' The man laughed,

holding out a hand. 'Why, the whole town knows. Can you not hear the bells, lad?'

Pieter de Hoed, with his usual sharpness, had already warned young Mei that she would have to become a more attentive chambermaid than ever, by the look of things, because the lady in his master's company bore an expression which no one could have called indulgent. Mei was therefore quaking in her stout leather shoes as she led the two guests up a winding wooden staircase to the room that Meester Silas had indicated, the one overlooking the canal. Heartened by her recent success at communication with the starched lady on the boat, Cecily was ready to try it out again on Mei, and, with a similar system of symbols and smiles, came to a mutual understanding remarkably quickly. Hot water, clothes from their panniers, and food. Yes, thank you, she had noticed the linen towels.

Spreadeagled on the bed, Isolde was staring in silence at the delicate curves of a metalwork chandelier and the pattern of lines that rippled across the wooden rafters above her, bouncing like will-o'-the-wisps through the open window from the water. 'I shall grow fins,' she murmured drowsily. 'I shall grow a tail like the mermaids. None of this is real.'

'Nice room, though,' Cecily said matter-of-factly, closing the door on the two lads who had brought up the luggage. 'And big enough. Not like that box we had in York. What's the bed like?'

'Big,' Isolde agreed. She looked around her. 'Yes, it is. Nice.'

The bed-curtains of aquamarine velvet lined with silk were tied up into pendulous buns with moss-green silken cords, and the matching bedcover was large enough to drape its embroidered borders heavily on to the floor in a tangled strapwork of gold and green. A bolster and cushions were arranged across the bed-head of carved and pierced woodwork that made a line of pinnacles like spires on a distant skyline. Softly mellowed oak panelled every surface, cut into pierced trefoils on the tops of the window shutters and across the back of a bench where a green woollen rug hung in tassels over the seat. A convex mirror surrounded by enamelled roundels hung on the far wall to follow their every move.

Intrigued, Isolde swung her feet down to the soft pile of carpet where an intricate pattern of red, brown, green and blue covered it from edge to edge. A kneeling cushion of the same design lay on the ledge of a prie-dieu, and Isolde knew without being told that it had come by camel-caravan from the other side of the world, where people had been known to drop off the edge. Crossing to the prie-dieu, she knelt to look more closely at the *Book of Hours* full of glowing pictures like the one she had seen at Dame Elizabeth's house. Quietly, she turned over the stiff pages and began to search for a prayer for safe arrivals while at the same time studying each of the illustrations of daily life for the figure which had dominated the page.

At the time, Isolde had not taken her captor's promise of every comfort too seriously, and was therefore surprised to find that, after the deprivations of the voyage, he appeared to be making an effort to compensate for all that she had lost. Had he but known it, she had lost little in York except her father's approval of her behaviour; the Fryde family had offered no comforts to speak of, their hospitality being far worse than Silas's custody. Naturally, she had been careful not to make the comparison in his hearing, nor did she display more than a polite approval of the cool, clean, well-managed house and caring servants, the excellent food and restrained but unmistakable signs of affluence which were in direct contrast to the Frydes' ostentation.

It was difficult not to compare the two merchants, albeit they were years apart in age and experience. Yet here was Silas La Vallon with a beautiful house in Brugge and another in York, enough wealth to keep servants in both, and a ship with a permanent crew. Pride had not allowed her to show the slightest interest in either his merchandise or his clients, nor had the bales and boxes unloaded at Sluys given any indication of their contents, but she would have given much to know the source of his wealth. Was it in those carpets from the Orient? The spices? The grain? Or was it in the woollen goods that came to Flanders to be finished, then re-imported? This was a question that might have occupied her mind before her first day in Brugge had drawn to a close. But then she was introduced to Silas's visitor, which raised a completely different set of questions.

Chapter Four

'What on earth am I going to wear?' Isolde said crossly. 'If I'd had more notice, I might have been able to refurbish my best blue gown and find some new fur to trim it, but it's been screwed up in the pannier for a week. And what about my head-dress? It doesn't match, and I can hardly attend court with my hair loose at my age, can I?'

That was not quite what she meant, and Silas knew it. A loose-haired maid residing with an eligible bachelor would raise a few eyebrows. 'Shh! Calm down, Isolde. Come out here and let me explain what it's all about instead of getting worked up about what to put on your head. Come on!' He took her firmly by the elbow and led her out into the courtyard. The full moon lit their way through the rose-covered trellis and into the garden laid out in plots and grassy pathways edged about with wooden rails. The Flemings, it seemed, had a passion for tidiness. They found a stone bench and sat, Isolde rigidly upright, Silas hoping that by taking one of her hands she would soften. 'William is a very good friend,' he explained. 'He came over specially to tell us about it.'

'You, not me. He didn't know I was here.'

'Yes, he did. He'd heard. He wants you to meet the Duchess. Heavens above, Isolde, most women would leap at the chance of being presented to the Duchess of Burgundy. She is English, you know.'

'I know that,' she said. 'She's Margaret of York, the King's sister.'

'Margaret of Burgundy now. And it will be an honour for William to have another Englishwoman watch him present his new translation to her. He printed it himself, you know. Here, in Brugge, on his own press.'

'Printed? What do you mean?'

'Well, instead of having scriveners to write each book by hand, William has learned how to put sheets of paper into a thing like a great cheese-press which marks them with words, so now he can print a lot of pages all the same in a matter of moments. It saves so much time. He's been to Cologne to learn the method from a German printer; a clever chap, Master Caxton. Speaks several languages and translates books from one into another. He's a Kentishman himself, but you can still hear his twang, can't you?'

'How long has he lived here in Brugge?'

'Oh, donkey's years. You must ask him about it some day.'

'Then surely his wife will be there.'

'No, William has never married.'

She found this remarkable. William Caxton was a man of mature years, but courteous and obviously at

ease with women. As a close friend of Margaret of
York, Duchess of Burgundy, he must know many
women in the ducal household, yet he had not married.
'Oh. Doesn't *he* stand still long enough, either?'

In the darkness, Silas smiled, caressing her with
hand and voice. 'I'd make little progress with you,
maid, by standing still,' he teased. His hand moved up
towards her neck, barely touching the soft skin of her
throat with the back of his fingers.

Trembling, she held herself rigid, hoping that her
voice would not betray the melting of her insides. 'This
is foolish talk, sir. We were discussing Master Caxton's
invitation. You must see that there is too little time for
me to…' Slowly, her head was eased round to face him
and tipped backwards to rest upon his shoulder, and
before she could remember which words came next his
mouth on hers made them unnecessary.

With the same tenderness he had shown during their
nights on the boat, he closed her mind again to the
fears that plagued her, gentling her lips with all the
skill of a master. With the same care, he moved his
hands on to the fabric over her breast and held it until
she realised what she had allowed. Then, she caught
clumsily at his wrist, not knowing in that first moment
of awareness how to proceed. 'No,' she heard herself
say. 'Please…no.'

Obediently, the hand caressed and moved away.
'No,' he whispered. 'It's all right. You're quite safe.
You prefer to sleep with Mistress Cecily now you're
here in Brugge?'

'Yes.' It was a lie, but not for the world would she have said otherwise.

'Then you have only to tell me when you wish to change your mind.'

She could have protested that such a thing would never happen, but he sensed the conflict and his next kiss was long and deep, designed to prolong her confusion rather than to banish it completely.

'Now,' he whispered, keeping her head on his shoulder, 'let's talk about tomorrow, shall we?'

His argument was convincing, although to Isolde the price of acceptance proved to be uncomfortably high. She was, he reminded her, a stranger to Flanders, so how could she know what was being worn at court? Those women with enough hair of their own, he assured her, wore it in elaborate styles threaded with ropes of pearls and jewels after the Florentine and Venetian fashion. The French and Swiss were doing the same. Those who had not enough of their own hair were using false pieces: plaits, chignons, piles of it. She would not need any of that, with her abundance. Jewels? That would present no problem; he had enough for a dozen such coiffures.

Mei was skilled. She had dressed some of Brugge's Italian ladies until she had become pregnant when, to please Pieter the Hat, Silas had taken her on as chambermaid.

'Is that his name? The Hat?'

'De Hoed. Hadn't you noticed? That's his weakness. And women, of course.'

'And is that your weakness, too?' She looked away, regretting the childish slip of the tongue. 'What about my dress? Are crumpled dresses in fashion?'

Silas had made all three women in his household available to Isolde on the morning of the next day, steaming and smoothing the blue-grey half-silk and fluffing up the snow-weasel fur trims to look like ermine. Cheaper, and almost as effective. The collar made a deep V from shoulder to waist and, when she would have filled the space with a high-necked chemise, Silas turned its edge down with practised fingers to show far more of her bosom than ever she had shown before. She protested that she was in danger of being taken for a courtesan, but Mei indignantly joined forces to silence her protests. This was high, she said, compared to some of the court ladies. She stitched the edges of a wide satin sash tightly together behind Isolde's back, its top edge resting just below her breasts, supporting them from below and accentuating their full curves. When Isolde attempted to cover herself in a sudden gesture of modesty, Silas took her hands and held them away.

'You've nothing to hide,' he said. 'Have courage.'

On receipt of Isolde's first smile, Mei—named after the month—had come to the conclusion that Isolde could not be the forbidding creature of whom Pieter had warned her, and, with Cecily's help, made Isolde understand that she had never seen a head of hair as lovely as hers. It required four hands and occasionally five to devise an elaborate creation in which every strand was plaited with gold threads and tied at intervals with pearls threaded on silk. Thin plaits were twisted around thicker ones, coil upon coil, to fill out the back of her head in an intricate maze of red and gold, the smooth front adorned only with a strand of pearls worn like a low crown on her forehead. Finally, the wayward curls at the nape of her neck, which Cecily refused to allow Mei to shave off, were tied with golden cords into tiny bunches. The effect was spectacular. The butterfly had emerged.

The only jewellery she was allowed to wear was a fine gold chain with a trio of pearls suspended from it, the pearl-shaped pendant falling into the cleft between her breasts.

'Who does it belong to?' Isolde had asked. Again, she could have bitten her tongue.

'To you, lady.'

'Sir, I cannot accept—'

At that point Silas had taken her arm in his strong grasp, so that she had had to clutch at her long skirts to stay upright. He had drawn her with little courtesy into Cecily's small room next to hers and she had thought that he was angry, so stern was his face.

Holding her by the wrist, he had closed the door. 'Now, understand me, Isolde,' he said. 'So that our inevitable explanations are matched; you *are* in a position to accept my gifts. You are a guest in my house. You were my guest at York, also. Your father and mine are old friends. He is expected to join us here, by and by. If anyone asks if we have an understanding, tell them to mind their own bloody…no, tell them yes. We have. Nothing official yet, but, dammit, I'll not have those young court louts nosing about.'

'I shall say nothing of the sort, sir! The only understanding we have is that I am here against my will and against my father's will. Did you believe that by dressing me up and showing me off at court that would change things? I think they should know the truth right from the start, don't you?'

'Fine words, but which of us d'ye think they'd be inclined to believe? You or me? Do you not think you'd be taken for a hysterical woman after such an unlikely tale, looking as you do? I have a reputation as being a man of his word. What reputation do you have here?'

'A good question, sir! What reputation I once had is now ruined, thanks to you. My chances of marriage are gone. What could I tell anyone that they'd believe, after this?'

'That you're mine. They'd believe that, and you'd better start believing it, too. You have a half-hour before we go. Let me have your answer.'

He had given her no chance to continue the discussion but had left her to her own devices which, in the deserted garden, had brought her close to tears. The maids had shown her how to keep the excess fabric of her skirt in a bundle just below her bust, but all this preening seemed meaningless in the light of Silas's harsh demand. She was *his* only because he had stolen her; it would choke her to admit anything else.

She was watching one of the cats playing with an injured mouse when he strode into the garden wearing a deeper tone of the same blue-grey half-silk, gold-embroidered, white-furred, and with full sleeves that showed a slash of white shirt at the elbows. The wide shoulders needed no padding, nor the chest where narrow pleats radiated from the waist and the frill that cascaded over perfectly formed buttocks. His hat was an inverted plant-pot of velvet, its brick-red echoed again in his tight hose that extended at the toe into long points. The choice of colours appeared to reinforce his belief that he and she were a pair.

'Well?' he said, coming to stand before her, noting her stillness and moistened eyes.

Isolde watched how the cat took the mouse gently into its mouth and carried it off into a tangle of madder leaves. 'You look very grand, sir,' she whispered. 'You, at least, are making some kind of statement about our relationship.'

'Isolde.'

'Yes?'

'Your answer, if you please.'

She allowed her eyes to wander with some purpose over his strongly handsome face, partly to keep him waiting for every second of the allotted time. He was an exceptionally fine-looking man. Had he gone this far with other women? Was all this really for Felicia's sake? 'As long as my father keeps your sister, sir. That's all.'

A faint smile disturbed his lips. 'Or until you change your mind.'

But to that enigmatic reply she could find no answer, and so she stood like a creature at bay while he took her chin in his hand and kissed her, which she could have prevented, but did not.

'You'll like the Duchess,' he whispered, retaining her chin. 'She'll know exactly how you feel in a strange country. Just stay by my side, eh?'

The streets around St John's Hospital and the imposing cathedral of St Salvator's were cobbled and by far cleaner than any in York, but Isolde was thankful to be riding rather than walking. Along Silverstreet towards the street of the moneyers, the Duke of Burgundy's palace was but a short step, time enough for her to form an impression of narrow streets where the signs of silversmiths, harness-makers, lorimers and spurriers threatened to knock them out cold if they rode too near.

In contrast to the previous day, Isolde looked beyond her fears to what lay ahead, to the irony of meeting a woman who, like herself, was a Yorkist in Flanders. Isolde's blue-grey gown of half-silk was called Bridges satin by the English because of an early misinterpretation from the correct Brugge satin, and she wondered if the Duchess had done her part to remedy the language problem as Silas and Master William had.

Across courtyards, up flights of stairs and along galleries they swept in stately procession, through the vast Princenhof to where Master Caxton waited in an anteroom with his book-bearing assistant. The two men were in conversation as Silas and Isolde were ushered in, and the conspicuous blinking and widening of eyes revealed astonishment before the hushed but delighted greeting.

'Mistress Isolde…Silas.' Caxton's smile transfigured the otherwise sombre face, too used, Isolde supposed, to poring over manuscripts in poor light. His greying mouse-brown hair, thinning on top, was brushed forward to spout over his ears like rainwater out of gutters, and his eyes and brows had an apologetic downturn, like the corners of his mouth, that changed to wrinkles as he smiled. Predictably, his best serge gown reached the floor, as those of older men did, and the long vestigial scarf draped over one shoulder was like an anchor chain to a soft pudding-basin hat that hung behind. The hands that were held towards hers in greeting were still stained with black at the tips, and he laughed ruefully as they were turned over for viewing. 'Still hasn't come off,' he whispered. 'D'ye think her Grace will notice?'

Isolde placed her own upon them. 'By now, Master William, she'd probably be uncertain of your identity if they were pink.'

'Ah, d'ye know, I'd never thought of that? Well, then.' He beamed.

Yesterday, Isolde had wondered whether Master Caxton's Englishness had, like inkstains, eventually worn off, or whether he still practised the typically English manner of greeting with kisses. She had discovered, soon enough, that he was as English as ever and that he had no intention of forgoing the pleasure. His lips were thin and dry, but as eager as a boy's.

'This is such an honour, *damoiselle*,' he said, enthusiastically. 'To have an Englishwoman, a beautiful

Yorkshire woman, with me on this occasion makes it much more significant. Now…' he turned to his assistant '…I forget my manners. Allow me to present Jan van Wynkyn. I'd not be here today if it were not for him.'

A tall young man in his early twenties stepped forward, heaving a large leather-bound book easily on to one arm. 'Vat he means, *damoiselle*, is that if it were not for me, he'd have been doing this a year ago.' His accent was heavily German, his diction as immaculate as his appearance except for the inevitable stained fingers. Sweeping his large-brimmed and feathered hat off his head with a flourish, he used it like a scoop to draw Isolde towards him for the same greeting she had bestowed upon his employer, and had it not been for the large book between them, the kiss he took might have lasted even longer. 'I am agreeable for this English custom,' he said, seriously. 'Vee Germans have much to learn.'

'Then go and learn about it in Cologne, *minen heere*,' Silas replied, with the same seriousness, placing a supporting hand around Isolde's upper arm and easing her back to his side.

Master Jan's large full-lipped mouth stretched sideways almost to his straight fair hair, undismayed by Silas's protectiveness. He stepped back a pace with mechanical precision, nodded once, and rounded off his greeting to Isolde with, 'Meester Caxton told me of your beauty, *damoiselle*, but alas he has no vay *mit* vords.'

The quip, so charmingly delivered, was received

with some amusement, and so, when the door opened in the panelling and a young page beckoned them through, the smiles were still in place. With no warning of what to expect, Isolde had thought to find the Duchess surrounded by one or two of her ladies rather than the roomful of quietly conversing noblemen and women who confronted them. And though Silas had warned her of the stares she would have to tolerate, he could surely not have meant anything like this. As she had been bidden, she stayed close to him, and was interested to see that his bows were being acknowledged by several of the men in the room and, if she was not mistaken, by covert glances from the group of lovely young women also, though their eyes were lowered in perpetual modesty. This was not a trait Isolde intended to adopt.

The room was painted in a soft watery blue and hung with sunny tapestries between which were windows giving views of tiled rooftops, pinnacles and spires. At one end of the room was a high canopied chair cushioned with green, and a tall cupboard on legs displaying an impressive assortment of gold and silver dishes, ewers and plates. The colourful floor was chequered, monogrammed and cyphred, and adorned by two gold-collared gazehounds which, with heads on paws, watched Isolde with eyes like huge dark marbles. She smiled at them and watched their delicate tails whip the floor in unison.

What astonished Isolde most, however, was not so much the costly fabrics worn by every one of the women but the amazing truncated steeples upon their heads from which floated yards of shimmering gauze reaching almost to the ground. Pointed tents of velvet framed their faces, the edges hanging freely to their shoulders and, instead of showing an inch or two of hair on their foreheads, loops of gold and velvet lay upon the smooth skin where hair should have been. Not only had they plucked their eyebrows but their foreheads, too.

'Ah, Master Caxton!' A clear English voice rang through the low hum of voices, and a lady disengaged herself from one group, turning towards her guests and closing the space between them effortlessly, as if on wheels. Her gown was of heavy red silk shot with blue, reminding Isolde at once of Dame Elizabeth's turban. Undoubtedly, it was of the same fabric. The Duchess's immense train was held off the floor like a pile of bedding in her arms, and as she reached Master Caxton she dropped it. A young woman came forward to arrange it in a swirl around her feet and then retreated, but not before she had parted with a stare of open curiosity in Isolde's direction.

Attention was now focussed upon Margaret of Burgundy, the sister of the English king, Edward IV, who had been given in marriage seven years earlier to Charles, Duke of Burgundy, in the expectation of cementing the friendship and, naturally, continued assistance in England's troubles with France. Four years ago Edward had had to seek temporary refuge with his brother-in-law here, in Brugge, that much Isolde knew, though she had never expected to meet the woman on whom so much depended. The Duchess was petite and palely attractive, with the natural grace of one born to the position. Around her neck she wore a gold chain and pendant similar to the one Isolde wore, though the Duchess's wide expanse of bosom left by the V of white fur showed no contours of any great interest, despite the absence of a modest chemise in the triangle.

Master Caxton dropped on one knee, kissed the Duchess's offered hand, then rose to bring forward Jan Van Wynkyn, Isolde and Silas. The silence and the stares intensified as Isolde's name was spoken out loud.

'Mistress Medwin, this is an especial delight. Newly from England? From Yorkshire? I long to hear all you can tell me. Are you being cared for here in Brugge? With Master Silas? Ah, then you are in good hands.'

Isolde made a deep curtsy, taking her time over it if only to allow her steepled audience a good view of her own intricately modelled head. That it was not of the Burgundian fashion was now clear to her, but, rather than dwelling on Silas's reasons for suggesting it, she bravely decided to relish the distinction. When she rose, she was smiling, but the Duchess had already turned her attention to Silas, who was apparently well known to her.

It was clear that neither the Duchess nor her ladies were immune to his patent masculine presence: the coquettish tip of her head, the faintly flirtatious glance had not been performed for Master Caxton or his assistant. 'Master Silas,' she said, 'I'm relieved to see that you are safely returned.'

'Your Grace honours me by her concern. But you have recently returned from France, I hear.'

'Ah, France.' She sighed and looked away for a brief moment, as if not knowing what to say before so many ears. 'We had hoped to unravel a few tight knots with my brother and Louis, but alas we find that they've tied them even tighter. We had to leave.'

'And his Grace the Duke?'

'Decidedly unpleased,' she said, with a sad smile. 'But enough of that. What will you have to show me, Silas Mariner?' She tapped his arm, playfully.

'I shall be glad to show you my entire cargo once it's been cleared by customs. Next week, perhaps? Shall I send a message?'

She nodded, excitedly, then turned to Master Caxton, who had been waiting patiently to one side. 'Now, you must not keep me waiting any longer for this book. Come, let me see it, if you please. A romance, did you say?'

'Printed, your Grace.' Master Caxton knelt again, holding the book out to show her the title page. 'Translated into English from the French, the *Recueil des Histoires de Troye*.'

'Translated by you? Remarkable! Does this mean…?'

Isolde moved back to make way for those who crowded round to see the phenomenon. By this means, the scholarly printer was assured that word of his books would reach those who could afford to buy them, those who could read, and those who would appreciate them, and she had played her part, albeit a very small one. A soft hand was laid upon her arm and she half turned to find a young woman at her side, the same one who had arranged the Duchess's train.

This time there was a smile which did not quite reach her eyes but which showed the mouth and teeth to be perfect. The woman's dark-lashed brown eyes, however, had a hardness about them that warned Isolde of trouble, putting her instantly on her guard. Isolde smiled in return, preparing herself for a question in the French of the Burgundian court which she would have to ask Silas to interpret. But there was no need.

'Yorksheer?' the young lady said. 'This ees somewhere near where Meester Silas lives, is it?' Her English was good yet with a lilt of Flemish at the edges.

'York, the county town, is where Meester Silas has his business. He's a merchant there, you know.'

The woman's eyes roved over every detail of Isolde's dress, her hair and the pearl pendant. Her own gown of black velvet and gold satin was patterned with sinuous plant forms, catching the light with a sumptuousness that made Isolde's grey-blue half-silk appear dowdy in comparison. Her tall steeple head-dress was patterned with chevrons of gold thread and seed pearls, and her deep collar was a mesh of gold links and flowers with centres of diamonds.

'I know that,' the woman said, coolly. 'How long have *you* known him?'

This was the time, Isolde thought, to put a few questions of her own. 'You have the advantage of me, *damoiselle*. You heard my name, but I didn't hear yours.'

'I am Ann-Marie Matteus, one of her Grace's ladies. My home is in Antwerp. Is this—' she looked pointedly at Isolde's confection of plaits '—what the ladies of the English court are wearing these days?'

Isolde knew it was meant to disconcert her, but she had already seen it coming. If Ann-Marie Matteus had been with the Duchess in France at the meeting of the English and French kings, she would know what the English women were wearing.

Twitching her eyebrows, Isolde shook her head in mock pity. 'Then you didn't accompany her Grace to France? You'd have seen them there, I feel sure.' She lifted her arms in an extravagant gesture. '*Huge* creations! But not for me, I assure you. I rarely follow the fashion in such things unless it suits me. I find the Florentine styles so much more flattering to anyone with a good head of hair.'

'Really. How interesting. Are you staying here in Brugge? At the Marinershuis?'

Ah. Silas again. So, she had interests there, did she? 'Yes, I am Master Mariner's guest. He brought me over on his ship from York to see something of Brugge. It's a beautiful town. I long to see more of it.'

'So how long do you intend to stay?'

The question was blunt and to the point, and Isolde was relieved to be joined at that moment by Silas, who placed a tiny skinny monkey to sit on her armful of gown. It wore a collar studded with diamonds.

'There,' he said. 'Seen one of those before?'

Isolde saw that any reply would have gone unnoticed during the meeting of Silas with Ann-Marie Matteus, for the woman's attitude changed from hostile to winsome at the bat of an eyelid. He bowed formally but, rather than take her hand to kiss, kept his fingers on the jewelled pommel of his dagger. *'Damoiselle,'* he said.

'Silas,' Ann-Marie simpered. 'You came as soon as you returned. I'm so glad to see you again.'

'I came here to accompany Master Caxton at the presentation of his book to the Duchess, *damoiselle*, that's all. You and Mistress Isolde have met, I see.'

'Yes. She tells me she's staying with you. Is that so?'

'You are asking me to verify what Mistress Isolde has told you?'

'Ah…no, of course not.' Ann-Marie's face struggled into a brittle smile. 'But is it wise, Silas? You know how people talk. I shall be pestered by people asking me what's going on. What am I going to tell them?'

Intuitively, Isolde understood both the gist of the woman's insinuations and Silas's predicament, and, though she had no sympathy to waste on either of them, she did not intend to stand as pig-in-the-middle while they batted denials over her head. Even to a blind man it was obvious that the woman was doing her best to inform her of some previous relationship and that her choice of this public place was sure to cause the most immediate damage. But, whether it was true or not, the woman was not going to score at her expense, in public or in private.

'Tell them whatever you wish, *damoiselle*,' Isolde said in her sweetest tone, before Silas could draw breath, 'but the truth saves a lot of effort in the long run. Tell them, whoever they are, to mind their own…oh, no!' She peeped up at Silas. 'Tell them that we have an understanding. Nothing official, yet, but our fathers have been friends for years, and…' she made it sound like a search for the exact wording '…and…er, oh, yes, he's allowed to make gifts to me. This is his latest.' She took hold of the pearl pendant and held it forward. 'Isn't it a beauty? Oh, and *this*?' She held out the bewildered monkey.

Ann-Marie Matteus snatched the creature from Isolde's hand and held it tightly against her. 'Is mine!' she said, all smiles now gone.

'Ah, he gave you *that*, did he? And do you and Master Silas have a similar understanding? He's a very understanding man, is he not?'

The woman knew when she had met her match. Looking at neither of them, she stooped to pick up her flowing veil and train in one practised sweep, and left them.

In some concern, Silas took Isolde's arm. 'Do you want to go home?' he said.

Refusing to meet his eyes, Isolde copied the same graceful gathering of her gown. 'Home? No, indeed. I'm just beginning to enjoy myself, I thank you.' She bent to caress the silky white ears of the little gaze-hound that had come to lean against her legs. 'Why, little thing,' she whispered, 'you are trembling more than I am.'

That was the extent of Isolde's compliance. The young court louts who, according to Silas, would come buzzing, were allowed to swarm like bees around a new queen, after which the Duchess, her duties discharged, took Isolde to her green-cushioned dais, an honour which Isolde could have boasted of for the rest of her life, if she had chosen to.

The whole experience, though exciting, was akin to skating upon thin ice, and the mental agility required to avoid mention of the actual circumstances of her presence in Brugge did even more to boost Isolde's confidence than the earlier acrimonious interview. Afterwards, she could not explain why the thought of a woman being close to Silas, any woman, should bring such a rush of ill feeling to her breast, but she would not ask him for details. No, she'd *not* give him so much satisfaction.

'So, should I have congratulated the lady, then?' Her sideways assault was easily hidden in the babble of voices as they prepared to mount in the courtyard of the Princenhof.

Silas had been particularly subdued, in the manner of one who expects an inevitable volley of questions at any moment, and now, when the first salvo appeared, his defence was over-prepared. 'Who?' he said, leading her towards the mare.

'The one with the diamond-studded monkey.'

His mouth twitched. 'No, there's nothing I know of there that deserves congratulations except for being a troublemaker. You could congratulate her for having a father who's a diamond merchant, but that's about all I can think of.'

'But you gave her the monkey, I take it?'

'No, I didn't. I sold it to her father. Anything else?'

He lifted her into the saddle, setting her sideways and arranging her skirts. When she made no immediate response to his invitation, he gathered the reins and held them out of reach on the mare's neck. His chin was on a level with her elbow. 'Well?' he said.

It was her place to start the attack, so what right did *he* have to issue a challenge? Anyway, there *was* something else, but with Master Caxton and his young assistant looking on he knew full well that this was no time for her to develop the theme. 'Are you going to give me the reins, or shall I be led?' she muttered.

He was laughing, she was sure, as he handed them over, but she refused to look and, for some considerable time, had to acknowledge her own bull-headed approach to be the prime cause of her aggravated irritation.

It was Saturday, and their detour through the thronging streets soon took them into the Market Square, dominated by the massive tower of the belfry which she had seen in the distance the day before. The Cloth Hall, where good Flemish cloth was prepared for export, was pointed out to her, its façade littered with cutwork, picots, and snippets of stone lace. On this busy market day, calls and greetings came at them from all sides, waves of feathered hats and whistles of admiration which, Silas told her, were certainly not for him. Nevertheless, they were obliged to stop more than once as they threaded a path through the stalls, giving Isolde and Cecily a chance to see the sugar loaves and spices, the cross-legged tailors, the barber's stall cheek-by-jowl with flagons of good sweet hippocras and the merry customers who reeled from one to the other. In many ways it reminded her of York, except that this was more compact and therefore appeared larger, but her eye was caught by similar sights: billowing sails of cloth hanging from lines, mirrors, leather shoes, belts and girdles, purses, carved boxes, combs and skeins of coloured wools.

Isolde winked at Cecily and together they sidled away from where the three men were being accosted yet again by acquaintances. Lengths of velvet and veiling, fine woollens and linens lapped like brilliant-coloured waves and, hypnotised by the sight, they moved nearer, eager to feel, compare and choose.

'I'll hold the mare,' Cecily mouthed to Isolde over the din. 'Go on, slide down...oh!' Her warning was unheard.

Isolde shuffled herself forward from her sideways seat but was restrained by a firm arm from behind, holding her back. 'What...?' She turned, angrily.

'No, mistress,' Silas said, leaning towards her from his greater height. 'It's a long way down, and you could injure yourself. And I have far more interesting fabrics to show you, if you can wait.'

Frustrated yet again, Isolde could not believe the boast. 'What, better than these, sir? Look at the colours. I need...' She pointed.

'Yes, I know you do. I intend to put the matter right, I assure you.' He took hold of the mare's bridle and turned her through the crowds to Bridlestreet, which linked the Market Square with the equally impressive Burg. Alone, they could have kept up a hostile silence,

Isolde sulking, Silas uncompromising, but with Master Caxton and Jan Van Wynkyn still bubbling after their appointment at the Princenhof and their expectation of a midday meal at the Marinershuis, she had little choice but to resume her pseudo-sociability.

More than willing to act as tour guide, young Jan pointed out the most interesting landmarks as they approached Silas's house from another direction, and, angry or not, Isolde was moved by the secluded nests of buildings and courtyards, bridges and glimpses of water opposite the Church of Our Lady. The sun sparkled beneath the smooth curve of St Boniface's Bridge, and reflections shone across the water in busy green and brown willow-patterns, making Isolde squeeze her eyelids as they turned to enter their own courtyard.

'You did not enjoy?' Meester Jan held up his arms to lift her down from the saddle.

But before she could respond Silas's arms enclosed her waist from behind and tipped her, slowly and gently, into them. 'Put your arms around my neck,' he whispered, 'or I'll give you to that wordy printer's assistant. Shall I?' he threatened.

'No.' She obeyed, wishing with all her heart that he would kiss her again here, before them all. But he did not. Instead, he carried her into the cool house, where all was dim after the bright daylight, and placed her upright to continue the acting-out of good relations.

The effort was almost too much for her, and by midafternoon, when the guests had departed, Isolde had reached the end of her tether. Almost before the sound of the hooves had died she paced back into the house across the black and white tiles, where she rounded on Silas like a whirlwind, her voice almost screeching with pent-up provocation.

'You *knew*, didn't you? You knew that woman would be there. You knew they'd all be wearing steeples on their heads, not as you said at all. You wanted to—'

'That's enough, Isolde.'

'To humiliate—'

'I said that's *enough*!' He closed the door and stood with his back to it, as he had done before, creating a barrier not to be broached. His voice, cutting but hardly raised, demanded her instant obedience. 'Sit down, maid, if you please.'

Defiantly, she stared back, eye to eye, until a quick glint of anger gave her all the warning she needed. She sat.

'Now,' he said, swinging a stool beneath him, 'you will tell me in a civilised manner, not like some screaming fishwife. Your range is most impressive, but I prefer to hear the lady you showed me this morning. She was truly astonishing,' he said in wonderment.

Chastened, Isolde was inclined to fume in silence, but that time had passed. 'Why?' she croaked. 'Why didn't you give me some warning? You obviously knew there'd be questions, but you didn't say I'd have to explain to a woman who clearly has some claim on you. That was the most humiliating charade I've ever had to play; every bit of it a complete and utter lie. How could you?'

'I'll tell you, if you'll listen.'

'No more lies. Try the truth.'

The cutting tone was resumed. 'I have every intention of trying the truth, so *you* try putting your preconceptions aside and believing what I tell you, for a change. First, the woman has no claim on me, nor has she ever had. Her father, Paulus Matteus, and I have done business together for years, and he once suggested an alliance between myself and his daughter, which he foolishly mentioned to her before he discovered my inclinations. She apparently approved, but I didn't, and she's obviously having some trouble coping with the hurt of rejection. Her father was at fault; he should never have mentioned it to her. That's all there is to it. The possibility that she might have been there this morning didn't enter my head. Yes, I knew she was one of the Duchess's ladies; unusual for a merchant's daughter, but a diamond merchant has…well…an advantage over a mere mercer. But it was William who invited us there, not me, Isolde. It was pure coincidence, and you handled it—' the smile emerged '—with your usual courage. I was most impressed, and I have to thank you for saying to her what I could not have said. Not then, anyway.'

'Why not? Because of her feelings? You didn't mind mine.'

'You had the advantage, Isolde. I'd not intentionally hurt the lass more than she is already.'

'But she's keeping the possibility alive in her own mind, and that casts this so-called understanding of ours into some doubt, doesn't it?'

'Of course not. Everyone knows what the situation

is by now. You were the only one there this morning who didn't and that's why she was trying it on. For mischief. She knew I'd not bother telling you of something that didn't happen.'

'Wishful thinking. Doesn't it embarrass you?'

'No. She can wish all she likes. I don't even think about it, and I want you to do the same. Forget it.'

'I *can* forget it. I care not who you have an alliance with, but I *do* resent having to justify my presence here with a pack of lies.'

'It's not a pack of lies, Isolde, it's as I told you. You *are* mine, like it or not.'

'As far as the whole truth is concerned, sir—'

'And what was the problem with the head-dress? From what I heard, there was nothing but admiration for the way you looked.'

'Another lie. You told me, if you remember, that *this* was what they were wearing—' she pointed to her head '—and then I find—'

'Not lies! I told you, if *you* remember, that it was the Florentine fashion, and so it is, and it suits you a great deal better than those ridiculous pinnacles they're wearing. If they don't take somebody's eye out first, they'll all be as bald as coots if they go on like that. I'll not have you pulling your hair out, Isolde, and that's why I forbade Mei to tell you about them.'

'So, as it was, I was the odd one out.'

'As it was, maid, you were the centre of attention. What more could you have wished for? Eh?'

'And now you're going to tell me what to wear. Is that why I was not allowed to buy myself some fabric?

Do you prefer ten-year-old half-silks to Italian bro-cades, too? You saw their gowns?' She swept a scorn-ful glance over her own, then went to stand at the win-dow, looking out into the side garden that had so far escaped the gardener's attentions. The conversation had taken a milder turn, but nothing now could compare with the relief at his explanation of Mistress Matteus's behaviour. What he had said made sense; she could not doubt it.

Silently, he came to stand at her back, placing his arms around her shoulders and his hands upon the wide sash as if to help its supporting role. 'Yes, maid. I shall probably be telling you that, too, if you'll listen. I told you that I have fabrics better than those on the market, but you didn't believe that either, did you? So what do you think I trade in that interests the Duchess so? Did you not wonder?'

'No, I didn't. My curiosity about you doesn't extend even that far.'

'Little liar.' His hands moved carefully upwards to the full curve beneath her breasts and stayed there, lift-ing and holding. 'To proud to ask, aren't you? Well, then, I'll tell you. I deal in luxury goods rather than in bulk cargo, as most other York merchants do. Fabrics, mostly. I'll show you later, so you can choose some for new gowns, and I'll have them made up for you, and anything else you need. But there'll be no pinna-cles on your head, Isolde. Is that clear?'

'Are you bargaining, sir?'

'Silas, if you please.'

'Silas.'

'No, maid. I'm not bargaining. I don't need to, do I?'

Suddenly, the direction of the argument had turned as, relentlessly, he refused to provide the answer she had foolishly expected. There was no vulnerable spot she could recognise, utilise, or profit by. Acutely aware of being disadvantaged, mentally and physically, she twisted herself away in a panic, but he was ahead of her even in that and she was held against him by an arm that refused to let go. Gentle as ever, he took hold of the pearl pendant as an excuse to make contact with the soft skin beneath it, his knuckles fitting into the hollow where the pear-shaped pearl had been.

'Shh...hush,' he said into her ear. 'We'll bargain when the time comes, lass, not before. No merchant ever buys what he can obtain by gift; he only has to wait.' His knuckles caressed, closing the discussion.

As soon as he released her she fled upstairs to where Cecily was tidying her clothes, flinging herself upon the bed to release the tensions that threatened to break her. Knowing better than to ask questions, Cecily covered her with a shawl and left her alone with the jumbled thoughts and emotions and the overwhelming need to lie once again in his arms, to be rocked and held as she had been on the voyage. Last night, the first in this strange country, she had slept alone and fitfully, and now, when she believed he would be eager to kiss her, he had not done so.

Stealthily, on bare feet, she crept from the room and along the cool passageway to where his chamber door stood ajar. His bed was large and covered with a rug of smooth blonde fur inside an alcove curtained with white linen. Slowly, she dragged one of the white pillows towards her and bent to inhale its scent, finally burying her face deep in its softness as a wave of pure longing shook her with its force. Then, controlling the urge to lie where he would lie, she set the pillow back, removed the pearl pendant and laid it upon the white surface.

'We'll see who waits longest,' she whispered.

Chapter Five

Silas's Marinershuis, tucked into a snug plot beside the Arentshuis, could be approached from the canal at one side and, from the other, from a green and leafy street that led directly into the cobbled courtyard. Screened by buildings and trees, the gardens surrounded a surprisingly large brick house which had been extended so many times since its conception that the windows gave no positive indication of where the storeys were, although Silas's jest about the attics was based on fact.

Through a door in the panelling of the upper passageway, Silas led Isolde and Cecily up a narrow flight of stairs, passing tiny plate-sized windows at foot level. At the top, a large room lit on one side by arched floor-level windows was high-beamed with a network of rafters, the walls lined with wooden shelves, tier upon tier, where logs of linen-wrapped fabrics lay like shrouded bodies in a tomb, their labels dangling as miniature pennants. The absence of colour was countered by the large central table where ledgers were piled with leather-bound sample books peeping with jewels of gold and silver threads, a quick shine of peacock and azure, the brown gleam of bronze.

He took her wrist to help her up the last step, then turned to Cecily to do the same. 'These are the most precious ones,' he said, 'but there'll be many more when the new cargo arrives on Monday.'

'They were on the ship with us?'

'Er, no, *damoiselle*. They come overland from Venice and Florence and Lucca.'

'So what were we carrying? Not luxury goods from England, surely?'

'No.' He strode over to the table and lit the lantern for more light. 'No, we carried wool and wood and various other bits and pieces. Other merchants use my ship to carry their merchandise, you see. Now, come and have a look.'

Isolde thought his reply too dismissive, but said no more. What merchants got up to was their own business. Between the shelves, door after door revealed smaller rooms and closets stacked with more bolts of cloth, all linen-wrapped and labelled, and when Silas opened the end of one and peeled back its shroud, the small room was suddenly aglow with a brilliant patch of red and gold.

'Not your colour,' he murmured. 'Something a little cooler, perhaps.' He laughed softly, as if sharing a private jest, and Isolde blushed and backed out.

'These must be priceless,' she said to Cecily.

'Pricey, not priceless,' said Silas. 'Nothing here is priceless. Look over here.' He led the way to another small door, partly hidden by a set of swinging shelves. Unlocked, this led into a large windowless room where shadows danced away from the lantern's light and revealed shelves stacked from floor to rafters with the dull gleam of precious objects. There were stacks of leather-bound and gold-clasped books, boxes and caskets of carved wood and ivory, bundles of quills, vellum and paper, silver and gold plate, chalices, knives and spoons, salts and mirrors framed with tortoiseshell and gold, leather purses and sets of falconers' equipment with gold bells and rich tassels, amber, lapis lazuli and sandalwood, unicorns' horns and sweet-smelling wax. Lower down there were the shining breastplates, gauntlets and helms of engraved armour, swords and polished yew bow-staves and, further round, coloured Venetian glass goblets with twisted stems. He opened a chest to show them bags of pearls and metal threads for embroidery, and Isolde then knew where the ones she wore had come from. Below were leather shoes and boots of exquisite craftmanship, rolls of soft coloured leather and a mountain of furs, silver and shining greys, black, brown, red and gold, striped, spotted and worth a king's ransom.

Luxury goods, he had told her, yet she had not imagined anything on this scale, nor had she even known such things existed except in fairy tales. Unicorn's horn? What on earth was that for?

'Detects poison,' Silas said. 'Princes and kings use it on their food to make sure they're safe to eat.'

'Use it? You mean someone has to try it out?'

'Of course. It's reliable, rare, and therefore costly.

Can't get enough of it. Look at this.' In the light of the lantern, he held up a glass goblet and twisted it to flash a pale ruby fire, then replaced it on the shelf. 'And you were eyeing the purses this morning, weren't you? Well, look, you can take your pick of these.' The clutch in his hand were stiff with embroidery, metal threads and jewels, tassels and shining cords. 'Shall we choose some fabrics first, then?'

More gifts. As if it understood her inner contradictions better than she did, Isolde's hand searched for the pendant she had returned only an hour ago. The gesture and her hesitation were observed, but not remarked upon except by a hand over her wrist that drew her gently back into the main store; in the next moment, Silas was hauling out the heavy bolts and thudding them on to the table, peeling back their covers and drawing out lengths of scintillating gold tissue, cut velvets, taffetas, brocades and damasks until the table was a glowing furnace of colour, pattern and texture.

'Mistress Cecily,' Silas said, giving Isolde time to search, 'I think you will have to resign yourself to a little refurbishment too, you know. Something like this pale grey damask, perhaps, or this plum-striped velvet. This one is from Lucca. Excellent stuff.'

Cecily winced. 'A broadcloth, sir? Mouster de Villers? Something sensible?'

Yelping with laughter, Silas held on to the table. 'No, mistress. No broadcloth. No French stuff. No caddis or kersey, I'm afraid. You'll have to make do with a sensible silk or a good strong Levantine. I know just the thing.'

Accepting no words of protest, he draped them with silks, satins and velvets, cloths of gold and a cream-coloured samite. 'Samite?' he said, holding it beneath Isolde's chin. 'This one is perfect for you. Look, the coloured part is a mixture of silk and linen and the pattern is of gold, yes, pure gold thread. D'ye like it? Good, we'll keep that one, then. Now...' he hunted for another bolt '...you asked me which one the Duchess was wearing this morning. That was a baudekin that came originally from workshops in Baghdad, but all these secrets escape, you know. Warp of gold, weft of silk. Here's one for you, *damoiselle*.' He produced a bolt from beneath a pile which, stripped of its cover, was undecided whether to be gold or sage-green or turquoise. He flung a length across the table to show off its tiny gold pattern, then draped it over Isolde's shoulders, smiling at Cecily's face which was becoming very pink and damp. 'That all right?' he said.

A mountain of fabric was growing at one side of the table, one pile for Isolde and one for Cecily and another of fine Italian cottons, silks and cobweb lawns for chemises, astrakhan lambskins from Messina and Siberian squirrel for trims, cloth of gold for sashes, veiling and spangles for hair.

'Combs, purses, girdles,' Silas said, 'ah, yes, and shoes. We must see the shoemaker on Monday, too. Feathers? Buckles?' He watched the two women do their best to repay his attentions by rolling up and tying the bolts of fabric.

Protesting and laughing, Isolde bade him stop, partly because she was now fast becoming immune to the beauty of some fabrics which, this morning, would have made her gasp. Partly, too, because his generosity had gone far enough, even though he was enjoying it every bit as much as they were.

'Paper?' said Isolde.

'Paper, *damoiselle*? How many reams?'

She snuffled. 'Not *reams*. A few sheets and a quill or two. Am I allowed to write to my father and brothers?'

'I don't see why not. It can't make any difference now, can it? I shall see that you have paper, quills and ink immediately. Mistress Cecily, your needs?'

'Oh, no, sir, I have no needs, really. Except…'

'Except?'

'Well…er…pins and scissors, and silk threads to match…' She waved a plump hand towards the mountain, blinking at its gigantic proportions.

Torn between pity and the mental image of poor Cecily surrounded by a sea of wayward silks, velvets and paper patterns, frantically cutting and stitching for the next two years, Silas and Isolde were soon helpless with a mutual merriment that continued in spasmodic and uncontrollable squeaks all the way down the steep stairway.

The view from Isolde's waterside window had intrigued her since her arrival, her attention held at first as much by the water itself as by the craft. Now the day was drawing to a quiet finale and the water had become darkly mysterious, disturbed only by those who slid silently past to reach home before the curfew.

The low sun caught the outline of the buildings opposite, the solid bulk of Our Lady's Church on the left and, next to it, the house of some important nobleman, she assumed. To the right, the little bridge of St Boniface was now deserted except for one of Silas's cats that walked the lowest parapet across to the grassy path on the far side.

Assuming that it was Cecily who had entered the room and then left again, she remained at the window with her thoughts until the last rim of light had moved upwards to the tall spire of the church, and it was only when Cecily brought in a candle to light the others that she saw something that had not been in the room before. Together, they approached the linen chest where a dark box had been placed.

'A casket, love? When did this appear?' Cecily said.

'Just before you, I think. It's wood. The sides are carved, too. Bring those candles forward, both of them. It *is* carved; feel it.'

The casket was portable, but only by a sturdy porter able to lift a hefty piece of carved walnut with a deep lid and bound with ornamental silver bands. A silver key was in the lock that clicked softly at the first twist, and the lid made no sound as it swung upwards on silver hinges.

In silence, Isolde explored. In the centre section lay a thick layer of creamy paper tied with a blue ribbon, and in various blue leather-lined compartments were quills, a silver knife, two horn inkpots with silver lids, a sand-pot, a heavy silver seal and a block of sealing-wax with a roll of narrow linen tape. Carefully, she took the seal and held its base towards the light, studying its indented design.

'It's a ship. Look, a three-masted ship. And an M.'

'An M for Medwin?'

'Medwin or Mariner. It's beautiful, but I cannot accept it, can I?'

Cecily touched two silver knobs towards the base of the carved front. 'What's this?' she said. 'A drawer?'

Isolde pulled, sliding out a flat table-top covered with smooth blue leather and edges inlaid with silver and coloured woods. Extended, its silver knobs became feet that held it at an angle against the rest of the casket, a perfect writing-surface with a hole at each side to take the inkpots.

Shaking her head, she lifted out the paper to feel its surface and saw that the floor of that compartment was the lid of the one below, where private letters could be kept. A package was there, tied with more blue ribbon. Instinctively, Isolde knew what it contained, but was unable to suppress an excited gasp of laughter as the contents were revealed. The pearl pendant. A message on the inside of the wrapper was written in a large bold hand. 'With its owner next time, if you please.'

Isolde pulled in her top lip and held it.

Cecily watched. 'You're keeping it?' she whispered.

'Yes.' The word fell out, uncomfortably. 'Oh, yes. I think I might have to, dear one.' She wiped one eye, then the other.

'If you're weeping, love, don't drip on to that lovely clean paper.' To Cecily, the dilemma was already solved; to refuse or to accept was a simple matter of making a decision and sticking to it, and when a man had taken liberties with her mistress's freedom, as this one had, then she was entitled to some compensation. Cecily knew her mistress well, but she had never seen her in love before, or as the victim of an abduction. Nor had either of them been so suddenly uprooted from all that was familiar to them. It happened, certainly, but to others, not to oneself. Consequently, it was hardly surprising that the accommodating and unsentimental Cecily was unaware of Isolde's deeper fears, which were to do with losing what little control she had left.

To Isolde, the dilemma was nowhere near solved. Indeed, it had been easier to understand when she had felt nothing more complicated than anger, and some fear. She had known what to do about those. But since her first encounter with Silas things had changed, and now it was as if he knew how quickly she had begun to soften towards him, even to the extent of predicting the time when she would capitulate completely. Already he had put words into her mouth which she had, out of anger, used as ammunition to defend her position, issued in the one place where it would be broadcast most effectively. He must be well satisfied with that. Had she stood and yelled it from the rooftops it could not have suited him better. Next, she was wearing his gift, which had given credence to her statement, and now, trading on her petty gripe about her clothes, he was able to flaunt his generosity even more openly by getting her to wear the best of his merchandise.

Irritably, she recalled how easily she had given way

to his insistence, how quickly seduced by the glory of the colours, the richness of the fabrics and the reflection of herself in others' eyes, after which her simple request for paper had been transformed into this. She had never owned such a treasure, not should she accept it from one who was revenging himself on her father. Yet she could not bring herself to return this as she had done the pendant; to do so would reveal to him the course of her heart more than he knew already. No, it was time for her to practise a more artful game if she hoped to regain control of her affairs.

Their Sunday morning visit to Our Lady's Church just across the canal provided her with an opportunity. Mass was another half-familiar event that only partly succeeded in granting her some peace of mind, because her mind was more bent on retaliation. Not only that, but the beautiful white church provided every excuse for her to dwell on earthly matters, and even the gossamer-light singing lured her eyes around the upper regions, the arches, the clerestory and vaulted roof. Behind the windows of a richly carved screen set high up on one wall she caught a glimpse of faces.

Silas noted her rapt attention and whispered, 'That's the oratory. Lodewijk van Gruuthuse had it built a couple of years ago. It leads from there into his house.'

'He's next door?'

'Yes, the house opposite your window. See his coat of arms, with the Order of the Golden Fleece and the two unicorns in the middle? And the firing cannons at each side? Underneath, too…see, where the motto is?'

'It's in French.'

'Yes. *Plus est en Vous.* More is in you.'

Below this was a set of stone-carved lancet windows and a door with the same devices and fiery cannonballs exploding above them, the motto and symbols so in tune with Isolde's new resolution that her smile almost turned to laughter before she could catch it.

Silas studied her as the singing died away, but she chose not to attempt an explanation. 'Do you know him?'

'Oh, yes. But that's not him up there; that's his family. He's away from home.' The service ended and the congregation mingled its way through friends and acquaintances whose greetings put an end to her questions. The name of Lodewijk van Grutthuse had been introduced into the conversation with Master Caxton the day before as the one who had provided hospitality to King Edward a few years ago, when he had had to flee from enemies in England, but she had not realised that they were near-neighbours. Was there anyone not known to Silas?

Apparently not. Before they left the church, she was introduced to a friendly middle-aged couple who greeted Silas with affection and Isolde with undisguised curiosity. The gentleman was plainly dressed, but one could see that the dark burgundy pleated coat was well tailored; his hat of smooth felt on a fringe of dark straight hair was probably the most inconspicuous he could find. Quietly amiable, he had about him a contemplative air which Isolde too-hastily assumed was because of his wife's quick chatter. She was Anne;

the quiet husband was Hans, who, being successful in some respectable trade, was able to clothe his wife in stiff black brocade that crackled as she moved and a steeple head-dress that, swinging in Silas's direction, made him dodge in exaggerated alarm. Moving off, they insisted that Isolde must be taken to visit them.

'To find out more of what I'm doing here,' she muttered to Cecily.

Silas overheard. 'Well, she might want to,' he said, 'but Hans will no doubt want to paint you.'

'Paint me? With what?'

'Hans is an artist.' When Isolde stopped to stare at him, he elaborated. 'Hans Memlinc. One of Flanders's most renowned artists, and one of Brugge's wealthiest citizens.'

'He's…an *artist*?' As a mere nineteen-year-old, and therefore still distressingly short on perspicacity, Isolde asked herself how she was supposed to know who was who when all the names were so strange and when people did not dress according to their station. The man looked so *ordinary*. She said as much, but was not allowed to get away with it.

'Isolde, people don't wear labels around their necks with their professions written upon them. It may well be usual for people to dress according to their wealth, but many people prefer not to.'

'Why?'

'Because it allows them to see others' true reactions to them as people rather than as clothes-props. Your interest in Myneheere Memlinc as a person was not very great, but would it have been any different, do you think, if he'd been dressed like his wife in his best jewels? Would you have tried harder to make yourself affable?'

Stung by his criticism, she retaliated with childish petulance. 'I could not catch the names. I didn't even know how to address them.'

'That's not what we're talking about, is it, Isolde?'

No, he was right, as usual. What they were talking about was her too-hasty appraisal of people, and her preconceptions of what to expect from them. 'I'm sorry,' she said.

His smile banished her sudden penitence. 'Nothing's lost,' he whispered. 'Here's another one coming up for you to assess, if you like. A much more straightforward case, this. Ah…Myneheere Thommaso!'

A keen-faced dark-haired man in his early thirties sailed towards them in billowing gold and black and an excess of fabric that dripped from his hat and elbows as though his tailor had lost his shears. His frame was slight, but his posturing made up for that, and the flashes of gold from his hands were an example of the conspicuous wealth Isolde had been trying to justify only a moment before. Unlike Hans Memlinc, this man pretended not to notice Isolde, but greeted Silas with a patronising manner that made her cringe.

'They said you were back, Meester Silas. Shall we see you on Monday?'

'You would have seen me on Saturday, Myneheere Thommaso, if your offices had been open. I shall be there first thing; you may depend on it.'

'Good.' Here, a slight lean forward. 'And you made good progress in England?'

'Excellent, *minen heere*. I shall tell you all tomorrow.'

'Ye...es. Yes, of course.' The man had clearly hoped to hear more, but was too curious to leave. 'Ah, *damoiselle*! Your guest, Meester Silas?'

'Mistress Isolde Medwin. Thommaso Portinari.'

And no doubt because his shrewish wife Maria was not too far away, Thommaso Portinari bestowed upon Isolde the same lack of interest of which she had just been found guilty. He bowed, but not before his dark Italian eyes had reckoned her worth in Italian currency. 'Eenglish? I am sure Maria will be pleased to receive you, *damoiselle*, and to show you the sights whenever Meester Silas is otherwise engaged. She speaks your language quite well enough for that.'

Isolde curtsied, but this time said nothing at all.

When they had moved apart, Silas said, 'Well, *damoiselle*? Your verdict?'

She rolled her eyes. 'I cannot wait for you to be otherwise engaged, sir, so that Maria can show me the sights. He's either a brothel-keeper or a bank manager.'

'The latter,' Silas said, imagining the alternative.

'No. You're teasing.'

'I am not teasing. Thommaso is the manager of the Medici bank here in Brugge. Bank managers, you see, have to let everyone know how successful they are. Artists don't. And there's the difference, *damoiselle*.'

'So why do *you* have to see a Florentine banker?'

'Because I carry letters and packages and portfolios from other countries.'

'You run a courier service.' It was more of an exclamation than a question.

'I am both merchant and courier, and every one of my clients would kill to know what I'm carrying from whom, why, how much and where to. They're a nosy lot.'

'But how can you know the details of what you carry?'

'I don't. But they know I could make a good guess.'

'So they pay you to make good guesses?'

'Think. D'ye think they'd trust me with their business, knowing I was open to bribery? Just the opposite, *damoiselle*.'

'But I was right, wasn't I? Sometimes, Meester Silas, they *do* carry labels around their necks, you see.'

They turned on to the little bridge that led them homewards. 'Don't believe what the labels say,' he said. 'They write them themselves.'

Leaving aside the militant imagery of cannonballs, it was the motto 'More is in you' that remained in Isolde's mind. Although open to a variety of interpretations, it had a resolute ring that suggested hidden resources, the very same amenity that she had identified that morning. Apparently, even the great Lodewijk van Grutthuse needed reminding of it from time to time.

Her early-morning sin of omission was offered up for repair, however, when she was in the garden after the midday meal. The little plot she had studied from the parlour caught the midday sun but had been neglected in favour of the larger one nearest the courtyard, and whilst that one grew everything for the kitchen, there was little space for anyone to sit without having their toes run over by the wheelbarrow. This one, Isolde called to Cecily, should be a private garden, enclosed by a wattle fence and perhaps with a fountain of sorts that could be channelled into a pond, and, instead of formal pathways, a carpet of camomile, periwinkle, speedwell and ladies' bedstraw, with a screen of roses across…oh!

Isolde swung her arm like a weathervane, her finger coming to rest in the direction of Silas and his guest, Myneheere Hans Memlinc, whose grins appeared to anticipate her surprise.

'A mead, *damoiselle*?' Hans said. 'A flowery mead with a turf bench facing the sun? And a bowl of carnations? You *must* have carnations.'

'They'd have to be staked,' she replied, looking where he pointed. 'And I had in mind a three-sided turf bench, an exedra, where I could have a table within reach. You know, where we could eat.'

'I'm invited, Mistress Isolde?'

'Certainly you are, sir. Do you play, or sing?'

'Not when your host is around.' The two men came forward and she could tell, even without looking, that she had pleased Silas by her cordiality.

She placed her hands into the outstretched palms of the artist and sensed his understanding in their warm, dry grip. 'I was preoccupied this morning,' she began. 'Please forgive…'

He shook her hands gently. '*Damoiselle*, I have come here especially to ask your pardon for *my* pre-occupation this morning; if I don't get my say in first, Anne will never believe I tried.'

Isolde sneaked a look at Silas and heaved a dramatic sigh. 'I have something of the same problem, *minen heere*,' she said, 'and I haven't yet had permission to do anything to this plot. Perhaps you could put in a good word for me in the right ear? You've known him longer than I.'

'Blackmail? I could threaten to paint his portrait. That should do the trick.' Already they were falling into the easy language of friends that gave the lie to every one of her earlier impressions, such as they were. 'I have also come to ask if you would care to visit my studio tomorrow.'

It transpired later that Hans had also come to ask Silas if he would allow Isolde to pose for him. He needed a Bathsheba. In the nude.

'He asked *you*? And what did you say?'

'I refused. Politely, of course.'

'Without consulting me?'

'Without consulting you, maid.'

'And didn't it occur to you, sir, that I might have wanted to?'

'*Did* you?'

'I might have done.'

'Then before you decide, you had better know that the only person apart from Mistress Cecily who will ever see you stark naked is me. Now, let's talk about the garden, shall we?'

His reply, uncompromising as ever, both excited and annoyed her and strengthened her resolve to make some decisions of her own, a development of which Silas was aware and determined to counter by filling each of her days with some organised pursuit.

The tailor was the first to be summoned to the Marinershuis, an event that left little room for anything but designs and another search of Silas's stock to supplement what she had already chosen. He brought his assistant and, together with Cecily and Mei, the five of them used up with ease the hours of Silas's absence in the town on his business affairs. The consultation led them all into the sun-filled plot for some refreshment, the tailor's ideas on dress and garden design being similarly imaginative, but when another visitor was announced, the tailor bowed and took his leave.

This time yesterday, the name Hugo van der Goes had meant no more to Isolde than Hans Memlinc's, but since then she had been prepared for the tall figure who stooped on his way through the brick archway although it cleared his head by inches. Talk of him had syphoned through yesterday's conversation centring around artists and writers in Brugge, most of them personal friends of Silas. Hugo was spoken of with affection, concern and admiration but no envy on Memlinc's part, though they were rivals. Their description of him had been both friendly and exasperated by his conspicuous self-doubts: he even doubted his ability to clear the arch, Isolde noted with some amusement.

'Myneheere van der Goes, you are welcome, but I fear Meester Silas is not here to see you.'

The long, heavily folded face was difficult to read at the best of times but now, when he chose the shadows and when his head was concealed by a brimmed hat, Isolde saw little of his expression except two large, sad eyes and full lips that seemed unsure whether to smile or speak.

His unsureness gave her more courage. 'Will you wait a while, sir? Silas will be back soon, I expect.' She indicated a three-legged stool still warm from the tailor's backside, then made as if to seat herself.

'Ah, no!' The words exploded softly, taking her by surprise.

'No?'

'Er…forgive me…er, yes. Yes, I will, thank you, but please do not sit just yet.' He held out a hand tentatively. 'Could you, er, stand a while?'

'Of course.'

Without any warning of the artist's intensity, Isolde might well have been at a loss. With it, she stood quite still and with downcast eyes under an examination a hawk would have been proud of, wondering how artists could be so different, one coolly confident in his ability, the other so uncomfortable in it. His clothes, she saw, meant even less to him than Memlinc's did; the long faded blue gown was stained with wine and only his white shirt collar showed that someone took care of his laundry. He might, she thought, have been a few years older than Memlinc, perhaps fortyish.

His manner of speech was soft and rushed as words came out in a block, and he leaned forward with the tension of them. 'Thank you…er…thank you,' he said, searching for a name.

'Isolde,' she reminded him. 'Shall we sit now?'

'Yes…er…I think I knew your name. They say Silas had a…er…I mean, he has a guest staying, and they said you were very lovely and I had to come and see for myself.'

'You are from Ghent, I believe, but you work here in Brugge.'

'Yes, when my clients are here.'

'I've heard about you also, you see, about the great altarpiece for Myneheere Portinari. Are you pleased with its progress?'

His head jerked away, his eyes searching the rosy brick wall of the Arentshuis next door as if seeing his work there. Holding his knees with long tapering fingers, he sighed and leaned back. 'No,' he said, quietly. 'No artist is ever pleased…well, perhaps some are, but very few are *really* pleased with their progress. Sometimes I'd like to scrub the whole thing and start again. God only knows what the Florentines will say of it when it gets there.' He said this to the wall, but then turned back to Isolde with a smile that shone through his eyes. 'But I can't. Myneheere Thommaso would not be best pleased to pay for another lot of materials.'

'Or wait another two years.'

The smile disappeared. 'That's the problem. There

are so many ideas piling up inside—' his hands pressed upon his chest '—and yet I cannot work any faster for fear of spoiling what I do.' He looked at her in sudden anxiety. 'It matters, you see, that what I do is the best; not just the best I can do, but the *best*. No…' he flapped a hand '…it's not competition I'm talking about. I'm not competing with anyone but myself. I could never compete. That's degrading.'

'But you are a free master of Ghent, *minen heere*. Your reputation is second to none.'

Hugo shook his head. 'It's what one thinks of one-self that matters, isn't it? If my work pleases others, that's because they're easily pleased. I cannot trade on that. My own standards must be met.'

'But surely if they're paying you for time and materials, they're not *so* easily satisfied, are they?'

'Surface decoration. Cleverness. Likenesses. That's what they're after. I'm after something deeper than that, mistress. I need another lifetime, because this one's not going to be enough.' His zeal was introvert, more to do with personal ideals than with the reaction of others. His next remark took Isolde by surprise with a sudden directness. 'I need a model, Mistress Isolde.'

'Oh?'

He stood up to explain, feeling more at home on his feet. 'A Mary Magdalen,' he said, pointing to the right side of the wall. 'Over there. She stands beside St Margaret and behind Maria Portinari.'

'She's on the altarpiece, too?'

'Oh, yes, she's at one side and he's at the other, with their patron saints. Mary…Maria…we have to have the donors on it so that everybody knows who put up the money.'

'But supposing she didn't want me to be…?'

'She'll not recognise you,' he said, dismissively, as if to suggest that Maria Portinari would scarce recognise her own mother. 'I need someone with presence. Elegance. You're the right height, colouring, everything. Should I ask Silas first, d'ye think?'

That made her mind up more quickly than anything else could have done. 'No, indeed not, Myneheere Hugo. On matters of this sort, I can decide for myself. I would be honoured to be your model for Mary Magdalen. When do you require me to come?' She told herself she was doing it because he needed help, that the honour of being part of the Portinaris' altarpiece was too great to ignore and that to stand, even anonymously, behind the patronising Maria for all time was a delicious way of insinuating herself into the woman's constellation. Even so, she could not ignore the tingle of excitement at having so quickly discovered a way of retaliating against Silas's injunction, even though she doubted whether Saints Margaret and Mary would be shown naked.

Her concern that this agreement should be kept private was dispersed by the artist's memory loss when Silas returned a few moments later. The two men were pleased to see each other, though Hugo's naturally morose disposition made the presentation of bad news far more important than the good. 'Bouts is ill again. Looks bad this time,' he told Silas.

'Again? I thought he was recovering.' Silas, dressed

completely in black, stretched his long legs and followed their line with his eyes towards Hugo's wrinkled hose.

'He was. He's back in Leuven. Doubt if he'll be painting for a while.'

Silas turned to Isolde, taking in the perfect curves of her figure on the way. 'Dieric Bouts,' he said, 'is a painter. Dutch. Lives in Leuven, not far from here.' He was careful not to comment on his brilliance, which he could have done. 'Been ill on and off for some time. Sad. Shall you go and see him?' he said to Hugo.

'Yes, in the next day or so. I *must* go.'

'Don't go,' Isolde said.

'To Leuven? Why not?' Hugo said.

She saw that Silas was looking at her and she knew she'd got it wrong. 'Not Leuven. I was speaking about now—you've only just arrived.'

Hugo unfurled himself like a fern frond. 'Even so, I must be away.'

Isolde held her breath, but he made no reference to their assignment, which caused her some uncertainty about the artist's reliability but relief that she would not have to explain herself to Silas.

Hugo left by the water gate, and Silas's slow amble back to the house gave him time to ask Isolde about her morning. 'What did he come for?' he asked. As a Yorkshireman, he saw no reason to disguise his usual bluntness.

'To see you, I suppose. To tell you about Myneheere Bouts.'

'I doubt it. I expect he came to have a look at you,

like Hans did. News is spreading fast, *damoiselle*. I've already picked up three prestigious invitations to trade, if I'll take my lady with me next time they have a gathering. You're going to be good for business, Isolde.'

Inadvertently placing herself in the sun's full glare, she stopped and turned to face him. 'You cannot seriously think it,' she said, frowning.

'Think what?'

'You cannot believe that I intend, now that I'm here, to aid you in your business? Have you forgotten the rules? I'm here against my will, remember. You may be deceiving your acquaintances and friends, but nothing has changed between us, sir. Don't rely on my co-operation, if you please.'

Having reached the corner of the house where the courtyard began, Silas advanced, slowly backing her into the brick wall where there was no escape from the sun's rays or from him. Her throat dried as he took hold of her wrists and held them where, a moment ago, they had ineffectually been pushing.

'Tch, tch!' he whispered. 'Still fierce, maid? Did the tailor not perform to your liking, eh? Did you not find what you wanted?'

'You truly believe, don't you, that all this will make things right between us? That new clothes will change an abduction into a friendly visit. And now I'm supposed to show my gratitude by accompanying you to social events here in Brugge to boost your business connections. Is that really what hostages do, sir?' His body pressed against hers and she felt her knees weaken with longing for him.

'What you need, my lass, is something to keep you busy. A wee creature, perhaps? Something to lie in your arms and depend on you?'

Speechless with anger, she reacted like lightning to what she believed he was suggesting, but her frantic pushes were held and controlled, having done little except to provoke his laughter.

'Enough, lass.' He grinned. 'I should not tease you so, should I? D'ye want to see what one of my clients has sent you?'

'No! If it's a bribe to attend you as your lady, I want none of it,' she panted.

'Well, you'd better take a look at it first, because it seems to want you rather badly. Come, take my hand. I expect a better greeting than this after a morning's work.'

Again, she had half expected that he would kiss her and, though she was unwilling to admit it, she experienced an emptiness that only the warmth of his palm on hers did anything to fill. Curiosity having the upper hand, she was led through the cool passageway into the parlour where Cecily sat upon a cushioned bench holding something white in the deep folds of her lap. It bounced as she held up a morsel of cooked chicken, then yapped as Isolde drew near to look.

Tenderly, she gathered the fragile white satin body into her arms, laughing as it reached up to lick her face and adore her with deep liquid eyes. 'It's the same one

I saw in the Duchess's chamber, isn't it? Did she give it to you?'

'To you,' Silas told her. 'She says it went looking for you after we'd gone, and she says you must go and thank her in person before she and the Duke leave next week.'

'And you said I would?' She smiled at him, sheepishly.

'I told you *we* would. So now it's yours. For you to name.'

She smiled at the little gazehound and then at Silas. 'I believe we had already decided on that,' she said. 'Hadn't we, Little Thing?'

Chapter Six

'Falconer?' Isolde repeated, turning sideways to the mirror.

Mei nodded in approval. *'Ja…goed! Valkenaere.'* She smiled.

'Doesn't sound too noble to me. Must be thousands of falconers.'

'Well, don't tell Hans that,' Silas joined in, lounging upon her bed to watch the finishing touches. 'Ann de Valkenaere comes from a vastly wealthy family. She's a chatterbox all right, but she and her dowry have been an asset to Hans. Be polite to her, Isolde, for his sake.'

She turned slowly to be viewed and to view him also, purposely withholding any sign of agreement so that his eyes would seek it for a fraction longer. Still in his black doublet and hose, he now wore a long gown of black figured satin belted with a silver girdle of enamelled discs, the only colour on an otherwise sombre-rich garb. But the beauty of the fabrics, the brief shine of a silk lining, the narrow edge of brown fur and the smooth tan of his skin against the embroidered frill of white shirt caught at her heart and held it, setting the picture into her memory for the dark hours of night. The young gallants at the Duchess's court stood and moved in carefully calculated poses, one leg extended, feet at an angle, hand on hip. Not so Silas Mariner: his elegance was unstudied, his head set proudly above great shoulders that she had held and explored, though never beneath the shirt. His legs in tight black hose made soft valleys along her green coverlet which, if Mei did not smooth them away, would be left until she could lie in them.

'You may go, Mei. Thank you.' Isolde adjusted the gold net that held her coiled hair, still watching him. 'I'll be polite to her. I just find her overwhelming, that's all. But I'll try, for Myneheere Memlinc's sake.' And for yours, she would like to have said. 'Will they mind if I take the Little Thing?'

Without answering her directly, he undid the silver-clasped pouch that hung from his belt and drew out, very slowly, a fine leash of plaited coloured leather with gold mounts to match the wide collar around the gazehound's long neck. Clipping it on while trying to avoid the appreciative tongue, he handed the end to Isolde. 'Keep it well under control,' he said. 'Hans doesn't invite everyone to his studio.'

His thoughtfulness was like a reproof. 'Thank you,' she whispered. Later, she was to regret once more the impulsive workings of her mind that vanquished caution like a flame over dry tinder. Silas accepted her thanks in silence, but she knew what he waited for. The stillness of him as he made no move to leave, his

deep gaze so like the ones she had seen when a kiss
was imminent, caught at her heart a second time. It had
been almost four days—years?—since his last kiss, and
now it was up to her. A shout reached the room from
somewhere downstairs but hardly registered as she bent
to lay her arms across his shoulders, to link them behind his head and submerge herself in his dark, un-
blinking eyes. Was it triumph she saw in them just
before she tilted her head?

Almost leaping out of her skin with fright, she
straightened as the door flew open with a loud crash
against the wall, making the little gazehound hurtle into
her legs with a yelp. Silas was on his feet in one swift
movement, holding Isolde's arms to swing her behind
him and to face the intruder who filled the doorway to
prevent both Pieter and Mei from getting there first.

'Well! What the hell are *you* doing here?' Silas
snapped, dismissing his servants with a nod. They
closed the door.

'Your greeting, *brother*, gets a mite tedious. D'ye
think you could manage a different one for a sea-
crossing? And what d'ye think I'm doing?'

'Barging into a lady's bedchamber?'

'Like you, you mean?' Bard looked pointedly beyond them to the deep indentation on the velvet-
covered bed. 'Did you have to bring her all this way
for *that?* Couldn't you have managed a quick one at
Scar—?'

Silas's hand shot out like a bow from an arrow, gathering up a bunch of the grimy shirt beneath his
brother's chin and pushing it backwards until Bard lost

his balance against the wall. He was no match for Silas's greater strength. 'Shut your mouth, lad,' Silas growled, 'or you'll be swallowing your teeth for supper. You wouldn't know it, but this is a *lady's* bedchamber and this—' he tipped his head towards Isolde '—is a lady. And this is my house. Keep a civil tongue in your head.'

Furious still, Bard took hold of Silas's wrist in both hands. 'Let go!' he snapped. It needed no examination to see that the voyage had not agreed with him in any sense, that he was desperately tired, lacking in food and ready for a thorough cleansing. His usual healthy colour had paled at the constant truancy of his stomach, and the optimistic bounce that women found so attractive was sadly deflated. Nevertheless, his eyes lit at the sight of Isolde who, flushed from breast to forehead, became instantly desirable to him though she was obviously mortified by his untimely appearance.

She was also mystified. 'What *are* you doing here, Bard? Don't pretend you knew nothing of this plot. I'll not swallow that kind of tripe.'

'What plot?' Bard said irritably, pulling at his neckline.

'The plot to revenge your family for Felicia's abduction, of course. What else could I mean?'

'I don't know of any plot, Isolde. I've come to take you back because I'll not have big brother Silas taking my woman from under my nose. He's duped me once, but he'll not do it again.'

'I'm not your woman,' Isolde retorted. 'I'm not anybody's woman!'

'You expect me to…?' He caught Silas's eye and glowered with burning resentment, running a hand wearily through his unkempt hair.

Silas intervened. 'This discussion can wait, I think, until you've had some attention. You smell like a drain, lad, and you're not going to talk much sense until you've had some sleep and food.'

With a look of horror, Bard clapped a hand to his mouth. 'No, not food. A mug of ale will do. Ah, it beats me how you can stand all that sailing. The floor's still rocking.'

'When did you reach Sluys?'

'Early this morning. Cargo of timber and lead. Nowhere to sleep. What a nightmare!'

'Come on, I'll find you a bed.' Silas went to the door to call for Pieter, but Bard's anger still boiled and bubbled over again before Silas could restrain him.

'Do you realise that I've chased all this way after you, Isolde? I thought you'd surely be as glad to see me as you were at York. I waited there for the boat, and you all the while thinking I'd hatched a plot…and he told you…what *did* he tell you?'

'Later,' Silas said, thrusting him into Pieter's arms. 'Go on. I'll follow. We'll clear the matter up later.'

'You were going out?' Bard mumbled.

'Still are, if you'll do as you're told. Go on.' He closed the door and turned to Isolde. 'Wait for me. I'll get him some clothes and see him comfortable, then we'll be off.'

'He waited at York. He didn't know, did he?'

'Isn't that what I told you?'

'I didn't believe you.'

'That seems to be a habit of yours.'

'Can you blame me?' She looked away, unable to hold his eyes and intentionally making no reference to what she had been about to do when Bard interrupted. A moment or two later, and who knew what he might have seen? 'You think it's safe to leave him here while we're out?'

'Pieter and Mei will be here. He'll be asleep in half an hour, anyway. I doubt he'll wake till morning. I'm not going to lose the chance of being seen out with you, my lady, just because I have a brother visiting.'

Misunderstanding, she bridled. 'No, indeed. That wouldn't do, would it? Today's theme seems to be about men needing women, for one reason or another. Mostly to do with pride, naturally.' She cradled the Little Thing in her arms.

'You are not flattered that your conquest has traipsed all this way to get you back? Most women would be.'

'Bard is no conquest,' she flared. 'He's angered by your treachery, that's all. Who wouldn't be? But I cannot understand why you didn't tell him in the first place. It would have saved him a journey.'

'Yes...well, I must admit to being surprised at his doggedness, though I can sympathise with his infatuation.'

'Thank you. Infatuation. Well, well. You know about that, do you?'

He raised an eyebrow. 'At my age? Surely. Show me a man who doesn't.'

'And you are not annoyed that he's turned up?' She longed for him to say, even to imply, that he was.

'Not at all. It's inconvenient, I suppose. But his being here making cow's eyes at you won't alter my plans one bit unless you convince me that you want to return to England with him. Then I'll probably have to revise the situation. *Do* you?'

'Do I what?'

'Want him to take you back home?'

She beat her brain for something to wound him with. Quickly. 'Well, not until I've seen my new gowns, anyway.'

A smile hovered and flew away with a quick shake of his head. 'Good try, maid,' he said, softly, 'but it won't do. I told you, I'm not bargaining, and nothing's changed since then.'

'I'm sorry. That was unmannerly of me. Please forget I said it.'

'I'm extremely deaf on that side on alternate Mondays,' he said, with a smile. 'Wait a while. We'll be away as soon as I've seen to him.'

Being reasonably certain that the English merchant known as Silas Mariner would be about his business on this Monday afternoon, Ann-Marie Matteus gave her doting father a dutiful peck and thanked him for taking her in his skiff as far as the Marinershuis and, yes, she would be ready to be collected in an hour or so. Dear Isolde, she said, would be pleased to see her new friend again in a strange town, so far from home. They had so much in common.

Her maid, as skinny as Cecily was stout, helped her up the steps and through the gate which was not as familiar to them as they would have liked. Not recognising the young lass left alone to keep watch while Pieter and Mei were otherwise engaged, Ann-Marie demanded to speak to Mistress Isolde Medwin, and the lass, already halfway seduced by the handsome young Englishman in the kitchen, soon found her place usurped by one who would present more of a challenge, at least.

Bard had come through the cleansing ceremony with flying colours and, until the secondary diversion, had been ready to eat before sleeping. In Silas's shirt and hose, with points hastily re-tied, he presented less than a courtly appearance whilst resembling, in the most marked manner possible, something from Ann-Marie's wildest and most erotic dreams. Consequently, he found his tongue before she did.

He spread his hands and assumed his most beguiling apologetic face, ready to tackle an English-Flemish explanation. 'No Mistress Isolde. Only me. I regret...' His hand flattened on his chest, reminding him that the shirt was almost open to the navel. He looked down at himself in mock dismay, knowing that her eyes would follow to the exaggerated but fashionable bulge, the braguette, below his waist. Then he bit his lip in pretend embarrassment, his eyes brimming with laughter and the certainty of eventual conquest.

The inexperienced and vulnerable Ann-Marie had little immunity against masculine wiles as blatant as this. The young men at court were fops, but this one was minus the obvious trimmings and she was wide open to any semblance of solace to her wounded pride, in whatever form it was presented. 'You are English?' she said. 'From England?'

Bard smiled his most charming smile and left the hand on his breast. 'Ah! What a relief! I thought I might have to speak Flemish, or French, or whatever. Your English is perfect, *damoiselle*. Where did you learn it?' He took her elbow and led her as if she were thistledown across the warm stone paving of the kitchen courtyard to the plot where Isolde's benches remained in position. Still in his stockinged feet and with his hair darkly damp and unruly, he sat at a respectful distance so that she would have a good view of his calf muscles and wrists, the gleam of his skin and the sunlight in his wicked eyes.

The young kitchen lass, not completely giving up hope, brought out the cold food and wine that he had been going to eat, and, with extra goblets for Ann-Marie and her maid, it was not long before he was accepting mouthfuls like a bird from a captor's hand, flavoured with her pity for such a frightful journey.

'You came to take Mistress Isolde home? That was an act of great courage, sir, but if she is visiting your brother, why should she wish to return home? She made me believe she was content here in Brugge.'

Bard shook his head, sadly. 'That's what she would say, with him by her side, isn't it? What else could she say? That he's abducted her?'

'What? Abducted? Silas would not do anything like that.'

'You don't know my brother as I do, *damoiselle*,' he said, opening his mouth for another piece of chicken. 'It's to do with our family's honour, you see, and there he's quite ruthless, as the eldest. He has to be seen to be taking some action. It was inevitable.'

'What was?'

As if reluctant to explain, he sighed and looked away, but not for long; he had seen the glint of diamonds in the golden coils of her collar. 'Our families are enemies,' he said, unfolding the story with a touching hesitancy and milking it for every ounce of pathos. When he had finished, he noticed a tear glistening in the corner of her eye, ready to trickle down her nose. 'Why, what is it, dear lady?' he said. 'It's not for you to weep, but me. Isolde has always been in love with me, and can't stand the sight of my brother, yet it's no use letting the situation worsen. I have to try to persuade him to let her go. It may take some time, but I must make the effort.'

'And you? Are you in love with...? Oh, forgive me. I should not have asked that. What must you think of me? No, don't answer. I have no right to know.'

'I shall answer you, just the same.' Bard was well practised in The Art of the Sigh: this one came from the 'alas' shelf. 'I thought I was in love, *damoiselle*, when we were at home and undiscovered. Now I realise that, since she's been with my brother, my heart is moved more towards tenderness than love. I'm duty-bound to relieve her distress; even though she's a Medwin, I bear the family no grudge, as Silas does, nor do I believe my sister to be in any mortal danger. But when Isolde places all her hopes in me, as she did in York, what can I do but help?'

Ann-Marie wiped the tear away now that it had been noticed. 'He was to have been mine,' she whispered. 'If only things could return to the way they were before all this happened. If only I'd known of her distress when we met, I might have been able to show her more kindness.'

Bard stared at her. 'Your pardon, *damoiselle*? You say that Silas and you...?'

'Yes, it's true. My father and Silas do business together, but he'd certainly withdraw his support if he thought Silas was not going to keep to his promise of marriage. It was to have been in two years, because of my being engaged on the Duchess's affairs, but the agreement was made last year.'

'And your father? He's a merchant, too?'

'Diamonds,' she whispered, with downcast eyes. 'We live in Antwerp. I'm the only daughter.'

Even Bard had heard of Antwerp's diamond trade. 'Is that what Silas trades in? He relies on your father, does he?'

'Completely. It would be the end of him. My father must never know of this business, sir. You won't tell him, will you? He believes Silas to be above reproach.'

'So you still hope to marry him, *damoiselle*?'

Ann-Marie dabbed again with a pretty embroidered handkerchief. 'Like you, sir, I'm beginning to have doubts after hearing of his treatment of Isolde, but I shall do as my father bids me. Poor Isolde. So brave.

If she were to lose your love, the feeling of rejection might tear her apart.'

'Yes,' said Bard, meaning nothing of the kind. From what he'd seen as he burst unexpectedly into her bed-chamber, Isolde's impending rejection was not the issue, but her virginity. That had been intact when he'd last seen her, and very highly she had held it. If that scoundrel of a brother had changed that state of affairs, then he deserved all that was coming to him, for Isolde's precious commodity had been the reason for the pursuit to both York and Brugge.

It could not have fallen better into place if he had orchestrated it himself, Bard mused as he pleasured the kitchen lass as soon as Ann-Marie had left. Fortune was certainly on his side here in Brugge, showing him a way to get even with Silas and also the distinct possibility of taking both Isolde and the diamond heiress without either of them being any the wiser. Meanwhile, refreshed in mind and spirit, it needed only sleep to complete his physical needs, with no one to silence about his new conquest except the maid, and that was in hand. When Pieter and Mei appeared some time later, the maid was busily plucking a goose and, when Silas and Isolde returned, Bard was fast asleep in his small room at the back of the house, replete in every sense.

Isolde had been polite to Hans Memlinc's chattery wife but had not been assailed by her in the studio, where only Hans and his apprentices had been at work, and though she had been fascinated at the time by the processes involved, she could now concentrate on little except Bard's unexpected appearance. Silas might think of it as an inconvenience, but to her it was a catastrophe that kept pace in her mind with how pleased she had been to see him in York, how quick to flee with him. Rarely had she missed a chance to show Silas how unwilling she was to stay here; now he would expect her to behave consistently in Bard's presence unless, of course, he knew the secret workings of her heart on that issue also, which she could hardly doubt after his remarks about bargains and gifts.

They had sailed home through the sleek brown water that dived beneath low bridges and cut a path through tall anonymous buildings, and he had lain his hand over hers, whispering. 'Don't worry about it. We'll sort it out one way or another.'

She had not asked how he knew what was on her mind but, by her silence, showed him that he had guessed correctly, and she was able to find some comfort in his earlier remark that his plans would not be changed by having Bard with them. The expected confrontation, however, was delayed by Bard's deep sleep, which did not end until the next morning, after Silas's departure to the Lucca Merchants' House on Needle-street.

Isolde was in the little plot of ground in conference with the gardener and his lad, discussing the height of a rose arbour along one side. Trelliswork tunnels, they told her, were high fashion here in Flanders. Bard's patience with this garden talk was limited and, taking

Isolde by the elbow, he eased her away at the first sign of an agreement.

She frowned. 'Bard, I've not finished here. You go in; I'll join you in a moment or two.'

But Bard's misgivings had come alive again by daylight and needed instant clarification. He kept hold of her elbow. 'Come,' he said. 'I've not travelled all this way to wait upon the gardener's time. This way, if you please.' He seated her where Ann-Marie had yesterday come down off her high horse to feed him pieces of chicken and where his dishevellment could best be appreciated in the balmy warmth of a secluded corner. It had worked a treat. But Isolde was no Ann-Marie. His tricks were already well known to her, and, now that his brother had had her at close quarters, it would not be so easy to regain ground. But how close was close?

For Isolde, his attempts at charm had ceased to have any effect except irritation, and the inevitable comparisons between this shallow-minded young rake and his elder brother were present at every word and turn of head. How could she ever have been attracted to him?

He tried the tender approach, taking one of her hands in both of his. 'Well, *chérie*? We can speak freely now we're alone. You've had an ordeal,' he said, softly. 'Can you tell me about it?'

She stifled a sigh, knowing how he watched for every sign. 'There's nothing much to tell,' she said.

'Eh?' He breathed a laugh. 'You were together on a boat for days, and now here with him, and there's nothing to tell? Come on, love. You don't have to hide it from me. How long was it before he...?'

She removed her hand in some irritation. 'It was not like that. And anyway, you've no right to be asking me such questions.'

'I thought I had,' he said. 'Did he make you sleep with him?'

Technically, the answer was yes. 'I slept with Cecily,' she said. 'Ask her.'

'So you're—?'

'Bard, your brother has not harmed me in any way. He behaved like a gentleman.' She stopped short of 'the perfect'. 'If I appear to be upset by your appearance here, it's because I was sure you had a hand in the plan to abduct me and revenge Felicia, and my anger has stayed with me. I felt betrayed.'

Bard leaned towards her and captured her hand once more. 'Sweetheart, I was *so* relieved to find you safe here. I'd have walked it to reach you. I couldn't bear to think of you weeping, deserted…'

She had not wept. 'How did you find out what happened?'

'In York? Well, Silas obviously intended me to know, once I reached his house. He told me how to get there. It's a huge place on Coney Street, just by the wharf. But his servants just laughed: thought it was a huge jest, you know, brothers, and all that. They said he'd been to York the previous week, then he was off to Flanders.'

'What about Scarborough?'

'They didn't mention Scarborough. Perhaps that was a change of plan.'

'So then what?'

'Well, I tied the horses you'd borrowed from Fryde outside the Merchant Adventurers Hall after curfew, then I stayed overnight at Silas's house. And the next morning I went down the wharf to ask if Silas was due; the dockers at the Queen's Crane said exactly what his servants had said, that he'd been. They didn't expect to see him for weeks. I was furious, I can tell you. The bastard! Anyway, I found a cargo ship that was due to set sail down to Hull and then to Flanders and, as it happened, we had a fair wind but, oh, Isolde!' He clutched at his stomach and groaned. 'Never again! Next time I'll learn to walk on water.'

'You saw nothing of Master Fryde in York?'

'Not a thing. Did Silas send him a message, do you know?'

'Not that I know of. But he's sent one to my father.'

'Eh?' Bard frowned. That was not good news. It placed him in the direct firing line. 'He's told your father? He wants a ransom? Greedy bastard!'

'No!' Isolde said sharply. 'He's told my father that he'll keep me as long as Felicia's a prisoner, and let him know that I'm safe. I don't believe he's interested in a ransom, and anyway the only thing the La Vallons would be interested in would be the return of your sister, wouldn't it? And my father's not known for changing his mind. Quite the contrary.'

'Not even for his daughter's safety?'

'My safety's not the issue. But I don't know. I think I shall have to sit it out here in Brugge for a while.'

Bard's voice softened. 'Perhaps we could both sit it out here, *chérie*. It's as good as York any day.' He leaned towards her, caressing her cheek with a travelling finger that found a quick route down her neck and into the edge of her chemise. It was caught and held off, but Bard was undeterred. 'There's a lot of exploring to be done,' he whispered, 'and as long as he believes we're behaving ourselves, we could stay here in his little palace while he's out on his business trips. Housekeepers, eh? What d'ye think of that? If he's intent on keeping you here, I could be his assistant gaoler. I'd make a very sympathetic gaoler, Isolde.' His other hand sneaked round the back to hold her neck and chin in his direction and, as her eyes flickered and watched his, he believed he was winning back some of the ground he had lost. 'So,' he teased, 'what was all that I saw when I arrived yesterday, my lass? Getting ready to seduce him, were you?'

Slowly but forcibly, his hand was prised away from her neck and held by the wrist. 'No, Bard,' Isolde said. 'As a matter of fact, I was thanking your brother for the gift of a dog lead, nothing more. Does that answer your question?' Her eyes were wide open now, holding nothing of the languorous invitation he had been so sure of, and, although she was not even perturbed enough to move out of his half-embrace, neither was she anywhere near ready to give anything away.

Bard was not easily deterred, for this was one of the most enjoyable parts of the hunt: the pursuit of the prey. There were times, though, when persuasion had to take a more positive line, for if he did not take control of the situation as a matter of some urgency, it was obvious that his treacherous brother would. He had already seen the signs. Laughing, he allowed her to keep hold of his wrist, now lying over her shoulder, as this kept her prisoner, too. His other hand closed over her breast and so captured her within a circle from which she could hardly escape without an undignified struggle.

Undignified or not, Isolde was prepared to indulge herself, if need be, and although Bard was strong, her attempts to be free of him were meant to be taken seriously. 'Get *off*!' she snapped, twisting away.

A voice, unmistakably Silas's, came from nowhere. 'She doesn't like it, lad. I tried it myself, but she won't have it at any price.'

Relieved, but very irate, Isolde propelled herself sideways and somewhat off-balance into Silas's arms. Not prepared to explain, she would have quickly disengaged herself to head off towards the house, but he caught her around the waist and held her firmly against him, her face beneath his chin. Before she could guess his intention, his mouth was warmly over hers in a kiss of greeting that was clearly meant to impress Bard as much as her.

She had been starved for days with only the memory of her nights in his cabin to feed on. Pretence was beyond her, the need for it way out of range, and the kiss she returned could not have failed in its message of desperate hunger, a plea to him to relieve her yearning.

Silas was prepared for anger and some resistance, but hardly for this. Nevertheless, her response reassured him that the line he was about to take with Bard was just as acceptable to her, even allowing for her unpredictability, and his soundless message breathed upon her lips. 'Say nothing', was the only insurance he had time for.

Holding her to his side, Silas regarded his brother's displeasure with faint surprise. 'I could have told you,' he said, 'but you were asleep. I didn't think to wake you with the information, though I suppose I should have. You've been here less than twenty-four hours, lad…' he motioned to Bard to sit again and shared the bench opposite with Isolde '…and already you've had the kitchen lass, halfway there with one of the duchess's ladies, and now an attempt upon my woman. I have to hand it to you, you don't waste time, do you? Even after a voyage in a cog, you're going a fair way to beating my father's record, I'd say.'

By this time Bard's pallor was quickly being replaced by a mottled flush and an Adam's apple that yo-yoed alarmingly, turning his first words into a croak. 'How the hell did you know that?'

'What…about the *maid*?' Silas leaned towards him, frowning. 'How do I know what's going on in my own house?' he said, incredulously. 'Wake up, lad, for pity's sake. How the hell d'ye *think* I know? Did you believe I'd let you have the run of this place whilst my back was turned? You, of all people?'

'You've…you've not dismissed her, have you?'

'Of *course* I've dismissed her. I'll not have your brat carried around my home for nine months. I hire my servants to work, not to breed,' Silas said harshly.

'So what d'ye think those other two were doing,

then? What d'ye call 'em…Pieter and Mei?' Bard asked, petulantly.

'Watching to see what you got up to, lad.'

'No…they were—'

'No, they weren't. How do you think I know about Paulus Matteus's daughter coming here?' Silas felt Isolde flinch and signalled to her with a quick press of his fingertips on her waist. 'And who came with her, how long she stayed, where you talked? And did you really think she'd keep quiet about it, anyway? *Did* you?'

'She told you? When? I don't believe it.'

'Then don't. She told her father. Her father's a friend of mine. Has been for years. I saw him this morning. The poor lass was so full of you she couldn't help herself, but you could at least have given her the facts straight instead of a bowl of codswallop. He'll not let you marry his daughter, you know, if you can't stick to the truth. He's a canny merchant, is Paulus. One of the best. And he knows a diamond from a lump of—' He glanced at Isolde, restraining himself.

'Marry her? Is that what she said?'

'Well, the word cropped up somewhere, and I'm damned sure I didn't suggest it.'

Isolde could not keep quiet any longer. 'What was this bowl of codswallop? Do I not have a right to know, since it probably concerns me?'

Silas was quick with the denial before Bard could begin to dissemble. 'No, sweetheart. It concerns me. Bard believes—do you not, brother?—that he can get even with me for stealing you from under his nose by taking the woman who pretended to him that she and I have an agreement to marry.'

'She said it was so. In two years, she said.'

'She would. She takes her rejection hard, but I can't help that. You have it from me that it is *not* so, so you're running down the wrong track, lad. Now, I could have told her father this morning about her silly claims, but it would have upset him and got her into hot water, so I didn't. Besides which, he seems to think that the handsome young brother of his friend Silas Mariner who made such an impression on his daughter is like a new toy that he can't deny her, and I'm certainly not going to thwart that, if that's what she's after. It'll be something of a relief,' he muttered, giving Isolde a gentle squeeze.

'And that would be convenient, brother, wouldn't it?' said Bard, adopting some sarcasm of his own. 'I came here to rescue Isolde, and you pair me off with one of your rejects. Well, that's very neat.'

'Rescue Isolde from what, exactly?'

'From you.'

'And does she look as if she wants to be rescued from me?'

'You abducted her, man! You cannot take a woman like that.'

'Her father took our sister; I've taken his daughter. That makes her mine as long as he has Felicia. Isolde is my woman, like it or not.'

Bard glared from one to the other, then accusingly at Isolde, and, though she knew exactly what was passing through his mind, she also knew that, in Silas's presence, he dared not speak it. 'Are you warning me off, Silas?'

Silas leaned back, half-dropping his eyelids. 'Well done, lad,' he said. 'You're beginning to get the message at last. So, while you're in respective mode, understand this. If the idea of having a diamond merchant for a father-in-law appeals to you, you'd best begin to stick to one woman at a time, because Paulus Matteus is an indulgent but jealous father. Perhaps now is the time to weigh up the pros and cons before you get in any deeper. Oh, and by the way, apparently Ann-Marie believes you've almost seduced her already, but she doesn't take too happily to rejection. Gets offended rather quickly. You can stay here for the time being, though.' He did not add *as long as you behave yourself*, but it was clearly implicit in the offer and Bard was not so incensed that he felt bound to reject it, or even to ask for modifications.

It gave Isolde little pleasure to be wrangled over by two brothers, or even to be claimed by the one she wanted as if she were a piece of prestigious merchandise. She would prefer to have been wooed. Silas's use of the term 'lady' and 'woman' appeared to depend on the circumstances and, whilst the latter had overtones of possession and was therefore, in a way, exciting, she would have liked him to say that she was his lady, conveniently forgetting, of course, that she had recently denied it. Even so, Silas's uncompromising declaration of ownership removed in one fell swoop any need for her to find an excuse to stay, though, had she thought about it more rationally, she would have seen how immaterial were her wishes on that point. In a sense, that little crisis was over, for now Bard would leave her alone.

Bard was uncertain whether to laugh or to cry. His hastily made plans had come unstuck before they were dry and the wealthy minx Ann-Marie Matteus had him tied up before he could blink. He too would have liked a wooing. An hour in the garden could hardly be called a chase, and the possibility that he was the prey had never crossed his mind. He was therefore relieved when Silas charitably offered to take him to the Antwerp merchant's office for an informal introduction to Myneheere Matteus himself. The glitter of diamonds grew brighter, but the possibility of being able to score over Silas had now grown dim in the light of the two men's mutual trust. Bard's eternal self-confidence, however, cheered him with the warming thought that the diamond merchant's daughter was willing to perjure herself to get him. Vaguely, he wished Isolde had been as keen, and what a pity it was that she had not been at home to see her new friend.

'Came to see *me*?' Isolde laughed with Cecily as they stood side by side at the window of her room. 'Well, whatever she came for, they'll both get what they deserve.' Below them, the two brothers tucked their long black legs into the skiff by the water gate and slid silently away, turning to wave to her before disappearing under the low bridge. 'Quick, love! We've just enough money to pay the boat one way. We'll have to walk back. Come on!' Naturally, it had not occurred to her guardian that she might need money, and she had had to ask Mei to lend her a few coins to take them as far as Goldenhand Street where Hugo van der Goes had his workshop.

Twenty minutes later, Cecily was still tugging at the long bell-rope as Isolde's hopes and fears spilled out together. 'You don't think he's forgotten, do you? He said something about visiting his other artist friend who's ill in—where was it?'

'Leuven. Ah, listen! Someone's coming.'

It was at this point that Isolde could happily have turned away and pretended a stroll along the canal, where houses sent mirror-images into the water, to lose their identities. The Van der Goes workshop was on the far side of a cobbled courtyard across which men in sober gowns, scribes and errand-boys beat criss-cross paths of business, disappearing up steps and through doors with sidelong looks of curiosity at Isolde and her maid. In York, or at home, it was nothing remarkable for her to venture into the town chaperoned only by her maid; here, she was being made to feel like a woman on the loose, an escapee, perhaps. Just as well, then, that Silas did not know about it.

A young man showed them inside, wiping multi-coloured fingers down a stained leather apron and throwing a cheeky grin at Isolde. 'Mixing pigments,' he said in English. 'You come to sit for the Master?'

Isolde supposed that, because of her plain woollen dress and the absence of an escort, the lad felt able to dispense with the formality due to a lady of quality, but she saw no reason to foster the notion. 'Myneheere van der Goes is expecting us,' she said, looking straight ahead.

The smell of wood, canvas, oil and burnt candles drew them along the tiled corridor from which half-open doors provided glimpses of paper-strewn rooms, a garden, and a chamber where a half-made bed spilled rumpled sheets on to the floor. This disorderly prospect might have prepared her for what was to come, had she been receptive to the signs. But she had embarked upon this venture in order to make a point, and any serious thought of backing out now would have indicated a sorry lack of conviction. So, when the lad motioned them through one half of a large double-door, then closed it behind them, Isolde's comparison with the studio of Hans Memlinc suffered from immediate overload.

Whereas Memlinc's studio was orderly in the extreme, cool, light and spacious, loaded with the concentration of four apprentices and jewel-bright with unfinished panels, the workshop of Hugo van der Goes was a duplicate of the man's mind, cluttered and restless with an abundance of everything in an orderly chaos. Picking her way over the littered floor, Isolde looked up to see a group of people standing around a large panel, quietly discussing it. The next thing she noticed was that two of them were women, stark naked, and talking as naturally as if they had been clothed. Stark naked? Well, one of them wore slippers and the other a scarf around her neck, as if she had a sore throat, both were very lovely and in their twenties and both turned to study their visitor without sharing any of her embarrassment.

The three apprentices, the young assistant and Myneheere van der Goes next turned to look, adding to her sense of dislocation with blank stares which verified that the invitation issued on Monday had been quite forgotten by Tuesday. This was the second point at which Isolde's resolution almost failed her. But too late. Hugo van der Goes came forward, his voice still hesitant, wondering, 'Mistress Medwin?'

'We met yesterday. You asked me if…er…'

His eyes widened, then laughed. 'So we did, so we did. St Margaret, wasn't it? I remember.'

'St Mary Magdalen.'

'Yes, well…one or the other. It was kind of you to offer. Come…'

She hesitated on both counts, but Hugo spoke to his friends in a gush of Flemish. She had no way of knowing if his words were accurate, and suspected, understandably, that they were probably not. He took her by the shoulders as if, here in his studio, her consent had been taken for granted, and she was turned to them, this way and that, while her eyes swivelled to watch for their reaction, half expecting to see either apathy or hostility. Not for one moment had she thought to find anything like this.

Yet the critical appraisal of the new saint was not hostile, and even though she could understand none of their comments she could tell by the way Hugo tilted her head between his palms, then traced a line down her neck with his forefinger—which caused a visible reaction—that her audience was seriously contributing to the Master's vision, even smiling at her human response to the fingertip. The sense of isolation caused by the unfamiliar language was nothing, though, to the consternation of confronting two very unselfconscious nude women in the company of five men probably aged between fifteen and forty. Though there was no time for her to ponder, there was at the back of her mind a hazy sense of relief that, if this state of affairs existed also at Myneheere Memlinc's studio, she had something to be grateful for in Silas's prohibition.

She was as aware of Cecily's discomfort as much as her own. Isolde herself was familiar enough with the bodies of her female friends as they bathed in the river and swam in the forest pools, but Cecily was not used to the idea that artists needed to understand the precise structure of a body beneath its clothing, and Isolde could see, from the corner of eye, that poor Cecily didn't know where to put herself. She sent a smile of reassurance but received only a reproachful scowl in return before Cecily found a stool, tipped a cat off it, and plonked herself down in a corner.

Hugo introduced the group to Isolde, but the names eluded her. She was asked to stand before an easel where the light fell sideways through hexagonal panes of greenish glass and from where she was unable to maintain any relationship with the others in the room, except to hear their subdued remarks and the grinding of a mortar in a pestle or the squeak of charcoal. Already speculating about the unreliability of Hugo's memory, she was disconcerted but not surprised to find that he was not speaking entirely in Flemish, even to her, though she told herself sharply that it was she who would have to adapt, not them.

There was a decisiveness about him here which had been lacking in the garden of the Marinershuis, and when he gave her an instruction which she did not follow, his reaction was to do it himself. Without more ado, he eased down the fur-edged shoulders of her wide-necked bodice until they rested halfway down her upper arms, pinning her elbows at her side. Then, with equal assurance, and again without considering the effect his warm fingers might have upon the skin of her bosom, he drew downwards the white chemise that modestly filled the V of her neckline until she grabbed at his hand a split second before the fine fabric was lost to view. As if she had intended to help instead of to obstruct him, he took both her hands and placed them flat on to her ribs pushing them upwards to support her breasts, taking not the slightest notice of the flush that burned into her cheeks and throat. Hardly daring to breathe, and certainly not daring to protest before all these worldly Flemings, she looked down at herself and prayed that the next breath would not be the undoing of her.

Had she been alone with the other two women and the Master himself, she would have felt like part of the furniture, but with four other men standing by and a calamity about to happen, her unease was at its zenith. She wished with all her heart that she had not come, that Myneheere van der Goes had found another Mary or Margaret, and, most of all, that she had not felt it necessary to go to these lengths to make a show of control over her life. Surely there was a more comfortable way?

If there was, it did not present itself in time to save her more distress, for Master Hugo's command in Flemish, which was clearly for her to keep her head up, coincided with a distant clang of the bell, doors opening and closing, and a cool draught of air on her bare back. Someone had entered; the artist's nod of acknowledgement was to someone he knew well. The visitor waited a while in silence and then, moving slowly along one side of the room, came within Isolde's view and lounged against the wall, where he could see both the artist's sketch and his model, and Isolde knew, without a second glance, that he was enjoying the sight of something she had been at great pains to keep hidden. Enjoying it, and revelling in her chagrin.

Finally, when the Master stood back for longer than usual without speaking, and when she believed she could not bear the tension a moment longer, Silas moved across to his friend behind the easel to discuss in Flemish the image on the paper, not once catching her eye to convey either amusement or anger. Nevertheless, she had no doubt that she would soon have to deal with the latter.

Without waiting for permission, she hurriedly readjusted her bodice and sought Cecily's company before accepting the firm hand that was held out to her. 'I believe the Master will release you now,' he said. 'Or do you wish to continue?'

'No,' she whispered, holding a hand to her flaming cheek.

'Then I suggest you take your leave of the company. I have a boat waiting.'

Chapter Seven

They did not, after all, have to walk home from Goldenhand Street, which was just as well, for Isolde's legs had ideas of their own and made no resistance when Silas picked her up in his arms to place her in the boat by his side. Only once did she catch the direct beam of his eyes, but once was enough. Their homeward journey was silent and fraught with tension, and with an underlying relief on Isolde's part that the ridiculous appointment had concluded decently, though with only seconds to spare.

As for Silas, he had had time in Hugo's studio to comprehend the reasoning behind Isolde's typically intuitive behaviour, and had correctly deduced that it was a direct response to his refusal to allow her to pose for Hans Memlinc. Not for one moment did he believe that she had wanted to pose naked, nor did he believe she had expected to expose most of her upper half, whether to easy-going artists or their models. Heaven knew she had guarded herself well until overruled by a determination not to be dictated to, but it had brought her little comfort, by the look of things, especially after his appearance. He tested the temperature of her discomposure with a sidelong glance: still furious, but chastened too, perhaps.

But Silas's real concerns were twofold. One was that, as a stranger to Brugge, its language and customs, and also as a woman open to possible reprisals from those seeking her return, she had put herself foolishly at risk by venturing out unescorted by at least one man. He was angry with himself for not having read more into Hugo's silence on the matter yesterday. But for Pieter's sharp eyes spotting her entering the house across the courtyard, he would not have known she was abroad. Forbidding her to leave the house would have been like a red rag to a bull. The courtyard off Goldenhand Street was also where many of the foreign merchants had their offices, including Paulus Matteus, who had received them moments before Pieter's news.

The second concern was just as serious, and probably accounted for Hugo's failure to go through the proper channels, as Memlinc had. Silas had seen no reason at the time to explain to Isolde that, by giving Memlinc permission to ask her to sit for him, he would have been obliged to do the same for Van der Goes, or suffer one of his notorious self-deprecating rages which had afflicted him more and more over the last two years. Earlier this year, Hugo had entered the monastery known as The Red Cloister near Brussels for treatment and to find some inner peace, and had only recently returned to work, having dismissed himself on the excuse that he had to catch up with things. His masterly altarpiece for the Portinari family was well overdue and preyed on his mind night and day. He was a brilliant artist, but his behaviour was becoming more and more unstable, his unpredictable and violent outbursts now well known to his friends and colleagues. Only last month he had tried to strangle one of his models: that was not something Silas wanted Isolde exposed to. In short, she had been in danger from all sides.

The obvious conclusion to the uncomfortable episode would have been, Isolde was aware, a blazing row instigated by her if not by him. When Silas said nothing that allowed her an opening gambit, she picked up the Little Thing, who bounced delightedly to greet her, and went up to her room, followed closely by Cecily. And it was the maid who turned on her mistress before the unsuspecting lass had removed her shoes.

'And what d'ye think your father would say to that, then?' Cecily hissed, closing the window that opened onto the canal. 'It's one thing getting into a tricky situation, young lady, but it obviously takes more sense than you've got to get out of it before it worsens. Just what d'ye think you've gained then, eh?'

'Oh, don't *you* start!' Isolde snapped, unwilling to be ruffled further.

'Just answer my question, Isolde Medwin. Or if you can't find any answers, start asking a few of your own. Forget my embarrassment, if you like. I'll recover from that. But ask yourself what you're getting out of this charade. I can understand you wanting to have your own way, child, but that option isn't open to you here in Brugge, remember. You're a hostage, and you told me you'd agreed to abide by the rules.'

'Rules? You knew what I was doing before we set out, Cecily, yet you chose to say nothing about the rules then, did you? If you felt so strongly—'

'I didn't say anything because I didn't know then that you'd be standing there half-naked before a crowd of strangers, did I? Men too, God help us! Have you no shame, lass? Have you done half as much as that for the man you talk about in your sleep? Is he only good for your resentment while a bunch of goggle-eyed lads get to look at your body? Is that how love goes nowadays? Does he have to give you the moon before you show him some affection, or have your attractions gone to your head of a sudden? Well, you've indulged your pride and look where it's got you. Nowhere!' Cecily hustled about, red-faced and bursting with indignation. 'If I'd been him I'd have dropped you in the canal to cool you off, young lady. Instead of that, he's too much of a gentleman and probably too confused even to remonstrate with you. And I'm not surprised. He's not the only one who's confused.' She stamped out, slamming the door and too far into her tirade to notice the tears that coursed down Isolde's cheeks.

Shaking, and almost blinded, Isolde sat with the little hound on her lap while it licked obligingly at the warm, salty drops. She thought of her maid's description of Silas and how he must be as confused as her to see the one he called his woman exposed to the stares of strangers when she had shied away from his lightest touch, even while she burned for it. Did either of them have any idea how much that statement of independence had cost her?

Crossing to her writing-box, she lifted the lid and paper to remove the pendant he had given her, clasping it with some difficulty around her neck and arranging the largest pearl to lie in the cleft that she knew had held his attention that morning. Then, carrying the Little Thing under one arm, she tiptoed out of the room, closing the door quietly behind her and entering Silas's room as softly as she had done before.

The white bed-curtains moved in the breeze from the window and the reflection of ripples danced across the oak-beamed ceiling and down one wall. A deep mustard-and-blue silk carpet covered with intricate patterns hung on one side, matching in colour the beautiful blond fur rug over the bed. There was a stool with carved sides, a deep chest, a small table with rolls of parchment and a silver sconce of great ingenuity that held at least eight candles.

As she had done on that previous occasion, she drew one of his white pillows to her face and, placing the little hound on the fur, inhaled its scent. Her nose was useless and tears still pricked at her eyes, so she lay with the pillow in her arms and her new pet in the bend of her lap, knowing that Silas would now have returned to Goldenhand Street. Then she slept.

She came awake slowly as the ground beneath her began to give way; the sky darkened with threatening clouds and a chill wind cooled her body. Silas's large frame leaned above her, carefully drawing away the pillow and scooping the Little Thing on to the floor. His fist beside her shoulder bore his weight as he lowered himself to sit by her, regarding her with serious dark eyes that, in shadow, she could not read. His voice, however, was softly teasing, deep and dark like the river pools she had just been visiting.

'So, you've come to me at last, have you, maid?'

'Silas,' she whispered. Her arms came up to reach for him as they had never done before, though yesterday they had come close and, as if he knew the significance of that simple act he slid his arms beneath her and pulled her across his lap, meeting her mouth with his and slaking a thirst that had grown more intense with each passing night.

Tears welled up again. 'I'm sorry, beloved. I let you down.'

'You've been weeping? There's no cause to weep, sweetheart.'

'I was so glad to see you.' She tasted his skin, took his ear and hair between her lips, breathing him in in deep lungfuls. But he caught them before they could stray further and kept them prisoner until he had taken his fill again, swinging her across the bed so that he could pull her under him as they had been on his narrow cabin bed. His fingers on her throat found the pearl pendant.

'You said to bring it back.' She smiled.

'Wilful little baggage. But I have your measure now, my lass.'

'And how much longer could *you* have waited, sir?'

'Oh, I could easily have waited two more seconds.'

She smiled. 'Yet you returned to Goldenhand Street?'

'No, I didn't. I've been here all the time. Popped in here a couple of times to watch you as you slept.'

'Truly?'

'Truly. You'd better start believing what I say. Why did you go to Hugo's? Simply to thwart me?'

'Yes. It was stupid of me. I wish I hadn't. Cecily was furious. If I'd known…' She turned her head away, recalling the scene and her acute discomfort.

'If I'd known what I was going to see, I'd have arrived sooner.'

'Those women, you mean?'

'No, maid. You.'

'Oh.' She placed her hand over his mouth but he held it away and, lowering his head to her throat, teased the soft skin with his lips and tongue over the pale triangle made by her gown, deep into the place where her chemise called a halt. He had ventured so far only once before, when she had protested violently, hanging on to her virginity for dear life. But here, on this bed, it seemed only natural that he should taste what he had gazed upon with such obvious hunger. He reached her lips again and she felt the full weight of his body as he rolled her sideways, cradling her against his chest and rocking her, gently.

'Nice,' he murmured against her mouth. 'I've hung pearls on it, seen it, tasted it. Now, am I allowed to hold it?' His lips kept hers well occupied while his hand searched the soft fabric of her bodice and, taking advantage of her raised arm that lay upon his shoulder, caressed in practised sweeps that quivered something low down within her. Then, giving her no time to consider, he held her arm away behind her back, slipping the gown off her shoulder as Hugo had done but this time releasing the full roundness of one beautiful breast to his waiting hand. He held it, tenderly, looking into her half-closed eyes for some reaction. 'Well?' he whispered. 'You're not going to fight me off, maid?'

She made a sound in her throat that began as a word and ended as a sigh, and he knew that she could not answer him.

'I want no one to see this other than me,' he said. 'This belongs to me. So, are we agreed on that now? At last?'

She understood what he was asking of her. He had already said that she was his property, to her and to Bard, but lacking her agreement his assertions had had a one-sidedness that she knew would not satisfy him permanently. Her own attempts at independence had not been exactly successful, nor had they been aided by her bodily need of him, which now burned beyond her control. Was it time for her to yield, to give as well as to accept? She could not remain still under his searching hand. 'Property?' she whispered. 'Your woman, or your lady?'

Refusing to compromise, his reply was prompt. 'All three. You are a hostage; that makes you my property while I hold you. And while I guard you against other claims you are my woman. When you become my consort, to be with me wherever I need you, then you will be my lady. You are intelligent and courageous and very fair, and I want you by my side and in my bed, Isolde. I have never asked as much of any other woman, nor have I ever taken any other woman against her will. But I took you because it was a chance I could not miss, and now I need your agreement before I proceed any further.'

'You took me so that you could revenge yourself on my father and so that you could upset Master Fryde, didn't you? Surely anything else takes second place to that?'

His hand halted. 'What makes you think I want to upset Master Fryde?'

'I heard you and Bard talking out on the quay that evening.'

He watched her eyes in silence, then said, 'What else?'

'That Dame Elizabeth must not know I'd been staying with him at York. So I took care not to tell her. Why, Silas? What has he done?'

'We were talking about you, sweet maid. I'll tell you some time about the other matter, but don't think you can wriggle out of an answer by changing the subject. Well?'

'As a hostage, I can understand being your property. Your woman, too, for that matter. But does a man like you take a lady to his bed and risk getting a child on her? And does an unmarried mother ever get the chance to marry decently after that? Or does she hide away in a convent, perhaps, and fade from memory? Yes, Silas Mariner, I am intelligent enough to have thought of that. I will be your woman and your lady because I cannot hold you off any longer; you must already know that. But I think I deserve some guarantee of a future, perhaps when all this bargaining is over and done with?' She saw that she had struck a note of conscience, and waited for an answer while he restored the shoulder of her gown to its former position, arranging the neckline with careful fingers.

'While you are a hostage, sweetheart,' he said, rolling her back into his arms, 'the position will be unpredictable, for your father could release Felicia at any time and oblige me to release you in turn. I would have to comply with that because that's what I've agreed to do, though if you were to tell him that you prefer to stay with me, then that would change things. That would be something you, as a dutiful daughter, would have to agree with your father. He might forbid it.'

'But what about…?'

'Yes, I'm coming to that. I'm asking you to become my mistress because that's the most dignified position I can offer you until the problem of ownership is settled. There's nothing shameful about being a man's mistress. Married, you cease to belong in law to your father, and then I lose my bargaining power, and that's not the object of the exercise. The idea is to take something he holds dear and keep it until he returns what he holds of mine.

'If you should have a child, sweetheart, that child will belong to me. It will be a La Vallon and your father may not have it, not for Felicia's exchange nor for anything else.'

'You believe he'd want it?'

'Feather-headed woman!' He kissed her nose. 'Of course he'd want it. His first and only grandson? A young La Vallon being brought up in his household? Think how that'd rile my father, especially as it would be *his* only grandchild, too, by me, his eldest son. But it would not come to that. Any child I get on you belongs to me, and I should not return you then, Isolde. You'd have to stay, like it or not, and Felicia's freedom will be out of the question.'

'So your bargaining power, as you call it, would be my child.'

'My child. Ours.'

'And I'd still be your mistress.'

'Mistress, wife, whatever you choose. You too become my property then, for all time.'

'And you are proposing that I enter into that kind of agreement, knowing that such events might follow?' She did her best to keep her voice even.

'Yes. Is it such a risk?'

'Yes, sir. It's a very great risk. It's risking Felicia's happiness as well as mine. But what's the alternative, if I don't like the idea of becoming your mistress?'

'I thought we'd agreed on that, more or less.'

'Did I? I didn't know I had.'

'Well, you agreed to be my woman and my lady. That's as near as dammit.'

'Mmm…'

Silence.

'Well, maid?' He took her chin and tilted it towards him.

'You said you'd not force me. You said it on the ship, remember?'

'Yes, I remember. You're afraid I might rush you?'

'I'm *not* afraid.'

'Yes, you are. Courageous in most things, but not in this.'

Another silence.

'How many women have you had?'

'God in heaven! You want me to list them?'

She snorted. 'No, thank you. If it's that many, you must know your way about.'

His chest heaved, and he rolled on top of her, kissing her neck. 'You want me to give you a demonstration before you decide? Is that it?'

She caught his hand just before it reached her knee. 'No, I do not!' She squirmed, but he held her still. 'Silas, what you're proposing is…look, let me go home now. This has gone on long enough.'

'No, it hasn't started yet. Now, are you going to accept or not?'

'Silas…'

'No. Listen, sweetheart. Listen to me.' He caught her again as she swerved. 'Any day now they'll be coming.'

'Who'll be coming?'

'Your father's deputies. Fryde's men. One after the other they'll come to threaten, bargain, try to steal you, perhaps. I can keep you much safer if we're of one mind on this, and if you trust me. We don't have to be enemies, Isolde.'

'I'm not your enemy, Silas La Vallon. You know

that I'm not that. But I cannot approve of your methods.'

'I'm not asking for your approval, but for your acceptance and trust. This is life, Isolde. Such things happen. It's unfortunate when women are caught up in their families' feuds, but at least you're safe with me. You know I'll protect you.'

She put up a hand to caress his face, unable to resist the persuasion in his deep, husky voice. 'Yes, I do know. I told my father so in my letter. Indeed, I may already have given him the impression that I'm not as unhappy as I'm supposed to be.'

'You didn't tell him that I beat you daily?'

'No.' She smiled, just before he kissed her. 'I'll try not to let you down again, truly, I'll try not to embarrass you. Only...I think you may be disappointed in... in...'

He smiled at what she could not say. 'In you? In your lovemaking? Nay, that's the very last thing that concerns me, my lovely mistress,' he said, noting the flush that rose at his use of the new title. He placed a warm hand over her neck, sweeping it over her breasts and waist, sending a tremor into her thighs. 'I shall not be disappointed. We'll take it slowly, eh? No hurry.' His kiss was tender and, when he lifted his head, she saw the softened expression of satisfaction in his eyes. His hair fell in silken swathes that he swept back with his fingers, and the cleft in his chin barely responded to the inquisitive pressure of her forefinger.

'What's that for?' she whispered.

'To keep your attention, maid.'

'It doesn't work then, does it? What time is it?'

'Suppertime. Can't you smell it?'

'My nose isn't working too well, either.'

'Then take my word for it. My brother will be home soon, and he's bringing Paulus Matteus with him for the meal. He wants to meet you.'

'God's truth!' She pushed away from him, tangling in her skirts as she pushed a way off the bed. 'What are we doing here like this when we have guests for supper? Why didn't you wake me?'

'I did,' he said, adding in an undertone, 'I think.'

The well-timed agreement gave Isolde a new framework upon which to build her tangled emotions. Never one to do things by halves, she accepted the role as mistress of the house as the occasion demanded, it being akin to the one she had just vacated at home and therefore not new in that sense. What was different was the confidence that cocooned her like a luxurious garment worn with more pride than ostentation, the former sinfully permeating every pore at Silas's bellow of laughter as he led his guests from the table to a shady corner in the garden. He had changed at the speed of light into a chestnut-brown brocade patterned doublet with gold tracery around each motif and this, with the frill of white at his neck, accentuated his dark good looks as no vibrant colour could have done. He was every inch the sober but affluent merchant. She had only to look at him to feel her knees turn to water, and to pity the diamond merchant who had wanted him as his son-in-law.

She understood, as soon as they met Paulus Matteus

at the water gate, the reason for his choice of Silas, for
the two men were compatible in everything but age
and, possibly experience. Myneheere Matteus was
older than Isolde had expected, which put into per-
spective the resentment of his beautiful daughter when
her father had not been able to secure for her what she
had badly wanted. In his youth, he would have been
handsome and bold of feature, though now his chins
were multiple and his heavily lidded and lined eyes
were dark with the softness of indulgent fatherhood.
Beneath the upturned flowerpot of dark red felt, his
grey hair was at odds with the beetle-black eyebrows
which looked to Isolde as if they'd been stuck on in a
hurry. But he was gracious, having nothing of his
daughter's shrewishness, and his acceptance of Isolde
as Silas's mistress was respectful, courteous, even fatherly.

Isolde was particularly interested to see whether the
merchant's approval of Bard La Vallon was also genuine, but found nothing to suggest that Bard had spoilt
his chances in any way. He was, in fact, more subdued
and rational in his contribution to the conversation than
Isolde had ever seen him, and it was obvious to her
that he was taking the acquaintance seriously.

It was for selfish reasons to do with his own future,
however, that Bard was anxious to prevent Paulus Matteus from discovering about Silas's abduction of Isolde
or about their feuding families, for the sudden possibility of a close relationship with the diamond merchant had caused him to revise his earlier plan to dis-
credit his brother in revenge for his own loss of Isolde.

The indulgent father must hear no scandal about either of them now, and Bard wished that he had kept Ann-Marie as innocent of the situation as she had been before. Moreover, he knew that Paulus Matteus was far too well-mannered to make any enquiries about how Isolde came to be Silas's mistress instead of his wife. He need not have been concerned; Isolde wielded the facts like a juggler, leaving both brothers breathless.

To Isolde, Paulus Matteus was making a reply. 'No, mistress. Alas, I was widowed two years ago.'

'I am sorry for that, sir, but you have a lovely daughter and connections with the Duchess's court. Her eventual marriage will be a credit to you, I'm sure.'

He smiled without showing his teeth. 'Yes, though she liked the idea of marrying your Silas at one time, you know. Did the rogue tell you that?'

'No, did she really?'

'But Silas is constantly on the move and I'd have been sad for her to live so far from home. Your families...they know each other in Yorkshire?'

'Oh, yes, indeed. They've been acquainted since they were born, almost. My father had someone else in mind for me, but Silas had other ideas.' She shot a sly glance at Silas whose eyes widened fractionally. She could see Bard turning an apricot over and over as if deciding what to do with it. 'I suppose one might also say it was...'

'Well, you know, that's what happened to my late wife and I. Her parents had other ideas, too. They didn't want a merchant's assistant for their daughter, so I abducted her. Not against her will, I might add.'

'You mean it, sir?' Isolde stared.

Silas and Bard blinked.

Matteus crossed his gown-clad legs and chuckled at the memory. 'Yes, I did. Ran off with her to Antwerp to live with my employer and that's how we started our life together. Of course her father came chasing after us but there was nothing he could do about it. Lost four infants, then came Ann-Marie. Then her father relented and we got married. In that order. Unconventional, but that was the way of it. We didn't do too badly, after all.' He grinned again, lifting his chin to fondle the jowls beneath.

Isolde placed a hand lightly upon the merchant's arm. 'Excellent,' she said. 'Now we only have to wait. So, the only difference between our situations, then, is that I was abducted unwillingly, kicking and screaming all the way across the North Sea.' Merrily, her laugh made nonsense of the scene.

Matteus's large hand covered hers on his arm. 'Hah! Is that so, mistress? Does she tell the truth, Mistress Cecily?' He turned to Cecily, laughing, but Silas intercepted the reply.

'Mistress Cecily remembers only the first and last days of the voyage, sir. Everything else was a blank. But I can tell you there was no kicking or screaming. Mind you…' He began a mock search of his arms.

Matteus noted Bard's polite smile. 'And you were sent to bring them both to their senses, were you, young man?'

'Something like that, sir. I think Isolde's father sadly overestimates my influence over either of them.'

'A token, lad,' Matteus said, kindly. 'A token gesture. Parents have to do it to prove that they've tried. I'll find you a place in my office. See if you like the business, eh? Ann-Marie has taken a liking to you and she's got a good eye, my daughter has. A good eye.'

With fortune hammering at his door, Bard could not maintain his vexation with Isolde after the cordial supper at which some of the crooked facts had straightened themselves out most satisfactorily. Even so, he felt it would have been easier if she had told him how it was in the first place, without all that maidenly coyness. He took advantage of Silas's last private words with his guest.

'A most accomplished performance, Isolde. May I call you "sister" now? Pity you could not have made the same effort to convince me, too. It would have saved me some embarrassment, wouldn't it?'

'You mean you'd have left the kitchen lass alone?'

'Oh, for pity's sake! Kitchen maids are fair game for anyone, and she wasn't exactly unwilling. You know what I'm talking about. I even asked you point blank, but you skirted the question time and again until I'd made a fool of myself. Did that give you some pleasure?'

'No, Bard. Forgive me. I should have made it quite clear to you how things were but…well…you see, the situation is new to me, too. And I still find it difficult to see myself as your brother's mistress when I disliked him so at first. Don't take it too hard, please. These are not exactly the most normal of circumstances, are they? And you'll do better with a Matteus than you would with a Medwin. Think of all those diamonds.' She watched the lift of his eyebrows.

'I would have liked a Medwin, Isolde, but perhaps I'm too greedy. Ann-Marie told me that Silas relies on her father for trade, but he doesn't, does he?'

'Oh, dear. She told you that? The minx. No, it's nowhere near the truth. And did you tell her a few of your…er…exaggerations?'

'Well, yes and no. I told her what I believed at the time.'

'Which was?' Isolde's heart sank.

'That you couldn't stand the sight of Silas.'

'And?'

'That you were in love with me.'

'Desperately, of course.'

'Yes, of course desperately. You see, you should have said.'

'So it looks as if you're going to have to explain to her that things have moved on.'

'You couldn't pretend…?'

'No, dear Bard.' She hung a brace of cherries over his protruding ear. 'If you think I can pretend to loathe Silas whenever she's around, forget it. Life's difficult enough as it is. Go back to her and explain my fickle nature. She'll believe it. Then sweet-talk her as you used to do with me.'

'You remember?'

'Of course I remember. How could I not? But for you I'd not be here. Nor would you.'

'That's true. But what makes you think she'll believe you to be fickle? You are friends, are you not?'

Isolde could afford to be generous. She could also imagine quite clearly how sick she would feel if Silas were to reject her in favour of another woman. 'Yes, love. We are friends. I'd even go so far as to tell her of your worthiness, in case she's missed anything.'

'Heavens, lass. She saw me for scarce an hour, but she makes up her mind faster than any woman I've ever met.' He removed the cherries and ate them with some complacency.

'A good eye, has Ann-Marie,' Isolde whispered, her eyes glinting, understanding only too well the other woman's line of reasoning. 'Ah, Myneheere Matteus. You must go already?'

'Alas, lady, it's going to be a race against the curfew, as it is. I don't want to be dragged before the burgomaster in the morning to explain myself. I've just been reminding Silas of the pageant on Saturday and Sunday. I'd like you to be my guests, watch the preparations from the burgomaster's house.'

'The same one you'd rather not be dragged before?'

'The very same, Mistress Isolde,' he beamed.

But for the approaching hour of curfew, Isolde would have persuaded him to stay longer, if only to delay the time when her last obstacle would yield, an event which Silas believed she feared and which Bard believed had already happened, while Cecily believed she should have been less precious about it from the start. She herself believed that the fear he suspected was more a natural reticence to yield her last possession to a La Vallon, of all people.

*   *   *

The curfew bell had long since died away with the last lingering light when, through her pillow, Isolde heard the sound of Silas's door closing. With a sigh, she turned over, sliding a hand over her breast as he had done and nothing that the gesture lacked the assurance of his, for it did nothing to remind her of the strange ache she had felt then. She was half asleep when his hand returned to brush lightly over the sheet and then, as she half-turned towards him, to slip searchingly on to the bare warmth of her waist and rest in its valley.

'I thought you'd forgotten,' she said, sleepily.

'Forgotten this?' he said quietly, his deep voice rumbling against her ear. His hand moved upwards over her breast, neck and face, deep into her hair. 'Nay, lass. This is something no one could forget.' His hand delved into the loose tangle of her curls, cupping her head in his palm and lifting it to meet his own so that, even if she'd been so minded, she could not have evaded the path of his lips that followed her throat down to where his hand had been a few moments before. 'Nectar,' he whispered into the soft mound of her stomach. 'Thou art like honey, Isolde. Like a ripe, luscious plum filled with sweetness. Will you give yourself to me? Can I have you now? All of you?' As he spoke, his hand slid softly into the cleft between her thighs, changing the word on her lips into a gasp.

'Link your arms around my neck. Hold on.'

She was lifted high up into the darkness against his naked chest and carried along the passageway to his cool room where the bed, scented with lavender, was peeled back in readiness for them.

'We don't want Mistress Cecily charging in thinking you're having nightmares,' he growled, laying her down. 'And, talking of intruders, look who's come to join us.' A fragile body leapt on to the sheet beside her but was scooped up and deposited on the rush matting. 'Thank you, Little Thing, but she won't need your assistance. Stay there and dream of big gazehounds.'

They lay as they had done on the ship that had brought them here, almost able to experience again the rocking and the rhythmic whoosh of the sea as it speeded past, and Isolde was content to succumb to the slow caress of his hands, which now had licence to roam without hindrance. In a blissful state of surrender, she absorbed the wholeness of him along her body, exploring the taut muscles, the swell of his shoulders and thighs, the startling hardness of his arms and back which previously she had only guessed at. She listened, smiling, to his soft-spoken praises of her first evening as his lady, to his pride in her elegance and wit, her adroit handling of the merchant's story, her exquisite social graces. Quite a step, he teased her, from their first tempestuous meeting.

She whispered into his neck, feeling the dense forest of hair above her nose. 'I hated you on sight. You didn't want me there, did you?'

'I wanted you here, maid, like this. From that moment I wanted you in my bed here, under me. You knew it at the table, didn't you?' He pulled her under him with a hand beneath her hips, and for a brief moment let her feel the full weight of him on her body and the sensation of his skin almost enclosing her. 'You did well to fight me off, sweet maid, but now the time of reckoning has come. I'll take no more delays.'

'Silas…you know…?'

'Shh, of course I know. It's all right. We'll go slowly…slowly…like this.' Matching his hands and lips to his words, he gently coaxed her body's responses as if by magic, stroking and fondling in leisurely forays over surfaces which, until now, she had thought of as only functional, never as a source of delight or pleasure. Seduced by his lingering touch, she allowed herself to be rolled on to her stomach to expose her back to the caress of his lips on her neck and shoulders while his hands explored as if to make good the times she had held him away. When she could bear the suspense no longer, she swung round to reach for his hand, taking him by surprise.

'Kiss me…please…kiss me again.' Her plea was intercepted and, with every sense craving fulfilment, she came alive against his mouth, consumed by her own hunger. Pressing and lacing herself around him, she sought new experiences of her own devising without knowing how they would be received or how to restrain them, and it was almost with relief that her frenzy provoked Silas into taking control again, wrapping her in his arms and kissing her until she was breathless. Then, with masterly skill, he stoked the flames of her desire with the penetrating caress of his hand between her thighs that brought her to the very brink of rapture, until she felt helpless, like a boat adrift. She opened herself greedily.

His possession of her was both the release and the capture for which they had both waited so long. Intoxicated with the effort of restraint, Silas eased himself with infinite care past the point where her body convulsed and softened again, past her almost soundless gasp that mingled shock with ecstasy, past her mewing cries towards the slow voyage that would lead them to the inevitable destination. From a distance, they both heard her calling to him, over and over, but Isolde was lost as soon as the voyage began and she was unable to define the incredible sensation of holding the one she loved inside her, possessing him while being possessed, fusing him to her. Blissfully, she lay on the tide and let it take her on, further and further, savouring every detail of the new experience and loving Silas for his blend of tenderness and domination.

Even as a complete novice, she became aware of a growing urgency deep inside her that raged quickly out of control, and, not understanding its significance, she cried out to him in panic. 'Silas…oh, no!' Pushing at him, she fought to take over, but was held without mercy by his arms and the relentless rhythm of his loins that knew better than she how to ride out the storm.

Sensing her consternation, and knowing that there was no time for explanations, he guided her, exhilarated, through the whirlpool for which she was so unprepared and out into calmer waters, joining her in a shout of triumph.

Never having received the slightest indication that there was anything other than sheer exhaustion which brought to an end this incredible activity, Isolde was confused by what had happened, not least the massive tide of emotion that had shaken them both. 'What was it?' she whispered. 'You didn't tell me, did you? Why didn't anyone tell me?'

Silas raised his head from her shoulder, indicating by his unsteady voice that he was struggling with laughter. 'Sweet, wonderful Isolde. They don't tell you about that because…hah!' He buried his face in her neck, kissing gently. 'Because, sweet thing, no one's come up with a good enough explanation. Yet. Could you describe it?'

'Well…er…no.'

He moved his lips upwards and over her chin. 'So that's why they don't even try.' He took her mouth and lingered playfully, remembering her animosity and her fear of him and wondering at the fierceness this experience had brought her, a passion that had excelled all his expectations. She was rare, exotic, responsive and finely tuned. He'd be damned if he'd let her go, whoever they sent to claim her.

Chapter Eight

Sir Gillan Medwin, Isolde's father, had been optimistic in his hopes that the two men would reach York the day after his bidding. They did, but only by taking the shortest route and the briefest of rests for their horses. As it was, the city gates were ready to close on the last few breathless travellers who had no wish to beg for shelter in the suburbs. John Thatcher and James Broadbank were not quite of this ilk, being well dressed under a fine layer of dust, well-mounted and well-spoken. The badge that decorated the harness of their strong beasts was also repeated in the embroidery on their saddle-cloths, a leather bottle with a halo of honey bees to signify the sweet fermented honey drink that no poor man could afford. Medwin: mead-friend. One did not close the gates too soon on men such as this.

'God speed, sirs. Come a long way, have you?' said the man at the Walmergate Bar.

'Aye, man, direct us to Alderman Fryde's house, if you will.'

'Keep straight on, sir, till you reach the minster, then

turn left into Stonegate. You'll not miss Master Fryde's house. It's the biggest.'

James Broadbank nodded and passed him a half-penny, wondering if Fryde's supper table would match the size of his house. James was a pleasant-faced man of thirtyish, with an honest nature that could not conceal a certain pleasure in his mission that offered a night or two away from home. Duty to his master came first, but visits to York were rare and, with any luck, this business might take a few days.

John Thatcher, older, quieter and more sober in every respect, was Sir Gillan's steward, who did not intend to stay in the great city a moment longer than was necessary, or heaven only knew what they'd get up to in his absence. Or what his flighty young second wife would get up to, more particularly. He was lean, and nimble, and efficient. This matter would be cleared up in no time. They soon saw that the gatekeeper had not exaggerated: Fryde's house was indeed the largest, hanging over the cobbled street in tier upon tier, every window glazed and polished, its large courtyard even now being swept up before a pair of horses had reached the stables.

A lad ran up to hold their bridles before the two men had chance to declare themselves. 'God speed, sirs. Master Frith will take you in. Supper's being served. I believe the master is expecting you.'

James Broadbank quirked an eyebrow at his companion. 'Is he?' he whispered.

'Course not. How could he be?' Thatcher frowned.

'Lead on, Master Frith, if you please. The water pump
will wait upon our appetites.'

For a private town house, the merchant's hall was
large and full enough for them to have slipped into one
of the benches at the far end unnoticed, but Master
Frith the hall-steward was there to do his duty, and,
despite the clamour of diners, the discordant blast of
musicians tuning up and the yapping of hounds, he
announced and seated them midway along one side,
where bottoms shifted to give them room. Their own
formal greeting was a formality unheard by Master
Fryde at the top table, or by any of his companions
whose shouts to each other passed for conversation. At
one side, Mistress Fryde watched the arrival of the
newcomers with some interest and, seeing her husband's preoccupation, beckoned Master Frith to her,
receiving his whisper with a nod and an instruction.

The supper, alas, was not as great as Master Broadbank had hoped, nor was it palatable. Thin, greasy
gruel bobbed with rock-hard dumplings in which the
strong taste of sage and rancid meat fought for domi-
nance. The manchet bread was of hard brown rye and,
in John's case, flecked with blue mould, his knife balk-
ing at the task of dissection.

'God's truth!' James growled. 'Is this what York's
wealthy merchants eat?'

John Thatcher snorted, pushing away his wooden
bowl and reaching for a spitted bird so small he thought
it must have been a sparrow. It was. 'Well, James. If
we can't have food, we shall have to make do with
music. We'll find a tavern later on.'

'And a pie shop. You don't think he'll invite us...?'

'Nah! Course he won't. Shh!'

They would have been content to listen, clap, sing or even to stamp a little in time to the troupe's rhythm, which reflected Master Fryde's acceptance of second-best to save money. At best, they were noisy and rhythmic; at worst, their zeal had more boisterousness and vulgarity than musicality, though the master of the house appeared to appreciate the performers' gradual decline through coarseness into indecency, an appreciation shared even by Broadbank himself, if his bellows of laughter were anything to go by. Thatcher preferred to watch Mistress Fryde, whose attempt to leave the table with her lady had been physically prevented by her husband. Few would have heard what he said to her, but it was a command she dared not disobey, and she lowered herself to the bench in acute embarrassment.

There were two women in the troupe whose dancing consisted of taking a dagger in each hand and balancing, upside-down, on the points, with their feet where their heads should have been. To begin, they had pulled their skirts between their legs but, to the growing crescendo of stamping, the skirts gradually fell, assisted by anyone who could reach, until the women were completely revealed from feet to waist, the balancing on daggers overlooked in favour of the display. Eventually they fell, and were pounced on by the rest of the troupe in a tangle that sent the hall wild with delight, except for Mistress Fryde, who pretended deep conversation with her lady.

John Thatcher gripped his friend's arm and yanked him up. 'Come on! We've come here to do business, not to wait on this kind of performance. Hey!' He called to a servant who passed with an ale flagon. 'Tell your master there are two who come from Sir Gillan Medwin. We'll await him in the courtyard.' They made their exit unnoticed, unsatisfied and, in Thatcher's case, disgusted. If this was how a future sheriff kept his house, then God help the city of York, he muttered to himself.

They had not long to wait in the darkening courtyard. A hound yelped in pain, a door slammed, and Alderman Fryde, accompanied by a younger man, appeared at the top of the stone steps that led to the great iron-bound and studded door, giving him the advantage of a greater height from which to address his two visitors.

'How the hell did you arrive without me knowing?' he barked. Standing, he had little height but plenty of breadth, a mass of quivering jowls making a solid pedestal for his ruddy sweating face. Lank locks of greasy hair fell on to his shoulders from beneath a ridiculously large and lop-sided turban.

John Thatcher would not reply directly to his question. 'If I'd known the like of your hospitality, Master Fryde, we'd not have bothered arriving here at all. It was not difficult, I assure you, but nor is it difficult to get into a whorehouse.'

The young man at the host's side gave a yelp and stepped down one step, his hand on the hilt of his sword. 'By God, sir!' But he stopped halfway when he saw that the two men were not intimidated.

'Yes?' Broadbank said. 'Know about God, do you?'

'We've come to take Mistress Isolde Medwin back to her father,' Thatcher continued. 'I presume you've found her by now, though I see she's not being forced to watch that display as your lady wife is, thank God.'

Fryde's colour deepened like a ripening strawberry, his lips compressed. 'A new troupe. I'd no idea they were lewd. I shall turn them out.' He threw a command to the young man on the steps. 'Get them out, Martin! And get your mother here to tend the guests. Your pardon, sirs, she should have been—'

'Mistress Fryde will not be required, sir. Sir Gillan sent us only to retrieve his daughter. She will be safer at home, after all.'

'At this time of night?' Fryde blustered, clutching at the stone banister to steady himself as he waddled precariously downwards. 'Really, there's no need.'

'She is with you, I presume?'

'Well…er…she will be, soon enough.' His blend of pompous dignity and agitation were almost comical. 'No need to be alarmed.'

The two men met him at the base of the steps. 'You are saying, I take it, that Sir Gillan's daughter is still missing. Is that correct?' Thatcher said.

Fryde took a deep breath to make himself taller. 'Well, the horses she took from my stables were returned only—'

'When?'

'Two days? Yes, on the day I sent the message to

Sir Gillan. They were left outside the Merchant Venturers Hall and I've not been able to discover how they got there, except that it indicates she must still be here, somewhere in York. But no message. Nothing. I've got men searching, asking, but no trace yet. We're doing our best.' His smile was nervously apologetic.

'I'm sure Sir Gillan will be relieved to know you're doing your best.' Thatcher's tone was loaded with sarcasm. 'Your concern is obvious. Does the city council know of your *massive* efforts to recover the lady? Are they assisting you?'

'Eh?' Fryde quivered. 'No…er, not yet. There's no need for anyone to be alarmed. A girlish prank…eh?' He smirked.

'Mistress Isolde is a woman, sir,' Thatcher snarled, 'as I'm sure you must be aware. And while you're sitting cosily at your board, watching whores show off their private parts before your entire family, Mistress Isolde, daughter of your friend, is no longer in your safekeeping but who knows where or in what danger. And you are, I believe, expecting to be elected sheriff next year. Well, sir, they'll be a tolerant lot if they're impressed by your efficiency over this business, believe me.'

The man almost fell over himself on the bottom step, his attempts to placate the two visitors now wearing thin. 'Look here, I've told you the matter's being taken care of. I have men searching night and day.'

'Where?'

'Eh?'

'Where are they searching, exactly?'

'Look, my man, don't take that tone with me. Go back to Sir Gillan and tell him that—'

'We shall do no such thing, Master Fryde. The first thing we'll do is alert the sheriff and obtain his assistance, since you've not already done that, I take it?'

Martin Fryde stepped forward again to forestall his father's negative reply, his florid face and unruly lips reminding Broadbank vaguely of a pile of uncooked sausages. His pale prominent eyes were cold and angry. 'You've heard what my father said. The matter's in hand, but perhaps if Mistress Medwin had been better disciplined by her father none of this would have happened to embarrass our parents in the first place. She was here only a week or so, yet her behaviour was anything but dutiful, sir. My lady mother's had a time of it, I can tell you.'

She appeared at that moment at the top of the steps, and in the dim light both men could see the magenta and green bruising along one cheek and around one eye. It was to spare her a place in the discussion that John Thatcher brought the fruitless interview to an end. Even so, he would not allow this spotty young whipper-snapper to have the last word about Isolde Medwin.

'Do not speak to me of discipline, young man, after the performance I've seen in your father's supper hall. Sir Gillan will be more appalled to hear of that than of his daughter's attempt to remove herself from such influences. Mistress Fryde is to be pitied of the time she's had of it. Sir Gillan will be in touch with you, no doubt. And with the city council.' He and Broadbank turned together and there was no reply either of the Frydes could make that would have altered the ugly mood of the debate.

Both Thatcher and Broadbank knew, of course, more than Fryde did about Isolde's friendship with Bard La Vallon, and had already decided that it was this young man who was responsible for Isolde's disappearance and also for the return of the horses. Though they had no intention of doing Fryde's investigation for him, they were duty-bound to do their utmost for their master, and so, at first light on the following day, they made enquiries along the wharf that ran parallel to Coney Street. From a series of encounters and clues, they managed to glean the information that a young man answering to Bard's description had indeed gone aboard a northern cog full of lead and timber down river to Hull and then, presumably, to Flanders. But, no, he had had no young woman with him. This was an inconclusive state of affairs they had no wish to relate to Sir Gillan, nor did they trust Master Fryde with this information after witnessing what had doubtless provoked Isolde's hasty departure. Nor could they jump aboard the next ship, which might not leave for several days, on a wild-goose chase to Flanders.

They sat in the sunshine outside the Crowned Lion on Micklegate, closing their ears against the strident shouts of apprentices and the hungry buzz of wasps around the sticky table, their problems unresolved.

'Drink up,' Thatcher said. 'There's nothing for it; we'll have to leave it in the sheriff's hands.'

Broadbank stood, relishing the idea of Fryde's impending disgrace. In every one of their enquiries, the name of Henry Fryde had exposed a barrage of dislike ranging from mild disgust of his cheating practices to outright hatred of his power and corruption far beyond the common shady deals in which most merchants indulged. No one had had a good word for him.

'Master Thatcher!' A call cut through the din, making both men turn. Mistress Fryde's bruised face was shaded by a wide-brimmed felt hat, her figure swathed in the plain dull garb of a working woman, and it was obvious to the two men that she did not wish to be recognised. Her eyes, which had once been large and soft, were now bloodshot and wary, though the trust which had once appealed to her husband was still apparent in some measure. 'Can we talk?' she whispered, approaching them like a furtive mouse. 'Privately?'

The men were concerned by the risk she was taking.

'Mistress Fryde,' John Thatcher said, 'this is not wise. Come…' he held out a protective arm '…away from the noise and prying eyes. You must not be seen with us.'

They could not have known, nor could she, how accurate their fears were, for no sooner had she parted with her information and left them than two men of the Fryde household suddenly appeared at her side to escort her back to Stonegate and directly into her husband's forbidding presence.

With a more exact picture of Bard La Vallon's contacts during his brief stay in York, extracted by Mistress Fryde from both her pretty laundry-maid and one of the kitchen boys, who had been buying fish on the wharf the day of Bard's departure, Thatcher and Broad-bank were now set to return to Sir Gillan with a more credible tale. Not good news, but credible.

The day was too far advanced to start for home, the lodgings and the widowed ale-wife too accommodating for Broadbent to balk at another night's stay. So they lingered in the warm evening sun that shimmered on the river below the Ouse Bridge, leaning on the parapet between the buildings that clung like limpets to the sides, watching with narrowed eyes the last of the day's activities on the Queen's Staithe where men prepared to grease the great crane. A lone rider plodded wearily along Skeldergate, passing the Staithe and heading towards the bridge with a head of deep copper hair that glowed in the sun's pink rays. As he turned on to the bridge, neither of the two men had any doubts about his identity, for they might have been watching Sir Gillan thirty years ago, and, if they had not greeted him first, he would probably have stopped to ask for directions.

'Master Medwin? Well met, sir. Welcome to York,' they called.

The rider pulled up and swung himself down, covering the last few paces on foot. His horse dropped his head, snorting in relief. 'Well,' he said, 'I certainly didn't expect a welcoming party.' A grin of recognition spread across his handsome face, creating an even greater resemblance to his father. 'Well met indeed, Master Thatcher...Master Broadbank. You are on the same mission as myself, I take it?'

'We are, sir. If it had not been too late to set off for

home, we'd have missed you. As it is, the situation may yet be saved by your presence. Shall we take you to our lodgings, sir, and tell you what we know?'

'Is my sister safe?'

'We have no way of knowing that yet, sir. She's been taken by the elder La Vallon. The merchant. He has a ship heading for Flanders.'

Allard Medwin stopped in his tracks. 'What? Ye mean Silas? She's with *him*?' The frown of incredulity misled his two companions into thinking that he was angry. 'Are you sure?'

'Yes. In a roundabout manner, we had it from a lass who spent a while in Bard La Vallon's confidence—'

'I'll wager she did. Another bairn next year for York's taxpayers.'

'And she was told that Bard's brother had deceived him. Run off with his woman.' The story was recounted as the two Medwin servants, unable to contain themselves, spilled out the tidings that Allard, Isolde's student brother, had come all the way from Cambridge at his father's summons to discover for himself.

Early the next morning, Thatcher and Broadbank headed for home with news that was still not good, but getting better, while Allard Medwin scoured the wharves for sea-going vessels with a space for a passenger. The only one he could find bound for the port of Sluys would not be leaving until the next day, just enough time for him to light a candle at the shrine of St William, sell his horse, and stock up with some warm clothes and food for the journey, with enough left over for his lodging and the weeks ahead.

The first of Isolde's new gowns to arrive was perfectly timed to coincide with her second visit to the Duchess of Burgundy, where she was to offer thanks for the gift of the Little Thing. Secretly, Isolde believed the summons to be an excuse for another chat about York, but it gave her the chance to dress up at last, and she shook the magnificent fabric free of its folds like a child with a new toy. Even without this newest delight, her face was radiant after the night spent in Silas's arms; with it, her happiness shone like a light that sparkled in her green-brown eyes against the sage, turquoise and gold of the shining silk. The large pomegranate motifs emerged as the fabric fell, linked with twisting stems and scrolling leaves, shimmering and rich. The tailor had sewn tiny bells along the hem of velvet, a green band echoed on the cuffs that reached over her knuckles in the latest fashion. Two wide velvet bands fell over her shoulders to the wide sash, the square neckline filled in by a finely-embroidered underdress that revealed the beautiful swell of her breasts.

Silas linked a wide collar of delicate goldwork studded with turquoise and pearls around her neck, removing at the same time the hand that flew modestly to cover the expanse. 'I want it to be seen, sweetheart,' he said.

'Which, it or me?'

'Both. Just enough to make an impression. More

than that would be unfair.' He smiled at her reflection in the mirror.

'More than that would be indecent.' She smiled back.

'You look ravishing. I think I might not let you go,' he teased.

'And if you insist on dressing to show every bulge, sir, you can expect to have a queue of Ann-Maries fighting to get at you.'

'Bulges, lady? Which particular bulge are you referring to, I wonder?'

Laughing, she turned to answer Cecily's beckoning finger to have her hair dressed. She might have had any number of bulges in mind, from shoulders to pleated chest, braguette to buttocks, thighs to calves covered in green silk brocade, patterned and plain. Under long hanging sleeves, a white embroidered shirt showed through a slit at each elbow, and a jewelled belt was hung with a gold-ornamented scabbard of finest tooled leather. Silas looked every inch the prosperous merchant, but, more to the point, he was also the handsomest creature Isolde had ever seen, masculine even in his finery, superbly healthy, lithe and strong. Last night they had not slept until dawn, when sheer exhaustion had claimed them in mid-kiss. Recalling his passion, and her own, the smile that played around her lips was not dispersed even by Mei's tug at the most sensitive part of her scalp. He was pleased with her, of that she was quite sure.

As before, her hair was coiled into a nest of jewelled plaits, threaded with gold cords and crowned with a plain gold circlet that dipped on to her high forehead. 'Exotic' was Silas's word for her.

Their entry into the Princenhof was less straightforward than previously, when Caxton and his assistant had met them. This time the courtyard was filled with the Duke's courtiers and their horses, who waited for him to appear. To be ushered through the throngs that lined the stairways and corridors to the Duchess's chamber was, to say the least, unnerving for Isolde, who could almost feel the stares upon her sumptuous attire. Protectively, Silas drew her arm through his, telling the little white gazehound in Isolde's arms that it must not think they were taking it back, to which it replied with a frantic whipping of its tail behind her elbow.

Unmistakeable in the dark blue figured velvet, the Duke of Burgundy was with the Duchess and her court as Silas and Isolde were shown into the room and, if they had hoped to wait quietly at one side, they soon saw that the Duke missed nothing. He turned to stare, haughtily receiving Silas's immaculate bow and Isolde's deep curtsy in a lingering silence that his wife eventually broke with a whisper, in English, 'Master Mariner and Mistress Medwin of York, my lord. You remember Silas?'

The interval gave Isolde time to regard the man whose seven-year-old marriage to Margaret of York would be celebrated during the coming weekend at the festival they called the Pageant of the Golden Fleece. At forty-two years old he was still good-looking, if a

rather weak chin could be discounted. His full and sen-
suous mouth had dimpled corners that betokened some
humour as well as the harshness for which he was
famed. He was known as Charles the Bold with good
cause. He was tall and well built, even forbidding in
his plainness except for the glint of gold on his padded
cote-hardie from the chain and pendant of the Order of
the Golden Fleece. A dark fringe of hair almost touching his heavy black brows was cut straight over grey
eyes, shaded by a huge velvet creation that could have
nested a pair of storks. His long legs were shapely in
tight blue hose that ended in extravagant points at the
toe, and his waist was neatly belted by a leather girdle
that flared the fur-edged pleats and slit-sides of the
cote-hardie over his hips. Only one ring adorned the
elegant hand that splayed its fingers over the blue bro-
caded velvet, a hand which Isolde had heard could
wield a sword and lance with the best warriors of Europe.

His English was near-perfect. 'So,' he said. 'The first
lady Silas Mariner brings to court, and she holds my
hound in her arms. Do you come to take the other one
too, mistress?'

Isolde was not taken in by the censorious tone; Silas's pressure on her fingers and his glancing smile
verified what she had already suspected. 'I have come,
your Grace, to thank her Grace the Duchess for her
gift, as one Yorkshire woman to another. Do I also owe
thanks to you, sir?'

The Duke's mouth tweaked, then he stepped to one

side, flourishing a hand in the Duchess's direction. 'To the lady first, I think.'

The warning of what was to come would have been impossible for Isolde to miss, for there was in the Duke's eye an expression that fed ravenously upon her beauty, unrelenting even while she placed the little creature in Cecily's arms. She came forward to enter the Duchess's gentle embrace, accepting her soft kiss to both cheeks. 'Thank you, your Grace,' she whispered. 'It was the kindest gesture to one so far from home.'

'My dear. She's taken to you?'

'Immediately.' Isolde's face lit with a spontaneous and ravishing smile. 'Both of us.' Whether the Duchess and she would have been allowed to say more at that point, Isolde never discovered, for then the Duke took her arm to draw her to his side with seeming impatience.

'Your thanks to me now, lady, since we are speaking in the English fashion.' There was no time at all between his command and the taste of his generous mouth upon hers or his hands on her arms obliging her to wait upon his pleasure which, to Isolde, seemed unnecessarily protracted for such a small gift. His release of her was similarly reluctant. 'Congratulations, Silas Mariner,' he said softly in French, tasting his lips. 'I think you and I have some business to do before the court leaves for Mechelin next week. Wait on me tomorrow, eh?'

Isolde could look neither at Silas nor at the Duchess, yet it was Cecily's eyes that told her the gist of the Duke's remark to which, observed from all sides, they could show no reaction. Although under the sovereignty of France, Flanders was ruled by the Duke who, like his father, Philip the Good, selected his mistresses without secrecy. They were always honoured, as were their husbands and families; not one of them would have dreamed of refusing the rewards that went with the status. No one ever recorded the Duchess's thoughts about the habit: they were trained in a more private warfare.

The Duke left shortly after that, leaving the Duchess free to indulge in conversation with her friends. With the sweetest smile, she invited Silas and Isolde to the ducal banquet on the second evening of the festival, and when Isolde told her they'd be watching the earliest processions from the mayor's house, she laughed prettily. 'Ah, you are using the English title, my dear. You'll have to learn to call him the burgomaster, you know. You must get Silas to teach you some Flemish. And French, of course.'

'Is it difficult, your Grace?'

'To speak Flemish is well-nigh impossible.' She laughed. 'But to understand, no, not at all. As for French, you'll soon pick that up. You're young.' In her smile was a complete understanding of Isolde's concerns, and the light squeeze on her arm lay a fraction longer than was strictly necessary. 'Two Yorkshire women,' she whispered. 'How's that for a coincidence?' Her delicate eyebrows lifted in secret delight, her blue eyes full of conspiracy and laughter.

Isolde was tempted to follow the Duchess's light-heartedness, and she smiled whilst inwardly applauding

the woman's courage, but as soon as the opportunity
arose they took their leave and, with characteristic
bluntness, Isolde's fears were loosed. 'What was the
Duke's remark?' she said.

'Which one?'

'In French.'

'Forget it.'

'Silas?'

He led her down the wide staircase, refusing to elaborate, and Isolde realised that she had mistimed her
enquiries.

Pieter de Hoed, who had ridden behind with mistress
Cecily, took his master to one side as soon as they
reached the courtyard of the Marinershuis. 'A moment,
sir, if you please.' He led Silas to the heavy wooden
gates, opening a crack just large enough to peep
through. 'Take a look, across there by the trees.'

Silas looked. 'Who are they?'

'They've followed us all the way from the Princenhof, sir. To find out where you live, I suppose.'

'Or where Mistress Isolde lives, more like.'

'You think they're English?'

'I expected it,' Silas said, closing the gate. 'Well
done, Pieter. Tell Mei to be extra vigilant, will you?'

Isolde held her peace on the matter of the Duke's
remarks. She would not even mention it to Cecily as
they strolled after the mid-day meal into the sunny garden where, at the far end, progress had already begun
on the new paths and raised beds, the wattle fences and
turf seats. The tailor was expected to return that after-

noon with Cecily's gown, and when men's voices were heard in the courtyard, the two women gleefully made a beeline for the archway, sure of being confronted by beaming smiles and mountains of pale grey damask and plum-striped velvet.

Silas's voice stopped her before they had rounded the corner; something in the tone rather than the words that warned her not to expect the tailor, after all. She waited, then, as the voices faded into the far room, she entered the passageway where Pieter stood guard. 'Who is it?' she whispered.

He frowned, but still managed to look pleasant. 'Someone who says he knows you, mistress. Fry, is it?'

'Fryde? Oh, no!' Isolde was horrified. 'Oh, surely he'd not come all this way. Big man, is he?' She held out her arms to the sides, letting the full skirt of her gown fall to the floor. 'Big jowls?'

'Jowls. No, this one is young.' He nipped his fingers together at the side of the mouth. 'Big lips.' He smiled.

The smile was not returned. 'God in heaven, Cecily—' she clutched at her maid's arm '—what am I to do?'

'You don't have to do anything, child. If Master Silas can't handle young Fryde then no one can. You could hardly be better dressed for a confrontation, could you? Pretend everything's as it should be.'

'I don't need to pretend.'

'Well, then.' Cecily nodded to the door. 'D'ye want me there, too?'

Isolde shook her head, assumed her most supercilious expression and asked, 'How's that?' She half closed her eyes for good measure.

'Perfect,' said Pieter.

'Perfectly terrifying,' Cecily said drily.

'Well, then.' Picking up her skirts and the Little Thing, she swept through the door that Pieter held open for her with the words, 'Silas, did you know that—?' already half-delivered before coming to an abrupt halt in simulated astonishment.

'Did I know what, mistress?' Silas said. On one shoulder, he leaned against the white wall that reflected sunlight on to his face and dark silky hair, his demeanour suggesting that he might have been discussing the latest Venetian cargo. 'Will it wait? You remember the gentleman, Master Fryde of York, do you?'

Martin Fryde had clearly not expected the vision in turquoise, green and gold who now stood before him; the last time he had seen her she had been very differently attired. Thrown off-balance by her magnificence, he exploded. 'Of course she does! She's intended for my...' The explosion died, prematurely.

'Intended for what?' Silas slowly returned his attention to the visitor. 'Your breakfast?'

Fryde ignored the wit, making a bow that was intended to impress them more for its extravagance than its lateness. 'Your servant, Mistress Isolde. As you see, I've crossed the ocean to rescue you.'

Silas groaned audibly. 'Oh, lord! This is going to get monotonous.'

'Rescue me?' Isolde said, before Silas could make

his predictable rejoinder. 'That's very civil of you, sir, but I've already been rescued once.'

'Twice,' Silas muttered. 'But who's counting?'

'I don't think I'm quite ready for the next one yet.'

Fryde's mouth tightened as he looked from one to the other for signs of levity. He had suffered as much as Bard from the voyage. His usual ruddy colouring had paled to a sickly hue that was not complemented by the magenta velvet doublet and paler cote-hardie of many pleats, and though his tall flower-pot hat was elegant enough, his rose blush was for the unwashed salt-sprayed hair of muddy blond that exposed his ears unkindly. 'What d'ye mean? Rescued once from what?'

'From York. Do you not remember my stay in your father's house on Stonegate? I prayed daily that someone would rescue me, and my prayers were answered. Do you not think that was fortunate?'

The sickly complexion deepened. 'You jest, mistress, I'm sure. That was your way, I remember, but you need have no fear of this man. My father sends you his assurances that no reprisals will be taken after your return. All you have to do is gather your belongings and return with me to my father's guardianship, after which he will let your father know that you are safe. Imagine how anxious he must be.'

'I don't have to. My father knows I'm safe.'

'Pardon? How can he know that?'

'Because Master Silas told him so.'

'Really. Well, Sir Gillan will hardly believe that, will

he? Not when you're in a La Vallon's custody. We all know—'

'Have care, sir. You are in a La Vallon house, you may recall.' Silas spoke softly, with no hint of a threat, but the point was taken. 'And Sir Gillan *will* believe it because he has my word. Which is why the lady will be staying in my protection.'

Clearly not enjoying the argument, Fryde resorted to his original complaint. 'But Mistress Medwin was intended for me, sir. That's why—'

'Really? Intended by whom and for what purpose?'

'By our fathers. They—'

Isolde broke in before he could expand the idea. 'Oh, no! That they did *not*! If my father had made an agreement, he would have consulted me first. They may both have voiced a wish to each other at one time, but—'

'There you are!' Fryde gathered up the morsel eagerly. 'There, you see, that's what I meant. They did both wish it, and so did you, mistress, if your behaviour towards me in York was anything to go by.'

'What?' Silas collected a stool in one quick swoop and set it down behind Fryde's legs with a crash, then drew Isolde towards him, seating her on the long bench by his side. 'Sit down, Master Fryde. That way you can make your accusations in comfort. Now, exactly what was this behaviour you speak of? Come on, man. Say it before her so that she can have it first-hand. We need to know of these things.'

'She's not told you?'

'Get on with it!'

However, Isolde did not intend to hear anything at

first-hand which she would be expected to deny. 'One moment, Master Fryde,' she said, reverting to the expression and voice she had prepared outside the door. 'Just one moment, if you please. If you have it in mind to suggest that my behaviour towards you in York was anything more than the most distant politeness, then I beg you will not perjure yourself. You know as well as I do, sir, that not by one word, look or gesture did I ever give you reason to believe that there could be anything between us, not even friendship, and if I had not left your father's house when I did, I would have left it some other way, for I had no intention of staying there another week. Now, sir, do not attempt to blacken my name or your own with lies of this nature.'

Fryde's eyes bulged angrily. 'Then ask yourself this, if you will. How black will the Medwin name be when it's known in York that you're living here with a La Vallon, unmarried and without your father's consent? If you care as much as you say for your name, then return quietly with me to my father's house where Sir Gillan can claim you, and no more harm done. Surely Master La Vallon will allow you some choice in the matter?'

Isolde opened her mouth to speak, but Silas was quicker. 'That seems perfectly fair to me. You can see how the lady pines for home. I lock her up in the cellar—'

'Attic.'

'Most of the time without any clothes—don't interrupt, woman—and with only a pet dog for company, so it's quite possible that by now she'll be glad to chase back to York to the comforts of the Fryde household. So, lady. The choice is yours. You may speak.'

'Thank you, my lord.' Isolde's demure expression hid her rising laughter. 'The truth is that I cannot decide immediately. A woman's privilege, you see. Besides, it's the pageant at the weekend and I'd so looked forward to seeing it, if you'll let me out of the attic—'

'Cellar.'

'By then, if I promise to be dutiful?'

'We'll see.'

'Thank you, my lord. So perhaps, Master Fryde, if I could give you my reply in a few days? Would one day next week be convenient?'

Fryde had already risen, not sure enough of either of them to know whether he was being made a fool of or accommodated. In the light of their deadpan faces, he gave them the benefit of the doubt. 'Then I have no choice, mistress, but I pray you will lose your fear of this man and give a thought to the direction of your future. Think of your father's good name as well as your own.'

'Thank you for your advice, sir. I pray for my father daily. Now, may we escort you to your horse? In the courtyard, is it?'

'I came by water.'

'Ah, so we shall attend you there.' They walked with him to the water gate, politely discussing the skyline of spires and towers and holding the boat close against the steps as he leapt aboard with unnecessary swagger. By some mischance, Pieter's hold of the boat slipped from him before the unfortunate Fryde's manoeuvre

was completed and, despite his wild clutch at the boatman's hand, his foot hit the slippery step below the
water, shooting out and depositing him on his bottom
between the boat and the bank.

'Oh, dear,' Silas said, tonelessly, guiding Isolde back
through the door on to the pathway. 'Pieter, I shall be
forced to dismiss you if you can't hold a boat still. Get
inside, man.'

'Yes, sir,' Pieter said, ignoring Fryde's dripping
form. He closed the water gate upon the yells of out-
rage, and bolted it.

'Now, woman. Is it to be the cellar or the attic?'

By mutual agreement, they could get no further than
Isolde's chamber before Silas swung her hard into his
chest and pushed the door with his heel. His kisses
were fierce and possessive, as if to reinforce their
agreement to fend off allcomers, though she could not
believe that, in Fryde's case, his concern was serious.
'What is it, beloved?' she whispered against his cheek.
'You don't believe what he said, do you?'

His eyes were black with desire. 'Of course not,
sweetheart, but *he* does, and I'll not give you up to the
likes of that little pinprick.'

She might have smiled at the description, but the
implications were more serious than that, and his
mouth was now on her throat, sending the deep vibrant
voice through her skin, diverting the flow of her
thoughts.

He unclasped the wide golden collar from her throat
and laid it on the chest, then tripped off his own doublet, unlacing her rich gown and letting it drop around

her feet like a solid aquamarine. His hands roamed over the fine cotton chemise, easing it over her shoulders and beautiful breasts, his eyes gazing, singing her praises in silence.

Isolde pulled at his points to release his shirt, drawing it up over his head as his arms came around her, and she felt again the heat of his skin upon her body and the strength of him as he lifted her. Even in their urgency, the ghost of a question drifted across her mind, but she stowed it away until this voyage was in calmer waters.

Chapter Nine

Reflections from the water flickered across the raftered ceiling, dancing madly after each boat that passed and reminding Isolde of how short and ineffectual her resistance had been against this man's siege. As insubstantial as ripples. Sated and exhilarated by his passionate loving, she could have found it easy enough to close her mind to the doubts that shadowed her, to live each day as if tomorrow did not exist, telling herself that the exclusion of the word love, which above all words would have been most comforting, was of no consequence. But the questions emerged again, persistent and carping.

She fondled the muscular neck and followed the slope of his throat down to a hollow that worked like a spring to open his sleepy eyes.

'What is it, then? Come on, you can let them out now,' he said.

'Let what out?'

'The questions, wench. They've been burning a hole in you since this morning, haven't they? Eh?' He picked up a loose half-plaited tendril and curled its end around his finger.

'How did you know?'

His slow smile was almost her undoing. Did questions matter, after all? 'You're not so hard to read, sweetheart. Your green eyes are like windows. You're concerned about the Duke, are you not?'

Isolde looked away. That, and other things. 'Less than a week,' she whispered. 'Less than a week.'

He was above her in one move. 'No, lass,' he said, gently. 'Calculate from the beginning and stop chastising yourself. You think I tried to make it easy for you to resist? With your fire I stoked it like the devil from the beginning, believe me. You were no pushover. You hated my guts. It could have gone either way if I'd not had a care. I'm not gloating over my conquest, but I cannot resist showing my pride for all that. Men do, you know.'

'And the Duke. What *did* he say to you that could not be said in English?'

'He wants you. It's as simple as that.'

She flinched at his bluntness. 'Is that the usual formula? In front of the Duchess? Just a word. No more?'

Silas rolled on to his back, pulling her into his arms and spreading her across him. 'I don't know what his usual formula is, sweetheart. How could I? All I know is that his mistresses are pleased to be chosen for the material advantages they gain. He's very generous to them, as he is to their kin.'

'So you would benefit if I became his mistress?'

'Certainly I would.'

'I see.'

'No, you don't. You don't see at all. The conditions I set out for you yesterday don't include anyone else, only ourselves and our immediate families. No Dukes, no painters, no printers, no merchants and their puny offspring. I thought I'd made that clear.'

'You did.' There was a silence. 'But I wondered if he might be an exception you could not afford to overlook.'

'There are no exceptions. The Duke may never have had a refusal, but he's not too old for new experiences. You will not become his mistress. Did you fancy the idea?'

She moved further over him, nestling her face into his neck. 'No,' she said, 'I didn't. But who are all these others?'

'Which others?'

'The painters and printers.'

'Memlinc, Van der Goes, that Wordy Wynkyn. They're all straining at the leash to get at you, lass. You'd only have to blink.'

'Oh, Silas! What nonsense.'

His hand smoothed over her hip and buttock. 'No, it's not. I can read them, too. But you're going to have to watch out for *real* danger, love, from now on.'

'From Martin Fryde? Surely not.'

'He didn't come here alone.'

Isolde leaned up to look deeply into his face and was met with a seriousness that made her frown. 'How d'ye know?'

'Three of them are staying at the English Merchants

House. I know exactly where they go and who they speak to. Young Fryde will know by now that it's no use coming back here for your answer. They'll try some other way to get at you.'

Briefly, she leaned her cheek against his, feeling the combined thud of their hearts. 'Silas. Don't let them, please.'

His arms came round her, rocking and caressing. 'As long as you stay close to me they don't have a chance. Trust me. But be on your guard and don't allow Mistress Cecily to go out on her own, either. This is not like Yorkshire, you know.' His kiss was warm and reassuring and, when it ended, she flopped breathlessly on to his shoulder.

'Doesn't the Duchess mind?' she said.

He chuckled, a deep vibrating sound that she could feel through her fingertips. 'She must be used to it by now, but she's devised her own compensations. She doesn't suffer too much, I believe.'

'You mean, she takes lovers?'

He made a sound that meant yes, but more than that, bringing Isolde instantly to a state of alertness. She straddled him, suddenly angry. *'You!'* she said. 'You've been her lover, haven't you? Don't deny it, Silas Mariner.'

Silas took her wrists and held them away. 'I don't intend to,' he said, coming close to a grin. 'Why should I?'

'And how long did *she* delay?' she snapped, struggling for possession of her arms. 'Did she hold you off for minutes, or was it hours? Did you make love to her here, on this bed, or was it between silken sheets?'

She was pushed over and held down, fighting him in a white-hot frenzy of jealousy. She had thought the Duchess to be pure and blameless, courageous, too. She had put Silas's obvious experience aside as being of no matter to her, yet the thought of the two of them together was far more potent than either of them singly. The *affaire* must have meant much to them, for they were a powerful couple. Was he being rewarded with the Duchess's patronage as the Duke's mistresses were? Was that why Silas was so successful?

Writhing and snarling, she fought without inflicting the slightest damage, and though her hands were freed, each of her blows was blocked by the paralysing hardness of his arms until he saw tears of fury well up into her eyes. Then he caught her, holding her immobile but unable to disguise his own enjoyment of her rage and her futile attempts to best him.

'Peace, my wildcat! Hush now; it was years ago, when I was a young man going about my master's business in York.'

'In York? Before her marriage? You lie, Silas Mariner.'

'No, sweetheart, I do not lie. She had a reputation well before her marriage to Burgundy. She's like her brother in that. 'Tis well known, love. I was flattered at the time, but now we're friends, that's all. No more than friends; I swear it. She's probably had dozens of lovers since then.'

'And you've had dozens since her! Let me go, damn you!'

'Not until you calm down.'

'I *am* calm!' she yelled. 'And I hate you! I don't want you and I shall go back home with Martin Fryde and Bard and I shall be the Duke's mistress and live in sin with *all* of them!' She choked on her hot tears and made only a token resistance when his hand slid softly down her body to gentle the dark red plumage that she had just relegated to others.

He did not answer her confused accusations and intentions. 'Beautiful thing,' he whispered, possessing her. 'Lovely, wild, passionate thing. You are my one desire. No duchess or queen could ever hold a candle to you, and no man shall take you from me. Not now. Not ever. I shall not let you go.' He made it sound like poetry with the emphasis coming on each thrust in a rhythm of new meanings that caught at her heartstrings, subduing her anger.

Dimly, it occurred to her in the tranquil and pulsating no-man's land when all talk had ceased, that she might not be alone in her fears, that Silas was by no means certain of her pledges, just as she had doubts about his reasons for keeping her, and that he intended to close every channel by which she might elude him. This one, of course, being the most effective and the most final.

An hour later, at supper, she remembered something. 'The English Merchants House? Is that where you store your merchandise?'

'No,' Silas said, 'not me. I have a place near the Grue.'

Isolde groaned. 'Oh, I'll never get used to these Flemish words. Where's the Grue?'

'It's the crane that lifts cargo out of the ships. I'll take you tomorrow. The Governor of the English House in Brugge used to be someone you know.'

She was quick to guess. 'Master Caxton? He was governor?'

'Yes, for many years. He was a mercer by trade. A man of many parts, is our William. You want to come too, Bard?'

Bard was in philosophical mood. 'Ann-Marie is indisposed. She's expecting me to behave myself. I'll come.'

Isolde was almost ready to feel sorry for him. 'Poor Bard. You're truly netted, then?'

'Mmm…the lady seems to think I have the makings of a good husband and her father believes I have a good business head, so…' he flicked a crumb off his doublet '…what more could I want?'

'Diamonds, lad?' Silas said, biting into a crispy apple. 'Nothing like a tray of diamonds to change one's mind about marriage, is there?'

Anticipating Bard's obvious retort, Isolde intervened. 'What will you do when Ann-Marie goes to Mechelin with the court next week, Bard?'

'I go to Antwerp with Myneheere Matteus. It's nearer Mechelin than Brugge and I'll be able to see her and learn the business at the same time.'

'So we shall lose you.'

'Yes, dear sister. You'll lose me. You might at least pretend to be heartbroken.'

They had already agreed on that, and Isolde's good-humoured silence was this time more comfortable than ever, for she was relieved beyond words that someone had found a way to halt Bard's interminable roving. At this point, she would almost have welcomed the chance to speak again with Ann-Marie, but the lass had kept well clear for her own good reasons, and Isolde would now have to wait until the court moved again before offering her congratulations. Or condolences.

The alleged understanding between Ann-Marie and Silas had been quickly dismissed as the fantasy of a young lady for a good-looking friend of her father's, but Isolde's attempts to shrug off Silas's admitted *affaire* with the Duchess was not nearly so easy, and the mental picture of the two of them together was as vivid to her as if it had been yesterday. Her superficial acceptance of his word that the connection was a thing of the past appeared to convince everyone except Cecily.

'What in heaven's name is the matter with you, child?' Cecily held a fistful of Isolde's hair in one hand, a brush in the other. 'You've snapped my head off twice now in as many brush-strokes. Is your head sore?'

'No, my head's not sore,' Isolde said. 'Plait it, Cecily, if you please.'

Cecily sighed. 'What is it, lass? You're worried, is that it?'

'No, of course not. But I wish I had news from

home, that's all. I'd have thought that if Fryde could send his son, my father could have done the same. I long to see Allard. I need his common sense, Cecily.'

'Then write.'

'I have done. But he won't get my letter until a boat sails. He might not get it at all.' She tried to keep her voice steady, but failed.

'But I thought your mind was made up. You seemed happier yesterday. You having second thoughts already?'

'God in heaven, Cecily!' Isolde snatched the vestigial plait away from Cecily's fingers and swung round on the stool to face her maid. 'I've hardly had time to set my first thoughts in place yet, have I?'

Cecily drew up a three-legged stool and sat, taking Isolde's hand in hers. 'I know, sweeting, I know. There, see, don't weep. It's all happened a wee bit sudden, hasn't it? Is that it? The suddenness of it? And a bit of jealousy, perhaps?'

'Oh, Cecily!' The floodgates opened. Isolde had never known jealousy until now, having never been in love. She had never known of its total unreason, its power, or its crippling pain. It seemed to make no difference that he had taken her for his mistress when the mere sound of his name, La Vallon, was enough to remind her of his family's reputation, and to taunt her that she had tangled with one only to be snared by the other. What assurance did she have that Silas differed from his brother and father except that he had apparently graduated from village girls to the nobility more quickly than they? And, in spite of his promises, the

whole charade was more to do with the La Vallon revenge upon the Medwins than with love. He talked at
length about possession, but then, he was a merchant,
wasn't he?

The words fell out in a disorderly array for Cecily
to make of what she could and, being Cecily, she did
not find the task impossible. At nineteen, Isolde was
old enough to give herself to a man, but that was not
the only element in the equation, for she was also a
dutiful daughter whose flirtation with the younger La
Vallon could hardly have prepared her for this. It did
not surprise Cecily in the least that Isolde was emo-
tionally unsettled: Silas La Vallon would unsettle any
woman, virgin or experienced, though Isolde was not
one of those flighty young things with shallow perceptions. She might be fiery, and somewhat impetuous, but
her feelings ran deep. She was like her father in that.
Cecily rocked her within comforting arms and said little: it was not advice or platitudes Isolde needed but
someone to listen, and Cecily had always been good at
that, too.

The visit to Silas's warehouse on the next day, intended to give Bard and Isolde some insight into the
La Vallon trading activities, gave Isolde rather more
information than she knew what to do with, nor did it
do anything to quell her misgivings about Silas's scru-
pulousness in all things. If she had not unconsciously
been searching for more fuel to add to the raging fires
of jealousy, she might have allowed him a chance to
explain before condemning him.

The Bridge of the Grue gave them a good view of the great foot-operated crane that winched bales, casks and boxes from the bellies of ships on to the wharf bordering the canal. A carved wooden crane of the bird variety perched whimsically on the highest arm of the contraption to look down upon the critical customs officers and expectant merchants, the stoic dockers and mildly insulting seamen whose seeming indolence was a front to cover their exhaustion. Amongst the rows of buildings that lined the canal with merchants' offices, Silas's warehouse was an elegant section stepped above its long dark windows with prettily carved gables and a door high up for accepting heavy goods into its upper storeys.

Its cool interior was cool and well ordered. An office was occupied by two diligent clerks half-buried in paperwork, and another for Silas's clients was lined with cupboards, shelves, pigeonholed papers, books and rolled charts, a set of exquisite Venetian glasses, and a large globe on a stand. His table was covered with a rug of glowing reds, browns and blues that felt like silken velvet.

'It is silk,' Silas said. 'It's come a long way over mountains and desert, seas and rivers. That's why it's expensive.'

'Hmph!' Bard snorted. 'What *don't* you deal in?'

'Slaves and fish,' Silas said tersely, leading them through into the rooms at the back of the house where two more men in leather aprons tied sacking-covered bales and nailed lids on boxes.

Isolde placed the Little Thing on the tiled floor and

laughed as it sniffed daintily at the nearest bale, then
sneezed. 'You're a gazehound,' she told it, 'not a sniff-
hound. Come and see up here, Little Thing.' They followed Silas and Bard upstairs to spacious floors
stacked with chests and large boxes that filled the warm
air with the pungent scent of cinnamon and cloves,
ginger and pepper. Bags of nutmegs sat alongside bags
of woad, one of which Silas opened to take out a handful of the hard black balls which, he said, would have
to be soaked before they could yield their blue dye.
There were chests of precious yellow saffron, madder
roots and indigo, sulphur, brimstone and liquorice,
alum, oak-galls and the shiny dried shells of beetles
that dyers used for red. Reams of paper were stacked
ready for Caxton's workshop.

'Meester Silas!' one of the men called from below.
'You have a visitor. Shall I send him up?'

Silas winked at Isolde. 'No,' he called. 'Tell him his
paper all went to the bottom.'

Master Caxton's face appeared, grinning sheepishly
beneath a felt hat with its trim turned up at the back
and a jaunty feather that arched over the crown like
the handle of a basket. 'Rubbish, Silas Mariner,' he
said, mildly. 'It comes overland from Fabriano and
you're hoarding it till the price goes up. I know you
merchants.'

The men clasped hands, smiling in the shared banter
of businessmen, and when Isolde had once again sub-
mitted to the eager kiss of greeting, she stepped back
to allow Bard an introduction. Their voices followed
her down the stairway and through to the room where

the men had been packing. Silas had not lingered here because, she presumed, the cargo was less interesting, and now the two men had vanished, leaving the lid of one long box lying half across it at an angle.

Lifting one end of the lid, she saw inside the leather-bound books and sheafs of unbound manuscripts that she knew to be from Master Caxton's printing press. Silas had said that he shipped them to England. But in the centre of the box, between the rows of books, were long bolts of linen-wrapped fabric like those stored on the upper floors at the Marinershuis, which seemed strange when Silas had told her that, for customs purposes, cargo had to be packed and labelled separately. Frowning, she replaced the lid and eased open the end of an untied bale that lay on a nearby bench. From between the springy white sheep's fleece, she saw the bright silver glint of a buckle, then the hard curve of a breastplate, the overlapping segments of arm and leg pieces. Quickly she closed the sacking and moved to another one, feeling the tell-tale resistance of metal amongst the fleece. In another box of what looked like rolls of plain linen, she found buried in the centre the soft black astrakhan lambskins that would evade customs duty at whatever port they were unloaded, the very stuff of the smugglers' trade. Moving across to a cask, she cautiously eased up the round lid that should not have been loose, discovering that the wine was held inside the wooden casing like a layer inside a false lining: the space in the centre was empty.

Isolde shook her head with disbelief. What was it he'd said they were carrying to Flanders? Wool, wood and other bits and pieces. So, what *did* he bring here, and what did he take back to England? Who did he sell to, and what else was he doing that was illegal? Did Master Henry Fryde have some connection with this, and was that why he must not go anywhere near Scarborough?

A burst of laughter made her jump. Quickly, she gathered the Little Thing into her arms, nimbly mounted the stairs, and was calmly inspecting a pile of rugs from the east when the men came through, still laughing.

'All right, William,' Silas was saying. 'So you may as well take the books yourself, if you're so bent on going.'

'Going, Master William?' said Isolde. A tightness in her throat forced the words out shakily. 'You're not leaving us before the pageant, are you?'

Apologetically, Caxton tilted his head. 'Indeed I must, dear lady. His majesty King Edward has offered me a station by Westminster Abbey where I can set up my press, and it's the chance I've been waiting for. I shall set off tomorrow before the autumn gales begin so that I can prepare the place to receive the machinery. Wynkyn is going to wind things up here and have it shipped over, and, if all goes according to plan, we may have it working by the new year. Just think, Isolde, it will be the first and only printing press in England.'

She could not resist a gentle hug, for his expression of pride was endearing on one so unassuming. 'There is no one more worthy of the honour, Master William.

You will make it a huge success, as you have done with everything else.'

'Except one.' He smiled. 'You must teach me what to do before I go.'

'Then come and dine with us, and I will.'

'Thank you. But this evening is my last in Brugge.'

'Come this evening. Is that all right, Silas?'

'Most certainly. And bring that wordy assistant, if you must.'

Caxton grinned, knowing the reason for Silas's reluctance. 'He likes to try his English out. He knows he's referred to as Wynkyn de Worde, but he doesn't mind. He knows his job, too.'

It was difficult for Isolde to conceal her discovery, the urge to question Silas conflicting with the cautionary voice telling her to wait. As it transpired, the choice was removed from her by a stream of visits from fellow-merchants and then by their own visit to Caxton's press before it was dismantled. Eventually, Isolde and Pieter de Hoed, wearing the newest extravagant creation, left the men to it in order to give the cook time to prepare an extended supper. She decided to speak to Silas in private at bedtime.

Inevitably, bedtime came late, and the guests' departure came some time after curfew, though the light that still lingered in the western sky was enough to make both men recognisable. The evening had gone well, and there had been times when Isolde was able to push the worrying discoveries to the back of her mind, but telling herself that Silas knew what he was doing seemed to have effect only for a few minutes until the penalties for smuggling pestered her like a recurring nightmare. Not only that, but the discovery appeared to strengthen her belief that all was not as it should be with the man she loved, and now she wondered whether she should confront him with the knowledge or not, suspecting that he would brush it aside and overpower her with his loving. Last night he had given her no chance to re-introduce the subject of his past, his abundant energy sweeping her away on a tide too strong to resist, robbing her of the will to reverse the flow.

The house quietened and the bells tolled out across the town, giving orders for the night. The water below her window rippled like dark satin and Isolde lined up the opening sentences of her confrontation, her heartbeats protesting at their feebleness. She began a turn away from the window when she was caught by a movement on the water. As she waited, a shallow skiff glided silently up to the water gate and stopped. Someone bent to pull the boat close to the steps, holding it while another figure prepared to disembark.

Isolde whispered to Cecily. 'Come…come here! Look, someone's coming.'

'At this time of night?' Cecily kept to one side, her head weaving from side to side to catch sight of the moving shadows. 'The only people to go abroad at night are the refuse boat, physicians and midwives,' she said.

'And smugglers.'

'Look, she's getting out. It's a woman, love. Nay,

it's not a midwife for young Mei, is it? You don't think…?'

'Shh…they'll hear.'

The figure was small and slender, her leap on to the steps graceful, and the generous lift of her skirts gave the two watchers a good look at the rich sheen of some exotic fabric. Her head was concealed by a loose hood, and the command to the boatman was high and imperious. The boatman sat: the woman disappeared through the water gate and out of their sight.

'It is, you know,' Cecily said, turning away. 'It's the midwife.' But her voice held little conviction.

'That's no midwife. Besides, she had no bag, and Mei's not—'

'Yes, she is.'

'Get me a blanket, Cecily. I'm going to wait.'

'Oh, do come away, love. Don't fret about it.'

'A blanket, if you please.'

The sky blackened and the bells marked one hour, two hours, before the gate squeaked and, in the darkness, Isolde could just make out the woman's figure, this time accompanied by a man. He spoke, but not low enough to escape Isolde's straining ears. It was Silas. From the water, the figure waved once, then disappeared: the gate squeaked softly again and the ripples lapped like echoes upon the deserted steps.

She lay in bed waiting, listening and counting the bells and then, near dawn, she tiptoed into Cecily's little room and slid beside her nurse's warm softness to be cuddled into sleep. Cecily left her to sleep on, and later was able to report that a message had come from the Duchess to summon Silas to the Princenhof without delay. He had taken Pieter with him and left a message that Isolde was to admit only the tailor, who had failed to appear yesterday. Bard had gone earlier to Paulus Matteus's office.

'We've got to go, Cecily. We can't stay. Pack our bags.'

'Tch! Oh, love…come on, now. There's no reason—'

'Yes, there is. There's a very good reason. I'll not stay.'

A grey sky lowered heavily over the town, the stiff breeze sending a vibration of black waves across the canal, firming Isolde's resolution and darkening her unhappiness. Jealousy, now augmented by the knowledge of Silas's illicit trading, held her in the very depths of its clutches, deafening her to reasoned argument and blinding her to the comforts, the prestige of her position and to the friendships she had already made. The fire Silas had lit now raged out of control, consuming her in the process. Her love, the first she had ever experienced, tore mercilessly at her tender heart, shaking her with a pain she believed only distance could alleviate.

The errant tailor emerged from the skiff at the water gate, looking the epitome of obsequiousness, his face already flushed with apologies and his arms loaded with boxes which he struggled to balance across the short step from boat to dry land. His tall auburn-haired

companion removed all but one from the tailor's arms,
strode easily across the steps and followed him through
the gate where Mei, clattering down the path to meet
them, greeted them as one.

'Ah, Meester Johannes, a good day to you. You were
expected yesterday, you know. Anyway, no matter, the
mistress is in her chamber. I'll take you up. You have
a new assistant, *ja*?' She turned to smile at the tall man.

'Er…well, not exactly. This…er…' He followed
Mei, who clearly was more interested to know what
was in the boxes than the identity of the man who
carried them, while he himself was more concerned
about his client's reaction to the clothes. Would she be
placated by the new undergowns?

One would have thought, from the look of astonishment on his client's face, that Meester Johannes had
been accompanied by the patron saint of tailors rather
than the kind stranger who had helped him off the boat
with the boxes, but as soon as the door was closed upon
the disappointed Mei he began to understand the reason
for the stranger's insistence. His client threw herself
into the man's arms and burst into tears.

'Allard,' she sobbed. 'Oh, you've come at last!'

Meester Johannes put the boxes down and waited,
noticing that the man called Allard was not in the least
taken aback.

'Dearest one. You knew I'd come. I came as fast
as—'

'How did you know? Did you get my—'

'Father wrote to me. It's taken me—'

'No, how did you know I was in Brugge?'

'I went to York and found out—'

'You must take me home, Allard. Now. This minute. See, my bags are packed already.'

'Now? Where's Silas? Has he made you unhappy, love? He's not injured you, has he?'

'Not injured, no. But I must go home now, before he returns.' She clung to him, barely able to believe that her prayers had been answered, and in the first jumbled hail of questions managed to discover that Allard had come from Sluys that morning and boarded the same skiff as the tailor. No, he had not eaten much, but that was not unusual.

All the same, he was perplexed. 'I had hoped to speak to Silas, Issy. Could we not wait a while?'

'No!' Isolde pleaded. 'No, Allard. He'll try to persuade me to stay.'

'But the dresses…all this…' He waved a hand. 'How could all this have made you so unhappy? Silas is not a bad chap. We used to—'

'You know him?'

'Well, of course I do. We're the same age. We used to fish together, climb trees for conkers, and—'

'And go whoring?'

'Er, well, not so much of that. That was Bard's pastime, I remember.' He looked at her sharply. 'Is that the problem? The La Vallon problem?'

She gulped and nodded.

'You've fallen for him, then?'

She looked away. 'No! I hate him. He's a La Vallon, isn't he?'

'He's a man.' Allard caught Cecily's eye and began

to understand. The fine clothes. The well-appointed room. Tears. Jealousy-hatred-love: all one word. 'Where's Silas now?' he said, preparing for the snarl.

'With the bloody Duchess!'

Another peep at Cecily, then the flick of an eyebrow. 'I see. I didn't think he'd be tarred with his father's brush. Where's her cloak, Cecily?'

'Ahem!' Master Johannes picked up his boxes with resignation.

But Allard detained him. 'Don't go yet, sir. We'll need you to get out again. Now, this is what we do.'

With four horses in the stable, it was not difficult. Mei was quite convinced by their need to visit the tailor's workroom; the mistress was well chaperoned; they'd be back by midday. Much to Master Johannes's disgust, their bags were stowed into his largest box and he was well paid to have the horses returned the next day from Sluys, where they hoped to find a ship bound for England. Allard sounded optimistic.

On a page of her white paper, Isolde left a message for Silas.

Silas, do not mind my going. I cannot be your mistress. It is not comfortable for my heart. I am leaving the Little Thing because I do not wish to be reminded. Please return her for me, with my thanks. And do not seek me, I beg you. I will care for your sister, God willing. God keep you safe. Isolde.

*   *   *

Until they reached the seaport of Sluys, Isolde had quite forgotten that it was Master Caxton's intention to sail that day for England; she had been intent on answering her brother's questions about all that had happened since leaving home, and before. To find her friend standing on the quay with his nose in a book while the small sturdy ship completed its loading was at first a fright, and then a godsend. If anyone could secure the three of them an instant place on board, he could. Although London was not their chosen destination, Isolde thought, beggars could not be choosers.

Predictably, he was amazed to see Isolde. 'Dear lady, you said nothing of your intention last night. And Silas not here to see you off?'

'A last-minute decision, Master William, to accompany my brother. My father has sent for me, and I must go to him.'

Allard Medwin, student of medicine at Cambridge, and William Caxton, student of everything, took a liking to each other from the start, striking up an instant rapport as if they had known each other for years. At Caxton's word, the master of the ship vacated a small cabin for Isolde and Cecily, asking no questions, taking the fee Allard offered, and hoisting sail out of Sluys with an eye to the freshening wind.

The two women looked back across the flat grey horizon of Flanders with different degrees of misgiving which were not the same as those they had brought exactly one week ago. But if Isolde had hoped to make use of her elder brother's sound common sense during the voyage, and to unload upon him those sorrows

which were still so new to her, her disappointment was
tripled, for he had found in Caxton an intelligence that
had not come his way in six years at Cambridge. The
other disappointment was Cecily's predictable malaise,
and the third was the early September gale that
screamed through the rigging night and day, lashed the
cabins, washed the decks and rolled the passengers
from wall to wall, keeping them confined to their cabins on a diet of cold food, cooking being out of the
question in such conditions.

On the few occasions she was able to communicate
with Allard not once did he grumble that he was being
obliged to suffer another voyage so soon after the first,
having the kind of nature that looks for the advantages
wherever they might be found, even while tending poor
Cecily. To her constant distress his advice was, 'Just
drink the ale, mistress. The food is so wretched anyway, you're probably better off without it.'

Huddled in blankets to keep relatively warm and dry,
Isolde was soon fatigued by the effort of staying where
she put herself, preferring to be wedged in the cabin
while losing track of the days and nights, caring for
her maid's needs. Far from regretting her impulsive
flight, she almost revelled in the possibility that the
ship might go down and she with it, for she could see
nothing beyond her arrival in a strange city and a life
without Silas. Longing for his arms, his mouth, his irresistible maleness, she managed to keep in touch with
her own need to control her life after being swept too
fast into a position where she was a tool to be bar-
gained with, a mistress of convenience, an unschooled

woman to be put aside whenever the more experienced one clicked her fingers. Alternating between anger, despair and humiliation, she rode out the storm in semi-isolation with misgivings that rose to panic each night at the thought that she may already be carrying a babe in her womb. He had said it would be his. But no; it would be hers.

The knocking on her cabin door roused her from dark thoughts. 'Isolde!' Allard called. 'Come and look. We're through the worst now. Here, let me help you.' He placed an arm around her, supporting her across the wet deck to where Caxton stood talking to the master, pointing towards the horizon. It was the first time she had seen either of the two men for some days, and so it was with surprise that she noticed the sling around the printer's arm.

'Master William,' she said. 'You're injured? What happened?'

He was pale and clearly unwell. 'I slipped on deck,' he said, trying to smile. 'Broke my arm. The good doctor here has splinted it. If I begin to ramble, don't mind me, it's the brandy.'

'Then you should be resting, sir. Thank God the sea is calmer.' A huge wave came up to soak them with its white spume, but by now they paid it little attention.

'I had to come out to catch the first sight of land. Look, the dark line across there: cliffs, then the white breakers below. See?'

'Oh…' Isolde shaded her eyes to focus them. 'Oh,

yes, I see. This is the south coast, then, where we approach London.'

The master smiled at her rudimentary reckoning. 'Nay, mistress, I hope not. Those are the east-coast cliffs of Flamborough and Scarborough. We'll be in harbour before nightfall, God willing.'

'What?' Isolde stared at him, sure she had misheard. 'You didn't say Scarborough, surely?'

'Aye, that's it. We've made good time with that bit o' breeze.'

She looked from the master to Allard, then to Caxton. 'But I thought we were bound for London. Isn't that where you wanted to go, Master William? You said you were going to London, not Scarborough.'

'Yes, dear lady. I *am* going to London,' Caxton said, smiling over her head at the master. 'But Silas Mariner offered me a place on his ship which was ready to sail with a cargo of my books for his English clients. He said I could sail with them, if I wished, since it'll be quicker to ride down to London from here than to wait for another ship to cross. There wasn't one due for another week.'

Isolde's heart leapt, making her suddenly breathless. Silas's ship? Scarborough? Then those boxes packed with books and black astrakhan furs were right here under their feet. What audacity. And unwillingly she had escaped on her lover's ship, bound for his chosen destination, with his friend and smuggled cargo.

Back in her cabin, she held on to the bunk where Cecily lay and buried her head in her arms, trying to control the shaking of her body and the spasms that forced torrents of tears from her aching eyes. Combined relief and frustration fought within her, confusing every attempt at lucidity. Then she splashed cold water onto her face, combed and plaited her hair and set about tidying the cabin, packing their belongings once more into bags. A seagull mewed from the rigging, sending her its mournful welcome.

Cecily moaned and turned her head. 'Get that cat out of here,' she said.

Chapter Ten

For the fourth time that morning, Dame Elizabeth Brakespeare peered out of her counting-house window overlooking the quay at Scarborough, where groups of men clutched at their headgear and tightened their faces against the driving rain. Ships of all shapes and sizes swallowed or disgorged their cargo on to men, resembling worker ants, who balanced along planks to load carts for quick transport to the warehouses. There was a frown on her otherwise serene face as she turned away. 'Searchers,' she said. 'I'm sure of it.'

At fifteen, John Brakespeare topped his mother's height by at least an inch, fulfilling his late father's thirteen-year-old prediction that he would be a giant of a man. Already his voice had deepened to correspondingly masculine proportions. 'Not the usual customs men, Mother?'

'No, they're strangers here, and it's obvious by their nosing about that they're on to something. They stayed last night up at the Ship.'

'How d'ye know?'

She smiled at last, with a lift of her brows, and John knew to ask no more. In a small port like Scarborough, everyone knew who stayed at the Ship. 'Has everything gone, John?' she asked.

'Yes. Everything.'

'Then we have no cause for concern, have we?'

'Silas is not due, then?'

'I don't know, dear. Do we ever? We can only hope that they finish checking on us all before he arrives.'

John sniffed. 'He puts us in danger, Mother. Especially you.'

Dame Elizabeth linked her arm into her son's. 'It's himself he puts in danger, John, not us. This is his house now, remember, and the roles have been reversed. I am *his* employee, and although I'm called merchant, he's the owner, and it's his goods that'll be forfeit if he's discovered, not ours.' Her voice dropped to a whisper. 'That's why we arranged it that way, so as to make him responsible. Silas would never take risks with us, John, you know that.'

John covered his mother's hand with his own. 'I wish you'd marry again, Mother. Would you not consider it?'

The smile this time was almost a laugh. Modestly, she hung her head. 'How could I marry and carry on Silas's business, love? He needs me to be here, not in another man's house. And it earns a good living, doesn't it? And you and Francis learning the trade. It would have to be an exceptionally understanding man who'd turn a blind eye to what we do. Do you mind so much?'

'I don't mind taking the risks for Silas, no. Without him we'd be nowhere, would we? I mind for you, that's all. You'd look well with a husband.'

His smile was so like his late father's, catching at Elizabeth's heart and starting the ache that thirteen years had barely begun to lessen. 'Yes, dear. So I would. Now, go and give Francis his instructions, if you will. He's downstairs in the big warehouse.'

The group of men had now moved further along the quay, waiting for a rowing boat to reach the steps. They had their job to do, their own methods, their successes and failures, and they knew of the lengths to which some merchants went to evade customs duty on goods from abroad. Even the most respectable of them was guilty of some deception now and again, when they believed they could win. Busily, Dame Elizabeth turned to her lists.

Later in the afternoon the high tide brought a drop in the wind, and the rain that had lashed against the windows now sprayed a fine veil across the harbour, lifting the seagulls sideways. John Brakespeare clattered up the stairs to the counting-house and, placing his head close to his mother's stiff white linen hood, opened the window to let in a blast of air.

She clamped her arms on to her papers. 'John! Oh, no!'

'Look!' he said. 'Look out there. What d'ye see?'

White sails bulging with wind and heading for the shelter of the harbour. Men already swarming in the rigging. 'It can't be,' she whispered.

'It is. It's Silas's little cog. It's his, I tell you.' He slammed the window and latched it, grabbing her woollen shawl and holding it ready. 'Come on.'

'Those men,' said Dame Elizabeth, wrapping herself closely. 'Where are they? I must warn him to have a care. This is ill timed, John. Quickly, you run on ahead. I'll lock up.'

The three searchers had watched the arrival of the cog with as much interest as Dame Elizabeth and the boys who stood by her side, searching the deck with their keen eyes for the one they hoped to see.

'No,' Francis said. 'He doesn't use this one himself much, does he, Mother? But there's Master Summerscale, and there are some passengers; no Silas this time. But wait...' he grabbed her arm '...aren't those the two women who came with Silas's brother last month? You know, the lady from York and her maid?'

'Good heavens,' said John, beaming.

'That's strange,' said Elizabeth.

No one would have guessed at her consternation as she waited at the end of the gang-plank to greet the passengers, her welcoming smile acting as a kind of proof to the beady-eyed searchers that this was what she had expected and little else. It could not have been a better diversion. 'Welcome back!' she called.

Allard came first, carrying Isolde, then Caxton, supported by a burly seaman, and then Cecily in the arms of the master, Summerscale. In turn each of the passengers clung to the Brakespeares as if they had expected to be met, which was far from the truth but comforting when their legs still felt the ground heaving beneath them.

'Dame Elizabeth!' Isolde almost fell into her arms, her face contorting with joy. Or was it pain?

'Come in...come in! Are these two gentlemen with you? No...please, leave the introductions till later. You look all in. That rough sea. Ah, you poor things, come.' Taking immediate control, she turned the four shivering passengers towards the house, calling to Master Summerscale over her shoulder, 'You'll sup with us tonight, master? Bring the crew, if you will.'

The three customs officers, however, had other ideas. 'One moment, mistress,' one of them said, signing the others to go aboard. 'This is your ship, I take it?'

'No,' Dame Elizabeth said, 'it isn't. It belongs to my employer, and this is hardly the time, Master Customs Officer, to start asking questions. Let it wait on the morrow, if you please, and give these good men some peace after their voyage. You can see what weather they've come through.'

'I beg your pardon, mistress, but any delay benefits you, not us. We need to know what you're carrying.'

Master Summerscale, halfway up the gang-plank, came to the point. 'I'm carrying four exhausted passengers, sir. What else d'ye need to know?'

'Cargo?'

Master Caxton stepped forward, imposing and dignified despite his pain, his face scowling at the hold-up. 'The cargo, sir, is books. My books. Printed on my press in Brugge.'

The searcher, his short well-filled neck overlapping

the good woollen cloak under his chin, turned his attention to Caxton with obvious sharpness. 'You were a passenger on the ship?'

'You know I was. You watched me disembark. My name is William Caxton, sometime governor of the Merchant Adventurers Company in Brugge and returned by command of his Majesty King Edward to set up my printing press in Westminster. Are you suggesting that I have travelled on a ship carrying contraband? Do you want to open each box to take a look?'

'Master Caxton? Er…no. No indeed, sir.' The man's eyes and mouth gaped simultaneously as he struggled to stay in command of the situation. 'My apologies, sir, truly. No need to trouble Mistress Brakespeare further. I bid you good day, sir. Mistress.'

'Not now or at any time in the future, I should hope,' Caxton added, severely. 'Whoever's sent you to investigate this lady's affairs had better look to his own, for this is a red herring if ever I saw one. A red herring, I say.'

'Absolutely, sir. Routine investigations, sir, no more than that.' The man called to his two hesitant companions and together they made haste up the hill towards the Ship, holding their dignity together over the slippery cobbles.

John Brakespeare stole a glance at Isolde and smiled shyly, removing the well-travelled bag from her hands so that she could support Mistress Cecily. Dame Elizabeth, overcome with relief and admiration, offered Master Caxton a genuine welcome, English fashion.

'We are in your debt, Master Caxton. I hope you

will accept our hospitality for as long as you need it. Silas has often spoken of you, but your timing was perfect. You're unwell, I see. Come, and you too, sir.'

'My brother, Allard Medwin,' Isolde said, 'and Cecily, oh…dear…!' As she spoke, poor Cecily sagged and was caught by Allard. 'We are indeed a sorry bunch. And an intrusion, I fear.'

But Dame Elizabeth was smiling as she placed an arm around Isolde's shoulders. 'You are the best thing that's happened to me all day. I mean it; the very best thing. Come, there is some tending to do. John, Francis, run on ahead and tell Cook. And tell Emmie to heat more water,' she called after them.

There was no denying that Fate had taken a hand in Isolde's affairs and left her little to do but accept the hospitality that she had, only a few miles out, decided to avoid. How could she impose a second time upon this good woman's generosity? What Fate had omitted to tell her was that Master Caxton carried a letter of introduction from Silas to Elizabeth, knowing that he would need at least one night's lodging before continuing his journey to London. Nor did Isolde understand that, over the years, Caxton and Dame Elizabeth had had their praises sung to each other so often that, except for an unbiased physical description, they were as well known to each other as if they'd been friends of long standing. Now, at last, they'd been brought together in the most auspicious circumstances. Caxton saving his hostess from deep embarrassment, as well as himself, whilst she was able to put him straight to bed with some broth and a dose of laudanum for the pain of his fracture. Needless to say, he went out like a light.

The riddle of how Isolde, her brother and maid came to be on the same ship from Flanders was a mystery that still had to be solved, but Dame Elizabeth's perceptions disallowed any questions about that until her guests had been made more comfortable, bathed, changed and, in Cecily's case, put to bed with the first nourishment she'd had for many days.

'No questions,' she told the boys. 'We do not interrogate our guests. Mistress Isolde will no doubt tell us, when she's recovered.' Nevertheless, she had not missed the tears filling Isolde's eyes which had been quickly brushed away, but her curiosity was not allowed to overcome her compassion. She met Isolde and Allard speaking together in low voices upstairs on the wide landing. 'Now, my dear guests. Do you have everything you need? I have dry clothes a-plenty, and some of Silas's things that would fit you well, Master Allard. He'd not mind you borrowing them, I know.'

Protectively, Allard kept hold of his sister's hand. 'Dame Elizabeth, your kindness is overwhelming. Isolde and I had intended to—'

'If you'd stayed anywhere but here, sir, I'd have been mortified. Now, I see that you lack some dry shoes. I shall get you a pair of Silas's.'

Isolde caught at Dame Elizabeth's hand. 'We owe you an explanation,' she said.

'No, dear. Not now you don't. First you must have

food, warmth, and a night's rest. Then we can talk. Yes?'

Partly from fatigue, Isolde's eyes brimmed again.

But the plan, devised out of kindness, had not allowed for Isolde's pressing need to unburden herself and to secure the approval of someone wiser than she, Cecily and Allard having been otherwise engaged. Far from diminishing over the distance, her anguish and uncertainty had grown, and now one more night was one too many. Wearing one of Dame Elizabeth's loose robes, and the cotton cover from her bed around her shoulders, she tiptoed down the staircase towards the soft light from the parlour, catching the same evocative aroma of beeswax, lavender and spices that she had noticed on that first occasion. It seemed like years ago.

Dame Elizabeth was standing alone before the great hearth, her face lit by the embers and piles of ash that spilled on to the stone, and Isolde was tempted to turn back so as not to interrupt her hostess's reverie. The hesitation was caught.

'Isolde, come in. I was thinking what a pity it is to cover the fire when it gives such comfort. Share it with me for a while. You are not ready to sleep yet?' She held out a welcoming hand and guided Isolde towards a low bench on the opposite side of the hearth.

'Forgive me. I know I should wait for a more convenient time, but would it impose on you too much if I were to tell you what happened, instead of waiting till tomorrow?'

'My dear, it would be no imposition. I was not ready

to sleep either. The day's coincidences are whirling around inside my head, and your account is probably what I need to explain them. Master Summerscale told me he brought you all from Sluys with a cargo of Master Caxton's books, so I realised you must have decided to go there with Silas, after all.' She threw a log onto the fire to revive it.

'Not quite,' Isolde said, watching the sparks fly. 'He told me he was going to York.'

'Yes, that's what I understood. Didn't he?'

'No, he'd been there before coming here. Did you not know that?'

'Yes, but he told me he had to go back there. It was a sudden decision, but it was important to get you back there without being seen.'

'It was a bluff. He didn't intend to take me there, or to meet Bard.'

'So he didn't…?' A crease appeared between Elizabeth's eyes. This was something she had not foreseen.

'No. He left Bard waiting and he took me straight to Brugge. He has a house there, you know, on the Dijver opposite the Gruuthuis.'

The log crackled under the licking tongues of flame and the wind roared in the chimney, pulling the blue smoke upwards. Dame Elizabeth's hand covered her mouth in utter astonishment, then dropped, slowly. 'He…he *abducted* you, Isolde? Is that what you are telling me?'

'Yes, he wanted me to become his mistress.'

'I see. And you agreed?' She had not meant to probe, but the question seemed natural enough, and when

Isolde's hands visibly shook, Dame Elizabeth moved to join her on the long bench, to place her own warm hands on Isolde's for comfort and to catch the first warm rain of tears that fell. 'Shh…I know. Don't say any more. He was attracted to you from the first; I could see that easily enough. But he's a powerful beast, isn't he, and I don't suppose he gave you much time to refuse? He's always known what he wanted, ever since he was a young apprentice. One could never call him impetuous, but when he sets his mind to something, he's not known for the subtle approach. My husband used to call him a young bullock.' She smiled at the memory. 'You decided to leave, then?'

Isolde was not sure how much Dame Elizabeth knew about the feud between the Medwins and the La Vallons and so, little by little, the full story emerged, during which the sympathetic listener had only to confirm what she already understood, or to prompt a detail. Yet when Isolde reached the part concerning Silas's connections with the Duchess of Burgundy, her voice grew incoherent with anguish, making questions concerning her love for Silas quite unnecessary. She shook with grief.

Dame Elizabeth allowed her to weep, then brushed the unruly mop of red hair away from her face. 'I think there is something you should know,' she said, 'though it might have been just as well if Silas had told you himself.'

'I know,' Isolde said, forestalling her. 'They were lovers in York before the Duchess's marriage.'

'He was no more than twenty, Isolde. Ambitious.

Confident. Irresistible to a woman like Margaret of York. She was only a year or so older than him at the time, and quite wild. My late husband had managed to obtain foreign goods for her that no one else up here could get; furs, books of hours, perfumes and silks. She's always loved silks. Naturally, she took a fancy to Silas. Everyone did. It was a very brief *affaire*. My husband put a stop to it, but it was enough to guarantee him a patron for life and exclusive links with her family who all wanted whatever he could obtain, especially books and fabrics. But it also made him a lot of enemies, Isolde, especially in York.'

'Master Fryde?'

'Yes. Fryde never had the same success in his trading as my husband, because for one thing no one could trust him, and he never managed to acquire the same kind of patronage as that which John had from Margaret of York.'

'You had a house in York, as well as here?'

'On Coney Street, alongside the river. It was convenient.'

'So Fryde was envious of Master Brakespeare's success?'

'Very. Especially when Fryde desperately wanted to take high office within the Merchant Adventurers Company and on the city council, because one needs a certain amount of wealth for that, you see. Even the lower positions require an outlay: bridgekeepers, for instance, must do their stint before they can be nominated for office. Granted, they get to keep the rents and tolls, but they also have to maintain both bridges out of that and their own pockets. My John never aspired to that, but Fryde loves the power it brings. Eventually, he brought my husband down.'

'Tell me, if you please.'

The lovely mature face showed soft lines for all the forlorn years. 'Henry Fryde was a councillor at the time. He authorised my husband to buy four hundred pounds' worth of luxury goods from Flanders for him and agreed to pay John five per cent commission. John was foolish to trust him, but he didn't see what could go wrong. On the way home from Flanders, crossing the North Sea, John's ship was caught by pirates. They stole the cargo, killed my John and sent the ship empty to York bearing his body. And young Silas. I was expecting our second son at the time. The cost of crew, handling, and cargo had cost us dearly, but Fryde refused to pay a penny compensation, not even as a gesture, and I was ruined.'

'My God! So that's it!'

'Fortunately, Silas had just completed his indentures, and Fryde offered to take him on as journeyman, but Silas refused. He's always been sure, you see, that those pirates were hired by Fryde himself, and that the cargo was taken on to York for Fryde to sell. These merchants keep an ear to the ground, you know.'

'There's a scar on Silas's forehead. Is that from the fight?'

'Oh, yes, he came home well-bloodied but full of remorse that he'd not been able to save John's life. He swore to me that he'd stay with me and the boys until I remarried and that he'd see Fryde brought down or die in the attempt. I've told him he stands no chance, but we went to the Duchess and borrowed money from her to repair the ship—that's the cog you sailed on to come here—and enough to keep me going until he could earn what he owed her. He's not stopped working, Isolde, not for a moment. He re-bought the house in York when he was accepted into the Merchant Adventurers and insisted I stay here in Scarborough so that I'd be well away from Fryde's attentions.'

'You mean, he's pestered you?'

'Indirectly. It was always Fryde's aim to marry me off to one of his merchant cronies so that he could take a hand in my affairs and make it look as if he'd done his best for a fellow-merchant's widow. Silas thought it would be best for me and the boys to be here, where I can run the second part of his business.'

'And a house in Brugge. He's done well. Is it all legal?'

Dame Elizabeth's blink was slow to recover. 'Ah...' she said on a sigh. 'Then you know, do you?'

'I saw something in Brugge. I wasn't meant to. They're with the books.'

'So you know about the courier service, too?'

'Between the Duchess and her brothers here in England? Yes, I can see how well he's trusted.'

'And enterprising, too. He's explored every avenue to make enough money not only to get ahead of Fryde but to keep me and the boys in comfort. His courier service extends to several members of the royal family here and to the Duke of Burgundy, the Medici bank, and any merchant who can pay him, except Fryde.

What you saw in Brugge that concerned you is Silas's attempt to prevent Fryde getting hold of luxury goods and bringing them over here. Silas *burns* to revenge himself on that man.'

'Which I suppose is why he saw me as a perfect bargaining tool. Did you know that Fryde sent his son Martin to find me and take me back?'

The dame's large brown eyes grew rounder and not a little concerned. 'No. Did he really? So, is he still there? If so, he's probably well primed to do whatever damage he can before he leaves.'

The silence was heavy with speculation, then Isolde's hand upturned to clasp Elizabeth's, caressing. 'So it could have been Fryde who sent the customs men up here to start looking. He suspects?'

'Oh, he's suspected for some time, I'm sure, but he's not been able to prove anything, especially in a place like this. You know how close Yorkshiremen are. He's left us well alone so far, because Silas is seen in York regularly and appears to make no secret of his merchandise, otherwise the Merchants Company would become suspicious. But Fryde can't complain because, in theory, there's nothing to stop him trading in the same goods. Only Silas himself, who has so many exclusive contracts. Fryde doesn't have his own ship, and Silas won't allow him to use his. Other merchants, but not him.'

'Isn't that against regulations?'

'Yes, but there's nothing he can do if Silas invents unacceptable delays or puts the price up too high or says he has no room. And the other merchants like

Silas, anyway. They don't care for Fryde, but he's one of them, so they have to lump it.'

'So how could he be elected sheriff, Dame Elizabeth?'

'Elizabeth,' she said, gently reproving. 'By moving up the ladder one rung at a time with just enough friends to push him up it.'

'And bribery?'

'Oh, of course bribery. That's where the money goes. You've stayed there. You've seen what goes on and what kind of company he keeps. That's the kind of bribery they like.'

'I've seen what he does to his wife, too.'

'So have I. I never disliked her, poor woman. I feel sorry for her because she's on the receiving end of the man's frustration against Silas. Everything Fryde tries to obtain from Flanders—goods that have come overland from the east or by sea from Europe—has to be done through his agent in Brugge, who happens to know Silas rather well. He lets Silas have most of whatever Fryde wants, and more, and Silas brings it over here to our Scarborough warehouse and sells it to Fryde's customers at a profit.'

'So Fryde wants astrakhan fur?'

'Certainly he does. All those fur-trimmed ceremonial gowns, Isolde. Just think of the impression, eh?' Elizabeth grinned, then became suddenly sober. 'I've no sympathy with him. He took my husband and my sons' father.' Her voice faltered. 'There's no wealth in all the world that could replace that, but Silas has done everything possible for us. He could have married a diamond merchant's daughter, but that would have interfered with his travels. He said he intends to keep going until Fryde's on his knees. Foolish, really.'

'Did he love her, the diamond merchant's daughter?'

'No. I've never seen him smitten the way I saw him with you, Isolde. You'd not have known it, of course, but I could tell. And you'd be quite mistaken to think that he has any real love for the Duchess, either. That was never love, and it was donkey's years ago. There's still affection, I dare say, but it must have been some urgent political business for her to have visited him at night, alone. That's the most likely explanation, my dear.'

'But he didn't come to me,' Isolde whispered.

Elizabeth squeezed Isolde's hand, unable to conceal a huff of laughter, however inappropriate. 'There have been times,' she said, 'when I've crept downstairs here to find out why he's not in his bed and he's still been going over my accounts, with candlewax dripping down on to the table and ice crystals creeping up the insides of the windows. I've also seen him asleep with his head on a pile of papers. His energy and commitment are quite astonishing, Isolde, my dear.'

The tears and laughter spilled out together. 'I know. Too much.'

'Ah, that's it, is it? You'd have preferred a lengthier wooing?'

Isolde nodded. 'No woman wants to be wooed as a weapon against someone else. He's never once spoken of love to me, only of bargains and possessions, so I have no way of knowing his true feelings. To say he wants me and intends to keep me is neither here nor there: one could say as much for a favourite hawk or a piece of merchandise. I love him, Elizabeth, but I'm not prepared to be a pawn in a game of war against Master Fryde or my father. Allard and I have agreed that I must go home, where I cannot be used so, even though I fear he'll find it inconvenient.'

'Who, Silas?'

'No, my father.'

'Then why not simply stay here?'

'Because I may be with child, and my father's house is the only place where it would be safe.'

'I see. So you discussed it? He said he'd claim it?'

'In no uncertain terms. He believes a child would be an even better weapon to use against my father. He'd not let either of us go then, at any price.'

Elizabeth took up the heavy iron fire-tongs and prodded the log viciously into life. 'I can scarce believe Silas could say anything so insensitive. Really! Was that supposed to persuade you to stay? It would have persuaded me to go. Silas in love is not exactly Silas in tact, is he?'

'Well, I suppose he was not so much offering me a choice of going or staying as whether to stay as a potential escapee or as his mistress, which he said would be more comfortable. And he was very generous, and never unkind, but he's not in love with me, Elizabeth. Revenge, not love. Any future with him would have got off on quite the wrong foot.'

'In that, you're probably right. It would; but even so, my dear, you could stay until you're sure, couldn't

you? We can send a message to your father to say that
Allard is here and that you're quite safe. Would that
do? I don't suppose Master Caxton will be going far
until he feels stronger. And as for poor Cecily, well,
she's suffered more than any of you, I think. She's
certainly very unwell.'

'Of course, you're quite right. I was thinking only
of myself. Cecily must be fully recovered before any
more journeys, but would you allow me to be of some
use while I'm here? I can do accounts, order a household, garden, work in the stillroom, the dairy, embroi-
der, write letters…sew…?'

She was gathered into a warm hug that rocked and
patted and soothed her with a surge of affection she
had lacked over the wearisome days of the voyage.
'Yes, of course you can help. See…' she held Isolde
away '…here's Emmie with warm possets for us both.
There, now. Let's drink to that, shall we?'

Isolde did not ask Dame Elizabeth, then or later,
whether she expected Silas to visit Scarborough again.
His small ship was now in the harbour and Caxton had
said that no other ship was due to leave Sluys for at
least a week, so that gave her time enough to tend
Cecily, to gather her scattered wits and to dry their
clothes, which were few, the rest having been left behind in Brugge. The conversation with her hostess had
helped, as nothing else could have done, towards her
understanding of Silas's drive for revenge, and it took
little time for her to deliberate upon the relative im-
portance of the two targets: Henry Fryde or her father.

Her brother Allard's views were typically unsentimental. 'What happens when it's known that Silas abducted you, then?' he said, leaning against the heavy oak door of the dairy. 'He'll be in a worse position than Fryde, won't he?'

Isolde skimmed the thick cream off a shallow bowl of milk and tipped it into a jug. 'There's a churn over there,' she said, not looking. 'It needs a strong arm. Knowing Silas, he'd probably say I went willingly and, although I didn't, he knows I'd not contradict that. He'd say that Bard rescued me from Fryde's disgusting home and that Fryde didn't know or care who I was seeing, nor did he even know where to start looking. He didn't, did he?' She stopped skimming to turn to him.

'Father's men said not, but he managed to get his stupid son to Brugge before me, so how did he do that, I wonder?'

Isolde wiped a finger across the rim of the scoop and licked it. 'I don't know,' she said.

'Well, I think I do. That frisky young brother of Silas's.'

'What, Bard?'

'Father's men were approached by Fryde's wife, who'd learned from her maid about Bard's plans. He doesn't lose a moment, does he, our Bard?'

'So Mistress Fryde told her husband. Surely not!'

'I don't believe she wanted to. I believe she was followed and made to tell what she knew, and then junior Fryde was packed off that night, before me.'

'And he's still there, Allard. In Brugge.'

'Yes, love. But you're not, so stop worrying. If Silas can't fix him, then no one can.'

'You like him, don't you?'

Allard came to her side and took a fingerful of cream to his mouth. 'Listen, love. I'm the eldest son, and so is Silas. If *we* like and respect each other, how can an age-old feud possibly continue? Whatever started it is long forgotten now. It's history. I don't truly believe that Father cares any more.'

'Then why would he take Felicia?'

Infuriatingly, he smacked his lips and headed for the door. 'Perhaps you should ask Father when next you see him. Or Felicia.'

She tried to take Allard's advice to stop worrying, but the image of Martin Fryde lying in the murky waters of the Dijver, shrieking and yelling while Silas walked calmly away, stayed uncomfortably in her memory all afternoon. Martin would not go meekly home after such an insult.

Fully rested and nursed back to comfort, Master Caxton found that his captive audience now included Dame Elizabeth's aged father, who was a scholar of astronomy, astrology, alchemy and mathematics, and whose deafness was a great burden to him. Closeted together for hours each day, the gentle white-haired old man and his two guests could hardly tear themselves apart for meals, and as each day passed the excuse was given that just another day would give extra strength to the broken arm which, in the privacy of the study, wielded a pen much as it had done before, if more slowly. Old Master Abbotson and Allard did their part to contrive at the slow progress of the healing, though Caxton himself was far from reluctant, being on the receiving end of Dame Elizabeth's concern. It was what he had lacked for many a day. Silas's praises of her had come nowhere near the truth. He was entranced. Captivated. And Dame Elizabeth lit up like a lantern whenever he came near. Even the boys noticed.

'I thought he was supposed to be going to London, Mother,' John said to her in the counting-house. The acrobatic young man was sitting on the window-ledge with his feet on his mother's table, leaning backwards out of the window to clean the salt spray off the thick greenish panes of glass.

'For heaven's sake, John, hold on!' she said, clinging to his feet. 'He *is* going to London, but he can hardly be expected to ride with a broken arm, can he?'

'Other men do,' he called, from a distorted greenish-pink angle.

'Well, he's not like other men,' came the defensive reply.

John reappeared, grinning cheekily. 'No, he's not, is he? We've noticed that, haven't we, Mother?'

'Exactly what d'ye mean by that, John Brakespeare? And take that grin off your face.'

He leaned his arms across his knees, filling the square of light with his frame. 'Has it not occurred to you that Cousin Silas sent Master Caxton here for a purpose? That he could easily have had him put ashore at the port of London before sending the ship up here to Scarborough? It would not have taken more than a couple of days to do that, you know. Would it?'

'No doubt Silas had his own good reasons, John.'

'Yes!' John clambered down, letting the sun pour into the room. 'I'm sure Silas had his own good reasons. I'm also glad he sent Mistress Isolde back.'

'John…come back here!' John was on his way out. 'Listen! Silas did not send Isolde back. And you must not pester her with your attentions.'

'Mother, I'm not pestering her. I'm simply being attentive, that's all. It'll give Silas a thing or two to think about when he gets back; it's time somebody took the wind out of his sails.'

Dame Elizabeth watched him bounce away and turned, tight-lipped, to straighten her papers. If anyone could take the wind out of Silas's sails, it was not likely to be young John.

Chapter Eleven

With time to herself at last, no demands on her emotions, no expectations, no restrictions to her freedom, Isolde came close to regaining control of the life which had been hers until so recently. One by one the constraints fell away, each new day bringing with it a peace that contrasted strangely with the glamour of Brugge, the hint of danger and intrigue, the competition that had so disgusted Hugo van der Goes. Here, there was no braiding and parading, no need to impress or to keep up the dreadful pretence of being secure in a man's love. Each day came with the sharp scent of September that lifted a veil off the sea and held it high above the corn-sheared fields, ripening the glorious brightness and drawing foraging bees into the harvest-laden air to bumble the late-summer blooms and fill the hives. Each day she took upon herself the tasks that had been hers at home, already quite certain in the way that women have that something had already taken possession of her body and that she was no longer one alone, but two. Her courses were two weeks late. Dame

Elizabeth had said it could be the voyage, the shock, her emotions, but Isolde knew, and was doubly thankful that she had called a halt, just in time, to the humiliating bargaining.

Purposely, she refrained from discussing Silas and his affairs, though from her upstairs window she searched each speck of white on the wide horizon and was torn between relief and grief that he was apparently making no mad dash across the ocean to claim what he'd insisted was his alone.

The messenger who had ridden to inform her father had returned days ago with a message to say that he would come to escort her home. He had given no indication when that would be, and from her seemingly innocent enquiry about the La Vallon woman, she learned that she was still there. Well, that would soon right itself, for surely their fathers would review the situation once it was known that she was home again.

Yet she was by no means as sure as Silas had been that her father would want a La Vallon brat to foster, and at such times of doubt she took to walking barefoot along the sandy coastline towards the rocks below the cliffs where, from Silas's ship, she had seen the breakers washing them with foam. Here, she could allow her losses and gains to fight it out while she called into the eternal wind what she dared not even whisper elsewhere. 'Silas…Silas…*Silas*!'

With the return of Master Caxton's strength and the excuses growing accordingly weaker, he set off for London, with Allard to assist him and a tearful departure to hold in his memory. Both Isolde and her brother were aware that the printer and his affectionate hostess regretted the empty years with only Silas's version of their virtues to go on, and Caxton's promise to return was, they all knew, not merely to recoup the joys of old Master Abbotson's company.

The house by the quay seemed desolate without them. With an eye to the main chance, young Master Brakespeare lost no time in stepping into the breach left by the two loved ones, and though his duty to his mother was never stronger, his infatuation with Isolde was beyond his restraint, as yet. Still in the dark about the mysteries of sexual attraction, he tried everything he could think of to engage her interest; flattery, attentiveness and a tendency to appear round every corner being the backbone of his repertoire. Finally, Isolde herself was driven to frenzied attempts to evade him: his friendship she could tolerate, but not this.

Telling no one where she was going, she sauntered to the far end of the busy quay and down on to the wide expanse of sand that curved like a sickle towards the shallow outcrop of rocks on the headland, slipping off her shoes and the ribbon that bound her hair. The tide was far out, no more than a silver thread underlining a hem of grey tissue, and the constant buffeting of the wind in her ears tore at the sea's distant murmur, at the mewing of the gulls and at the thoughts that wrapped an ache inside her breast.

The sand was hard and cool beneath her feet as she dragged a strand of bladder-wrack behind her towards warm pools like satin pockets, or mirrors to reflect the clouds. Clambering upwards, she perched like a hidden sentry, watching, willing, daring, despairing, placing a hand over her womb in the sudden realisation that the part of him there, inside her, was a solace to her emptiness, not a penance for her weakness.

Far out on the glittering edge of water, women pushed triangular nets on poles along the sea-bed to catch millions of grey shrimps and the occasional careless crab. Towards the town, children scampered, their voices lost in the distance, and a lone figure in a white shirt walked beside his horse, taking bites out of something in his hand. He stopped to throw it far out to sea with a powerful bend of his body and a familiar flick of the arm, an image so heart-stoppingly familiar that Isolde was riveted, her heartache tearing a sob from her throat before she could catch it. Her face crumpled, and she held it together with her two hands, trembling with black despair and forcing herself to look again through the tunnel of her hair.

He was tall and well built. His white shirt billowed in the wind and flattened itself against his chest and shoulders, tearing open a wide expanse of body and forearm. Black hair whipped across his face and, as he stopped to examine the distant rocks, he held it back with a quick slide of his fingers that shaded his eyes and focussed them. The rocks were grey, brown, green and draped with seaweed, but there, over there by that deep shadow, was a hint of red that fluttered, and two pink arms holding it back. But for that, her camouflage would have been perfect.

'Thank you, faithful Cecily.' He laughed, throwing himself into the saddle. The horse bounded forward.

The motionless figure on the rocks came alive in the blink of an eye, suddenly erupting in a flurry of moss colours that had, until that moment, been a part of the landscape. The red mass of hair lifted and streamed behind her as she leapt, barefoot, from rock to rock on to the sand, her howls reaching him before he could see that they were not laughter, like his.

He dismounted and ran, catching her in his arms as she leapt at him, burying her primitive wails into the cool skin of his throat, wrapping her slender form close to him with a ravenous greed too powerful for words. He rocked her and let her weep unhindered until he carried her to the flat slabs of stone, when her first words became recognisable as, 'Where's your ship?'

He settled her inside his arms, enclosing her with his long legs, and pushed back the wild tangle to find her wet eyes. She clung to him, wiping her tears on his shirt.

'It's at York, sweetheart. I met your father there. He's come for you.'

'He's here at Scarborough?'

'Yes, love. We came together by road.'

The grimace of weeping became a laugh. 'To rescue me?'

'To rescue you. We're coming in twos now, you see.'

'Oh, Silas!'

Their kisses were breathless and almost childlike in an effort to taste every reachable surface, quickly, before it disappeared. But now something else slipped through the kisses, almost colliding upon their lips. 'I love you…love you…love you! Ah, beloved.'

'I love you, Silas. I've been so unhappy without you. Why didn't you—'

'You'd not have believed me, would you? You doubted me, my motives. I *should* have told you, sweetheart. Forgive me, but you must have known that I love you. I adore you.'

'I was so angry. I didn't give you a chance to explain. Forgive me, love?'

'Angry about what? Explain what?'

'About the Duchess. When she came the night before I left.'

'That wasn't the Duchess, love.' His eyes twinkled into hers and he kissed first one eyelid and then the other. 'You thought it was…oh, God!'

'It wasn't?'

'No, it was Ann-Marie, bringing me a message. You saw her?'

'I saw, yes. But why would Ann-Marie bring you a message at that time of night? Was it to do with Bard?'

'No, Bard was in bed. It was more serious than that.' He sighed, and kissed her again. 'I'll tell you. She'd been sent by the Duchess to tell me that young Fryde had been trying to get his revenge, as I suspected he would. He'd sent a message to the Duke, telling him that the Duchess and I had been lovers in York before her marriage and suggesting that we still were.'

'Oh…no! She was warning you to flee?'

'No, not at all. There was no reason why I should. Apparently the Duke sent for young Fryde to appear at the Princenhof and to repeat his accusations in front of the Duchess. He had no option but to go, but he didn't dare repeat it to her face because he only had his father's word for it, and he dared not drag his father into it. What a fool the lad is! But the Duke was just as angry as if he *had* done, and he's thrown young Fryde and his two pals into the Steen—that's the big stone gaol, love. He's likely to be there for some time.'

'So the Duchess wanted you to know that?'

'She wanted me to know that the Duke was going to send for me the next morning to hear my side of the story. She had already denied it, naturally, and she wanted to be sure that I knew to do the same. She sent Ann-Marie because she knows that Ann-Marie's the only one who knows the truth and has my interests at heart.'

'So you denied it.'

'Certainly I did, for her sake as well as my own, and yours.'

'And he believed you?'

'It's in his own interests to believe me. He relies on me for messages to get safely and secretly to their destinations. He's far more inclined to take my word against young Fryde's any day, and he's well aware of Fryde's corruption amongst the Merchant Venturers. As soon as I heard you'd gone with Allard and William, I went straight to Antwerp where my carrack was berthed and came across to York; there the Venturers told me that Fryde's affairs were being investigated in great detail, both within the company and by the city council. The message I took to them from the Duke has instructed them that Fryde is now forbidden to trade in Flanders for good. He's ruined, sweetheart. He's getting a taste of his own medicine, at last. And not before time.'

'His poor wife.'

'Don't grieve for her: she's left him.'

'Left, Silas? Oh, where?'

'Gone back to her parents. Best decision she could have made.'

'Is it, Silas?'

He knew what she was asking him. He had come with her father from York, having met him quite by chance at the Merchant Venturers Hall. They had talked, amicably, with no trace of the feuding that had dogged their ancestors, and Sir Gillan proudly admitting that it was Felicia and her mother who had engineered a meeting between him and Silas's father that had ended in laughter and reminiscences instead of recriminations. Yet Felicia stayed with Sir Gillan, as Silas had known that she would. He would have to explain before she could see for herself.

She took his cleft chin between her fingers and slowly nibbled her lips towards his. 'Answer me, Silas Mariner. Is it best for a woman to return to her parents, as I intended to do? Or is there another way?'

His reply was prevented for some time, and when he raised his head as if to listen, she mistook his words of warning for a reply. 'The tide's turned, love,' he said.

Her hair stood on end. 'What?' she whispered.

'Look. The shrimpers are coming back. The tide's

moving in. We must move, too.' A quick glance at her eyes showed him how her emotions were on a knife edge, and instantly he picked her up, holding her fast against his chest with a fierceness which would have been impossible for her to misunderstand. 'God's truth, woman!' he whispered. 'Are you doubting me still? I've not come all this way just to take you back to your father. Did you think I had? You're mine! You always were and you always will be.' A sharp whistle brought the bay stallion back to him and, making a pad for her of his shirt, he sat her before him on the saddle, holding her securely with one arm. It was what she had dreamed of.

With the wind at their backs, he told her of the love Felicia and Sir Gillan had always had for each other and of how she had confided only in her mother and to himself on a solitary excursion to York. Her so-called abduction had been a desperate attempt to resolve an impossible situation in the light of his father's predictable refusal to release his daughter.

'So the decision to send me to York was to spare *my* embarrassment, or theirs? Didn't my father think I'd understand?'

Silas kissed her forehead. 'Probably not,' he murmured. 'But nor did he want you getting all cosy with Bard, nor would he have sent you to Fryde if he'd known what *he* was getting up to. He didn't know about Elizabeth's husband, who was my father's brother's son.'

'Yes, I knew he was your cousin, but I didn't know

what had happened until Elizabeth told me. But does my father intend to take me home, Silas?'

'He did, but not any more. They understood the message I sent them from Brugge, as I knew they would, but he believed it had not worked out when he received yours a few days ago. But I've asked his permission to woo you, sweetheart. That's been missing, hasn't it? And it's upset you, I know. It was undignified. So, when I've wooed you properly, then I shall ask you to marry me, because your father's agreed that I'm a proper husband for you. There, does that sound more civilised? Nay…nay, lass. Don't weep again. Ye're not breeding, are you?'

'Yes…yes, Silas.'

'Are you saying yes to the idea, or to…? God in heaven!' He reined the horse in and took her face in his hand, searching her limpid green eyes for the answer. 'You *are*?'

'It's too soon, but I think I may be. Does it complicate matters, Silas?' She sniffed, wiping a tear off on to his bare chest. 'Will it have to be a shorter wooing now?'

'Sweetheart, I know my timing is not half-bad, but this time it's damn near perfect, isn't it?' His laugh reflected all the joys of their reunion, ending with a bass whoop that lifted the stallion's head and those of the nearby shrimpers. 'The wooing *will* have to be curtailed, I fear, but will that be so very uncomfortable for you, my darling girl?'

'Not so uncomfortable as those days since I left you, beloved. I wished a hundred times a day that I'd told you of my love for you while I had the chance, but pride and jealousy got in the way and I deserved to suffer. I've never known a pain like it, Silas. It blinded me. How could I be so stupid when I knew even before we left this harbour that I loved you? I want to bear your child, Silas. And above everything I want you to be proud of me.'

'I am, my love. I was in Brugge, too. That reminds me; the Duke asked me for you.'

'And you told him?'

He tightened his arm around her as the stallion took the steps up to the quay. 'I told him no, in the circumstances. I dare say he'll understand when next he sees you, eh?'

But one whose understanding could not be relied on was young John Brakespeare. The sight of a half-naked man holding an obviously emotional and dishevelled young woman before him on his saddle-bow clattering into the courtyard could mean only one thing, when everyone knew how she had fled from his forcible abduction only last month.

Pushing young Francis aside, John ran to Isolde with arms outstretched, lifting her down before either of the riders had realised that the look on his face was of hostility rather than concern. 'Go inside,' he told Isolde, swinging her away to one side. 'My mother will tend you while I see to this.'

'What?' said Isolde. 'See to what?'

The quizzical half-smile missed John by a mile as he turned his attention to Silas who, swinging his leg over the horse's mane, was in mid-flight when John's punch hit him in the ribs. Momentarily, Silas doubled, warding off with his forearm John's next unexplained attack, but the young man saw only what was there before him, his rival with a tearful Isolde. He lunged again.

Torn between laughter and incredulity, Silas grabbed his shirt from the saddle and whipped it hard across John's head as the lunge went wildly astray. 'What in pity's name's got into you, lad?' he snapped. Stepping neatly behind John, he brought his forearm across the lad's throat, forcing the head back against his chest. 'What's all this about, eh?'

Isolde, half-inclined to laugh at these antics, now saw something of the problem in John's furious expression, and she came forward with an attempt to explain. But Silas scowled at her with a shake of his head, mouthing 'Go!' and with a sharp look at the doorway commanded her to reverse the direction of Dame Elizabeth at the same time. With a lift of her eyebrows, she obeyed, and saw how Silas released John with a push that sent him untidily into the stable door.

He swung round to face Silas with the low sun streaming into his blue eyes, spitting with anger. 'Get out of here, Francis!' he snarled at his younger brother. 'And shut the door. This is men's business.'

'All right,' Silas said, 'so you have a problem; I can see that. But men's business can usually be discussed rationally before violence. Blows usually come afterwards, you know, John. And I'm not so very bad at understanding, am I?'

Not to be outdone regarding the proper dress for a fight, John was stripping off his shirt. 'Then it's time you tried some of your well-known understanding on the lady, cousin. She made it quite clear last time you were here that she wanted none of you. Yet you took her to Flanders against her will and obviously made her so miserable that she couldn't wait to escape you. Now, you come chasing after her again, and while my back is turned, you…you…' he pointed at Silas's magnificent torso '…well, *look* at you! No wonder she's in tears. No wonder she wants nothing to do with you.'

'Has she told you exactly what happened in Flanders?'

'No, she cannot bring herself to speak of it, but she's moped ever since she's got here, and anyone can see—'

'No, John. There you're wrong, I'm afraid. If anyone can see what a woman's thinking from one moment to the next, he'll have to call himself God. They're not like men, lad. That's the first lesson you'll have to learn.'

'You cannot deny it, Silas Mariner! You cannot deny that Mistress Isolde couldn't stand the sight of you when you first met. Even I could see that.'

'No, I can't deny that. But that's now several weeks ago, John.'

'Weeks, months!' he yelled. 'What's the matter? She's *still* in tears at the sight of you. You don't change a woman's heart in weeks, do you? Even you can't do that, surely? You shall fight me, cousin. I've sworn to protect her against you and I shall rescue her from your clutches. Come on, fight me!' He balanced himself with fists aloft.

One would have had to look closely to see Silas's reaction: a slight tightening of the cheeks, a fractional lowering of the eyelids.

John was now in full spate. 'She's told my mother what happened, and my mother's given her comfort, so the least I can do is to offer her my protection. Put them up, man!'

At that moment, the door into the courtyard opened quietly to admit Sir Gillan who, summoned by Francis, hoped to mediate in the dispute. He stood with his back to the door as one who had seen this kind of thing before. 'Master John is the challenger?' he enquired.

'Yes, sir. I am,' said John, glowering.

'He is, sir. Should I accept the challenge?'

'If the lady's honour is at stake, then I believe you should, La Vallon. Is that the case?'

'No, sir,' Silas said.

'Yes! Yes, it is! You know damn well it is. She does not want your attentions forced upon her. She's been happy to accept mine while—'

'Ah, I see,' Sir Gillan said. 'Then I see nothing for it but to fight for the lady. You are well matched. Are you ready, both of you? Do you accept me as referee?'

'Sir Gillan.' Silas frowned. 'If you can persuade John to listen to me, I'm sure this can be settled without the need for violence. The lady doesn't want this any more than we do.'

'Speak for yourself, sir!' John said. 'If you're afraid, say so!'

Silas sighed. 'Tch! I accept the challenge. Come, let's get it over with.'

'The first to land three clean punches is the winner. Now, set to,' Sir Gillan called.

Within doors, Isolde could hardly believe what was happening. But Dame Elizabeth was philosophical about her son's need to prove himself in the eyes of adults. 'Silas won't hurt him, my dear,' she said, hugging Isolde to her. 'He knows what it's all about, and so does your father. They'll see he's not injured any more than he needs to be. It's his pride that's suffering most.'

And in that she was right, for although John's education in the ways of women was not completed in the fifteen minutes that followed, his pride was salvaged by knowing that Isolde was lost to him not by default but by force of circumstance.

Watching for Sir Gillan's signal, Silas put an end to it with only the minor disfigurement of a cut lip and a bruised eyebrow for John and some sore ribs for himself. The bucket of cold water was then the prelude to a cooling-off during which Sir Gillan tended the young man and gave him some much-needed fatherly advice about the wayward workings of women's hearts, citing his own Felicia as an example rather than Isolde. From him, John took it to heart and was obliged to shake Silas's hand with a good grace.

Silas eased a hand over his ribs and pulled on his much-mussed shirt. 'Another couple of inches, young man, and I shall insist on swords instead of fists. Are we friends again?'

John nodded, moving his jaw from side to side with his hand. 'What's Mistress Isolde going to think?' he said, thickly.

Lifting an eyebrow, Silas gave him a gentle thump on the shoulder. 'If you ever discover what Mistress Isolde thinks,' he said, 'you might let me and her father know, because you'll be breaking new ground. Now, lad, let's go and eat, eh?'

What Mistress Isolde thought about Silas's house on Coney Street in the city of York was not so difficult for anyone to see. They had taken their leave of Dame Elizabeth once again, tearfully and with much affection, but in complete agreement that it would not do to linger, all things considered. Now, an added delight was to meet Felicia La Vallon, who had been staying in York since her brother's departure with Sir Gillan the day before, and the tension that Isolde and Felicia had half-expected from each other dissolved at their first meeting, having so much more in common than their unusual relationship. They were to each other like the sisters neither of them had had.

The house was large, built around a courtyard and tastefully furnished, and staffed by three men and a woman who were overjoyed not only to see their master in love at last but to know that they would be living in York, with some months in Brugge during the summer.

In an upper chamber hung with autumn-red carpets, they watched a September gale lash the windows and bounce across the wide river that passed the end of the long garden. Silas's hands gently caressed her belly, his lips nudging at her neck. 'Scarborough too, eh? In the spring, perhaps?'

'You've lost Elizabeth, love. You know that, don't you?'

'To William? Yes, that was the general idea. I'd been wondering how to get them together for years. I've never known anything fit so well into place as that, and now he's established in Westminster, she'll go to him, I know it. The boys are ready to run the place now: John's longing to be left in charge.'

Isolde turned herself into his arms. 'And I hear that my brother Sean spends all his days in your father's library. I hope he doesn't learn bad habits.'

'What habits, wench?'

'Abducting people?'

'No! He'll not learn how to do that. That's a La Vallon specialty, remember. Reserved for difficult cases. Have you decided to marry me, lass?'

She took his hand and held it again over her womb. 'Both of us?' she whispered. 'You want both of us, Silas Mariner, for the price of one?'

'Priceless,' he said. 'I have nothing to offer except myself and what you've seen. It's an unfair bargain, lass, but I beg you to accept me. Mistress, lover, wife or what you will. Name your terms.'

'Wife, dearest heart. Silas Mariner's lady, if you please.'

She would have elaborated, but Silas lifted her and laid her with care on the great tawny-coloured velvet bed with its cover of gold-patterned brocade. He loosened her hair and took it greedily into one hand, letting it trickle through his fingers like red gold-dust. 'Mine,' he said, watching her green eyes half-close with desire. 'Mine. A real live Medwin.'

Epilogue

One month later, Silas and Isolde, Sir Gillan and Felicia were married at the little family church in Medwinsholme and, by coincidence, their firstborn sons were born within a week of each other the following May.

Young Sean went to join his brother Allard in London as assistant to William Caxton and his new wife Elizabeth, who had one daughter named Mary. Eventually Caxton's assistant, Wynkyn de Worde, carried on his master's printing business at the Sign of the Red Pale in Westminster, established in 1476. Deiric Bouts, who was ill in Leuven, died that same year and Hugo van der Goes was committed to The Red Cloister again, where he died a few years later. But the Portinari altarpiece, about which he was so concerned, was finished by then, shipped to Florence, and was acclaimed as a masterpiece, although Thommaso Portinari bankrupted the Medici bank by his misuse of their funds.

In 1477, the year after Silas and Isolde's wedding, Hans Memlinc fought for the Duke of Burgundy, was wounded, but returned to Brugge where he produced many exceptional pieces, some of which can still be seen there. The Duke of Burgundy was killed that year, but his widow maintained a glittering court at Mechelin, her need of Silas Mariner's exotic merchandise and Caxton's books being greater than ever.

Bard La Vallon took to the diamond trade like a duck to water and stayed in Antwerp with his wife and seven children, three more than his elder brother. But then, that was only to be expected.

*   *   *   *   *

MILLS & BOON®

Makes any time special™

Mills & Boon publish 29 new titles every month. Select from...

Modern Romance™   Tender Romance™

Sensual Romance™

Medical Romance™   Historical Romance™

MAT2

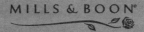

2 FREE

books and a surprise gift!

We would like to take this opportunity to thank you for reading this Mills & Boon® book by offering you the chance to take TWO more specially selected titles from the Historical Romance™ series absolutely FREE! We're also making this offer to introduce you to the benefits of the Reader Service™—

- ★ FREE home delivery
- ★ FREE gifts and competitions
- ★ FREE monthly Newsletter
- ★ Exclusive Reader Service discounts
- ★ Books available before they're in the shops

Accepting these FREE books and gift places you under no obligation to buy, you may cancel at any time, even after receiving your free shipment. Simply complete your details below and return the entire page to the address below. *You don't even need a stamp!*

YES! Please send me 2 free Historical Romance books and a surprise gift. I understand that unless you hear from me, I will receive 4 superb new titles every month for just £2.99 each, postage and packing free. I am under no obligation to purchase any books and may cancel my subscription at any time. The free books and gift will be mine to keep in any case.

H1ZEA

Ms/Mrs/Miss/Mr ....Initials.................................
                                                     BLOCK CAPITALS PLEASE

Surname ....

Address ....

....

....Postcode.....................

Send this whole page to:
UK: FREEPOST CN81, Croydon, CR9 3WZ
EIRE: PO Box 4546, Kilcock, County Kildare (stamp required)